ARC CONTINUUM

ARC CONTINUUM

PART I: FRATRES

Kira,

Enjoy!

Mark F. Worthing

MARK F. WORTHING

Library of Congress Control Number:		2011961062
ISBN:	Hardcover	978-1-4653-0720-0
	Softcover	978-1-4653-0719-4
	Ebook	978-1-4653-0721-7

This book was printed in the United States of America.

To order additional copies of this book, contact:
Xlibris Corporation
0-800-644-6988
www.xlibrispublishing.co.uk
Orders@xlibrispublishing.co.uk
302666

For Henry Charles Anthony

PROLOGUE

Light—white, pure, blinding, clinical, foreign. Not familiar light for hunting, feeding, fighting, and taking females. Not normal light-time.

Confusion—deep and undreaming sleep sliding away fast. Not normal sleep—just dark, unknowing, unthinking nothingness; black void—no thoughts, nothing.

Objects—not trees, not home. Where is forest? How can I not see anything? Eyes streaming with salty waterfall. Must see where I am, where to run, where to fight.

Discomfort—eyelids stuck together at corners. Limbs tied, numb, hot, tingling, immovable at my side. Wrists and ankles cut, bleeding, raw. Lying on strange rock. Flat, soft, skin like snake. How? Why?

Fear—intense, relentless, rising from chest, cascading up through head, faster, feeding greedily on itself, out of control. Much head pain now—front head pain. Head bursting with pressure like many tiny rocks pounding from inside. More eyes streaming, stinging with salty tears.

Gagging—mouth blocked; cannot scream. Alert the troupe, run, fight, or bite. Can't spit or swallow. Bitter, disgusting plant taste. Breathing through nose—difficult. Dry throat, want river, want sick.

Noise—unknown, too loud, repeating, high note. Not ape, not animal noise. Hurt ears, more head pain. Can't turn head. Head also fixed to strange rock. Now more light in corner of eye. Colour like last sun of day. Flashing same time as noise. Now more noise. Other animals here. No! Not animals. No fur, no feather, no scales. Floppy white skins on dark body. Large heads. Must run, escape strange new animals. Why can't move! . . .

Calm—total calm now; all is fine. No danger, no need worry. New animals friends, mean no harm. Calm my body, stop fighting against restraints, breathe slowly and easily. Strange animals will give medicine for wounds. Better to sleep. All will be fine. Back to forest, family, home soon.

He let out a sigh of pure relaxation. He felt so good, so in control of his body, and so alive. Life is good. 'Good to be alive!' he worded in his brain. At least he thought that it was him forming the words deliberately in his head, could it have been someone else? He did not feel alone and, strangely, it felt good.

He did not understand what this voice in his head was, but for some reason, its sudden presence did not concern him. Neither did it concern him that he was embracing thoughts, concepts, and words that he had never used before. His head was fuzzy, light, and the presence combined with his euphoria seemed to be taking him to a different plane of consciousness.

'I must sleep now. Yes, time to sleep, and when I wake up everything will be fine.'

Dreamless sleep flooded over him like a rogue tsunami of pure blackness.

CHAPTER 1

Secure transmission

From: Lt. Gen. Anthony McGill, 8 August 2063

To: Western alliance security congress level 5 eyes

Cc: General Lloyd, commander of alliance forces

Subject: Post-global scorching and inter superpower hostilities quarterly report no. 24

Ladies and gentlemen, please find attached a full report on the political landscape of our planet, the current state of our defences, and levels of water and oil inventory based on the recent data from our operatives and remaining satellites.

The highlights are:

Current global population

Our best estimate is approximately seventy-two million individuals, comprising

Western alliance—twelve million,

New Russian empire—fifteen million,

Chinese sector—twenty-five million

Remaining inhabitable areas—twenty million

Residual population:

This mainly comprises groups of South Americans located in the southern tip of that continent, which was formerly known as Argentina and Southern Chile. Additional small populations exist on Northern Antarctica, but these are believed to be only small due to the increasing inhospitable nature of the terrain. The area is subject to massive temperature swings and fluctuating ozone cover along with increasing incidents of tectonic and volcanic activity leading to inconsistent crop harvests. This sector is poorly organised, so it continues to pose little or no danger to our security; the threat level remains low.

Russian empire:

Most of the population remains located in three areas of what was once the U.S.S.R.; the major two being centred on the main freshwater supplies near Leningrad and Finland and the waterways of the Volga through Gorky as far south as Saratova.

The territory still extends from Scandinavia (as far south as Oslo and Stockholm) and the United Kingdom (a small population around northern English lake supplies) across Russia to the Ural Mountains, which are still defended vigorously against the Chinese to the east. A large force also defends the border of former Kazakhstan.

The European desert still encroaches from the south-west and reports are that Moscow has been finally evacuated.

We believe that some populations may still exist further south around the dwindling Aral water supplies, supported by multiple desalination townships on the shores of the Caspian Sea and the need to have defence posts against potential Chinese invasion from the south-east.

Chinese sector:

This confederation still holds the area that used to be Siberian Russia, to the west of the 200-kilometre radius nuclear fallout zone just west of the Ural mountain range, both factors acting as a hindrance to any potential Western European invasion plans. The largest population surround the Baikal water supply, still, by some distance the deepest and voluminous fresh water supply in the world. We are unsure if any Asians now live in the south of the Mongolian mountain range as desert conditions continue to encroach, rendering China's original land as uninhabitable. Pockets of population may exist in the Tibetan region though, surviving on the relatively swollen waterways there, these having benefited from the post-scorch melt-off from former Himalayan ice-locked supplies.

Both the Russian and Chinese sectors have an empty inventory of oil, having been beaten to the Middle Eastern 'clearance sale' by ourselves at the time of the scorching. Little or no oil remains in that formerly rich region with all drilling infrastructure being destroyed and allied to the 80 °C temperature during the day there. This gives no reason for an investigation on potential sources there. Both have to rely on once great but dwindling supplies of coal and natural gas, running at approximately one thousandth of their early century values and estimated to run out in the next ten to twenty years.

US alliance:

We have finally completed the evacuation and relocation of the last alliance citizens living outside of Canada and the Great Lakes' borderlands. The United States desert has encroached so much that the combined Missouri and Mississippi river system, once one of the longest and mightiest in the world, cannot support a population, thus forcing the retreat.

We must now rely on the Canadian-water systems from the Great Lakes, north-west through Winnipeg, Reindeer, Athabasca, Great Slave, and Great Bear lakes to provide us the water we need. This is our home and last stand now.

When completed, enormous damming of the water and the deployment of our new technology for slowing evaporation rates will help the decline in supplies from these lakes, but their volume is already only twenty-five per cent of early century levels. The rate of consumption is still high, and the area has had no rainfall for over two years to replenish the levels. Priority must be set for more research to promote conservation, recycling, and discovery of new supplies. The use of desalination stations on the Atlantic combined with infrastructure to pump this resource to our population centred around these lakes is expensive on our remaining Middle East and Venezuelan oil inventory. This stands at 100 million barrels and 0.03 per cent of pre-scorch levels. It is time for us to consider reopening the oil sand operations in Alberta to supplement this, which was not ideal due to the extreme heat and desert conditions in the south of this old Canadian province, making extraction difficult and hazardous.

In the meantime, a thorough review of the laws regarding water usage by our citizens is required, and an upgrade in punitive measures for miscreants should be put in place.

Finally, we now have no undercover-spy facility in either of our two enemy territories. The danger of being caught, combined with the increasing difficulty in conveying information back to us has led to the evacuation of our European spies from western England. Regrettably, no such option exists for our Chinese conglomeration team, whom we have not heard from for some months now. We presume that they have been discovered and either suffered execution or torture and imprisonment.

Additionally, it will not be long before the accuracy of our reports diminishes, as more and more satellites are falling out of orbit or being sabotaged by our enemies. We can no longer find loopholes to avoid their detection and subsequent jamming, rendering them useless. The continued viability of our network can be measured in months rather than years.

However, although we must remain vigilant, it is clear that our fellow pockets of humanity have the same survival problems and priorities as us and hence have larger issues to deal with than attempting any risky invasion attempts. Though we maintain a strong force on the west coast of the Great Bear Lake, monitoring for any Chinese plans from that direction, we think the possibility of invasion is small for the time being, perhaps, it will increase when their energy and/or water reserves are depleted.

*

Alex Clugston woke up suddenly, torn from his nightmare by his own terrified shriek of terror. He sat up in bed, automatically looking at the time.

'8.30, shit! Sodding clock!'

The truth was he had not been sleeping well. He had had the dream again, a familiar haunting; one that lingered at the edge of his consciousness. Some details retained to his waking state, but others, just remained held out of reach.

There was a boy. He was in pyjamas and was in a room. And there was something there with him—something not human, something neither evil nor good but definitely something powerful.

That was all he retained. He furrowed his brow in an attempt to retrieve the missing piece of the dream but failed once again. The further into his conscious day that he ventured, the further the image receded into a far corner of the subliminal areas of his brain.

He picked up his hand-held unit and looked again at the decoded transcript sent by Kenny. Mentally he scratched his head. '*Was it him or this message from his brother an immense amount of gibberish?*' He desperately hoped his younger sibling wasn't on the psychotropic chemicals again. He knew that he was very different from his often embarrassing and always odd sibling and that they shared little in common.

Alex was the jock, the athletic sportsman, the ladies' man, and someone who you always felt that you had to follow—a born leader. In this current global environment, it was hardly surprising that he had progressed to senior ranks in the alliance defence corps. On the other hand, his brother, Kenny, was what you used to call a nerd, possessing an enormous IQ, little character to speak of, and he was always locked away, working on some scientific experiment. He was now one of the most gifted but wasted scientific researchers in the alliance, not having the maturity to equal his scientific brilliance. If he had possessed the required sagacity, no doubt he could have progressed up the scientific political ranks and been able to really make an impact to change or even save our world, if that was possible these days.

Unfortunately, most of Kenny's theories were far too 'out there' and were immediately discarded by the scientific legislature. As a result, Kenny was confined to working on renewable energy research, which he hated. Consequently, he was disinterested in his job and not bothered to apply himself to make a difference and so was unproductive that he was never given much of a budget. He would much rather be extrapolating or disproving quantum string theories or getting his fingers dirty by running experiments in a related science, all of which was 'double Dutch' to Alex.

Alex sighed audibly. He was fed up having a go at his brother and just tended to leave him alone. They seldom even met socially now that Mum had died. '*How could two brothers be so different? He wasn't a bad bloke*', Alex thought, '*but he was just such a . . . what was the word . . . a "Pratt".*'

What did his message mean? Kenny, for all his faults, was usually intelligible, unless he was expounding one of his grandiose and lengthy theories on particle physics or confirming mathematical equations. He could get lost in monologues about long-winded mathematical calculations, which proved or even disproved some such ancient scientist's theories of relativity. It was all normally way beyond Alex's comprehension. He was interested sometimes, but the art was to slow down his brother's ranting and get him to talk at a decent pace in language that a layman could understand. However, this missive, although clearly in plain English, just didn't make sense.

'Axe, come to my lab now. Something awesome to show you. Been to new place, new world, new beginning. The power of this thing is world changing. It's huge, Bro! Need to keep lid on. Come soon. Don't ignore me, Bro, and come and see this thing urgently'.

'Axe'. How he hated the familiar nickname that his brother insisted on giving him. He was sure that he did it to deliberately annoy him.

Alex swung his legs into the cockpit of his electric buggy and placed the Alliance Network Secure Encoded Transmitter (forming the amusingly devised mnemonic 'ANSET') in its charging bay. All communications had to be made via this protocol these days since the scorching, as the Internet was disbanded along with all the mobile telephone networks and traditional land-line communications. The infrastructure that supported these forms of communication had simply collapsed with the implosion of civilisation as they had known it.

The buggy doors automatically closed and double locked against the outside world. He couldn't be bothered to encode a response to his brother. It would be much better he thought to just go and catch up with whatever harebrained scheme Kenny was up to, anyway. There was no point in arguing with his sibling, as his exceptionally thick skin meant that no was never accepted as an answer.

Alex firmly engaged the electric unit's lever into drive, applied his foot on the accelerator, and the vehicle jerked gently into a forward motion. He would soon be travelling at the exciting top speed of 42 mph. Overall, he couldn't complain, as his status as a level-two patrician of the alliance allowed him this luxury of motorised transport—a simple pleasure that the majority of the population were denied.

Having reached the rank of Colonel, the third highest-ranked officer in the British-controlled hydro zone hierarchy, he was hoping that soon they would authorise access for him to a diesel or even petrol vehicle. But then again, he was British, or at least originally came from Britain at the time of the scorching—was there still resentment from the American sector for the ex-European immigrant inhabitants of this expressly assigned zone. Any Canadians who decided to live in this area were also considered 'immigrants' even though New Deline, primarily a military defence town, was well inside the territory of what used to be Canada. Would being of British descent count against him for any further promotions or when perks were handed out?

Ah! He couldn't complain. Nobody from his sector could. They were all lucky to be there as opposed to being left back at home, when the Russians walked into Northern Europe amongst all the turmoil of that terrible time. His mother, younger brother, and he were lucky to find a boat out of Barrow in Furness when the Russians started to swarm across Britain; his father and elder brother were not so lucky.

The family had been parted when their father went to find his elder sibling, who had been lost in the melee of the escaping crowds, and get him to come with them; it was not such an easy task as Charlie was backward. His father had sent them on as he had refused to leave the boy (actually thinking about it, he was a young man, but because of his condition, he always thought of him as a boy), a surprisingly noble gesture for such a bastard. There was no love lost between Alex and his father. You can't choose your relatives; the old adage went. He missed his brother Charlie though and was sorry that he had been left behind, but he couldn't give a shit for his arsehole of a father.

At the time of scorching, the Americans had welcomed their old NATO allies from Britain, Scandinavia, and Western Europe and gave them refuge. However, with the continued decline of vital commodities, especially water, since that day, would they make the same call if they had to decide now?

How he missed the Mercedes that he had when he was a young man in his early twenties, a vintage, 2025 model that he would tinker for hours on. The global scorching and associated war, terrorism, riots, famine, and plague events that followed had a lot to answer for. Fossil fuel reserves were limited and were jealously hoarded by his government, the North American alliance. The best guess of intelligence revealed that the other powers, new Russia and new China, similarly hoarded their supplies of water, oil, and coal; but information was sparse and difficult to get hold of, with drastically reduced population, and a collapse in communications technology leading to a limited ability to intercept broadcast messages. Nobody actually knew what the population of the world was; it was just educated guesswork.

The vehicle hummed along the imaginatively named Main Street, a relatively busy artery of New Deline—the second largest town in the north-western hydro zone, an area of about 1,70,000 square miles in the lake area of what used to be known as the Northern territory of Canada earlier in the century. This was one of the three zones protected by the alliance, where all supplies of oil and coal were hoarded, and the natural but dwindling reserves of water were to be found. Additionally, their area was mined for Uranium, which was a main source of power for the American alliance. This sector was controlled by former European immigrants, mostly British and Scandinavians, and stretched in an approximate 200-mile band from the post-scorching town of New Deline on the west coast of Great Bear Lake to the south-east shore of Great Slave Lake—a distance of about 750 miles.

The Europeans used to have to patrol the area around Lake Athabasca, but resources had been pulled away from this lake due to dwindling water supplies, dwindling populations, and reprioritisation being given to the larger lakes in the north. The strategic military importance of their position also meant that army resources (including two battalions of US forces and an American General to spy on them) are needed to be deployed in New Deline. Supposedly, this was in case the Chinese attempted to make a military incursion across the enormous desert that stretched across North east China, an area stolen from Russia—the Bering Strait and Alaska.

However, in truth, it was unlikely that such an incursion would take place. The Chinese had their own problems, similar to theirs—along the lines of hoarding resources, controlling their populace, and just surviving—such a military attack would most probably suffer chronic supply-line problems and be resigned to inevitable failure as a result. Anyway, what exactly would they be gaining by such an annexation of land? Some oil, coal, and radioactive fuels admittedly, but little in the way of water.

The Canadians, whose land it was originally anyway, controlled the mid hydro zone encompassing the lakes of Winnipeg, Manitoba, and Winnipegosis. And the Americans controlled the Great lakes' water ways, which still contained the majority of the alliance's water supplies.

There were dozens of people milling around; some walking, but most cycling, to whatever they did at this time of the morning, work or otherwise. All were wearing their compulsory water-retention suits in an attempt to minimise wastage of this valuable commodity. Much had been learned and copied from popular science fiction novels of the twentieth century—mimicking the precautions of living on a desert world. The suits ensured that the liquid emerging from skin via water vapour or sweat or urine was collected and could be recycled and reabsorbed for the body's reuse. Penalties for not wearing your water-retention suit and recycling water were severe.

Cycles were very popular due to the lack of vehicles and vehicle licences available to the general public. Alex felt this society must have been what he expected China to be like in the last century, based on books he read as a child. Like China, but less water.

Jobs were hard to come by as well. Employment that merited credits was not available to all citizens of the alliance; but everyone was assigned some duty, large or small to help the survival cause.

This depended on the individual's skill set and capabilities, and participants, generally, were compensated fairly for time and expenses. Being in a state of martial law meant that repeated failure or refusal to comply with your allotted task normally lead to expulsion from the alliance hydro zone. And Alex had a special task-force monitoring all identified resources on a continuous basis.

This event was extremely uncommon, as forced expulsion from the zone normally meant almost certain death, usually from thirst or hunger, but occasionally by being murdered by any of the number of nomadic mobs living by their wits on the outside of the zones.

Alex felt uncomfortable as usual as he buzzed by in his vehicle. The specially decorated water-retention uniform of the alliance military stood him out as a primary upholder of the military stranglehold that was necessary to ensure no further occurrence of civil unrest. Martial law was in place so that their continent could have a chance, however slim, of surviving the rapidly deteriorating world climate.

The Sun was poking its unwelcome head over the horizon of the east now. Naturally, it was going to be another hot day—in the 40-50 °C range, with no respite, no clouds, and virtually zero chance of rain. This was the same as the last few hundred days and would almost certainly be the same as the next hundred days. The only difference over the course of the year was a variation in temperature. As they were currently in spring the heat was moderate, but in summer, temperature in excess of 50 °C were normal. The 'cooling' relief of temperature, in the mid thirties, during the brief winter months seemed a light year away.

There was a lot of concern that the enormous desert to the south and east of their zone, which had already swallowed up the entire region that used to be called the United States of America, was encroaching irresistibly on their alliance territories; and there was nothing they could do about it. The scientists, controlled by the military, were always putting out research, suggesting that things were not so bad, but not many believed this propaganda.

Their climate could be described as 'Mediterranean plus'—a climate that was in the early century, before the scorching, which was used to be prevalent, as the name suggests, in the countries bordering the Mediterranean Sea in old Europe. However, with average temperature increasing every year during each season and water supplies dwindling, it was impossible not to face the realisation that it was only a matter of time before this changed, and their country would become uninhabitable. That was around the time that the end would come. After all, what could man do next to save himself with no water?

Alex altered the setting of the infrared filters on the vehicle windows to 60 per cent, a setting that he would increase as the day went on. Simultaneously the car's climate control clicked on to begin the daily chore of maintaining a comfortable-enough climate for Alex.

The vehicle pulled over outside the renewable energy laboratories of the alliance foundation for scientific and medical research, and came to a halt as Alex applied the brakes. Alex engaged the hand brake, retracted all the wheels (it wasn't entirely safe to leave those exposed to potential public abuse), and to reassure himself that he was safe to disembark, he had a quick feel of his holsters to ensure that both his automatic pistols were there before releasing the door locks. In a state of full alert, in case of attack by someone from the desperate and disgruntled populace, Alex stepped on to the pavement.

At that exact moment, only thirty yards away, on the first floor of the building, the brick outer wall and window of the laboratory imploded with a colossal and ear splitting 'pop'.

He instinctively knew from experience that it was his brother's laboratory.

*

The large beast swung skilfully through the higher canopy—efficient and graceful pendulous movements of its long arms allied to highly developed hand eye coordination. Save for the whispering rustle of swaying branches and leaves, this combination of innate skills propelled the ape almost silently along. With concentration etched on his eyes—two carved out orbits on his hairy face contained vigorous irises that flickered energetically from side to side—he made split second decisions about his trajectory and the availability and location of suitable vines or branches.

He landed softly and paused momentarily on a large branch—thirty metres from the forest floor—swiftly got his bearings, and then resumed his graceful journey. With four beautifully constructed arcing movements across a field of vertically hanging vines, he instinctively found another thick bough and landed noiselessly, his small but strong legs cushioning his arrival.

He stood motionless, considering his location and reviewing his plans. The minor oxygen debt from his exertions impelled his chest up and down in controlled and steady heaving movements to alleviate these arrears. His eyes now moved in a much calmer and measured sweep of his surroundings. A hairy right arm, twice the length of his legs, steadied his balance by gripping lightly to an overhead offshoot from the trunk of the tree which he was on with his highly specialised curved fingers.

This was a fairly large ape for his species, standing 1 metre and 65 centimetres and weighing 110 kilos, almost the maximum size of his species' growth potential. That fact aside, he was a relatively young and immature adult male, who yet had not developed the tell-tale sexual flanges or cheek pouches that distinguished the roaming males of the territorial version. He instinctively knew that it was not yet the time for him to find, maintain, and defend his own territory. He was successful enough in mating with females and ensuring that his own genetic material was passed on. He did this without the hassle of maintaining his own marked space, by sneaking into the domains of territorial males and forcing sex with any females in those territories. In the process, he always risked instigating a fight with the incumbent territory's owner, but he always fancied his chances with his combination of height, weight, and experience.

His hand instinctively travelled to his left ear to rub the missing portion of his lobe. The memory of the brutal encounter during the recent wet season, when it was bitten off by a flanged male, was still fresh in his memory.

He looked up and saw some fruit growing abundantly above his head. He relinquished his grip with his right hand and tugged at a piece. Soft and yielding, proof of its readiness to eat, it came away; and he placed it between his teeth. The leathery skin was easily prised open by his strong jaw, and he sucked at the contents, his large tongue flicking at the juicy goodness.

He continued to reflect thoughtfully and resumed the planning of his raid into the territory. He knew a bit about the ape that laid claim to this patch of land and that it was probably wise to try and avoid meeting him, if at all possible. The last time they confronted each other, they were well matched, and he had to make the guarded decision to retreat and live to fight another day, albeit minus a chunk of his ear, acquired by the defending ape as a souvenir. However, this male must be getting old now, and if it came to it, he would allow another battle to commence, but he felt that it was always best to take the safe line unless absolutely necessary.

He knew that if there were any females passing through this ape's territory, they would normally be congregated, with their young, near a small pond which was located near the edge of his competitor's relatively large region. That was where he would make his foray today. As they would have to protect their children, the females would not be able to escape in a hurry, so he would be able to easily overpower one and mate with her. The region adjacent to the pond was almost completely wooded, and the canopy was especially thick and lush, which would help him to remain concealed until the very last moment. He set off again—a new spring in his steps.

Only moments later he was forced to come to an abrupt halt. The tree line, until recently undiminished, now stopped unexpectedly, and a new and large clearing lay before him. The small clearing that naturally made space for the pond and its specialised ecosystem had been expanded tenfold by someone or something's intervention. Hundreds of tree stumps stood where once a forest of vibrant forty-metre trees had prevailed. A pile of cut down trees laid at the edge of the expanse, their life terminated pointlessly.

The vast open space, totally alien to the primitive Hominid, screamed at his tiny mind causing a paralysing fear to spread over his body. After several minutes, when his mind had settled, he noticed that to the far end of the clearing were several structures, similar in construction and size, and were positioned in a circle around a glowing red and yellow heap of blackening, flickering, and smoking wood. Black clouds trailed away from this object thinning and fading as they progressed further into the sky. He had seen this before, when the sky gets wet and dark and strikes the trees with a deafening noise. It was something to fear; it was the animal with no teeth or body that eats the flesh and kills with pain and flickering colours.

The travelling ape became progressively more agitated and confused, and fear gripped the primitive animal's mind. His species did not have the mental capacity to grasp the appalling, inconceivable panorama before him. '*How could so many enormous and beautiful trees have disappeared, leaving only dead stumps a mere metre high? Was it the burning animal's fault*?' The young ape stood there on the edge of the clearing for several minutes, staring at the bewildering scene below and not knowing what to do. His simple mind was caught in a feedback loop beyond his command and comprehension.

The decision either to retreat back into the forest to the comfort of what he knew or to advance and investigate the unknown was finely balanced and out of his control. It was an adrenaline-fuelled battle between the twinned but contrasting autonomous responses of 'flight and fight' and the desire to procreate. His body, gripped with the uncontrollable natural impulse to mate, was telling him to advance, find a female, and continue his genetic line. He could not see any other threats, whether from competitor apes or big cats, and this eased his fear marginally. Slowly, his natural desires overcame his apprehensions and drove him forward. He climbed down from the tree, picking his way deliberately to the open space below.

He did not see any of the female apes. Maybe they were beyond the clearing on the other side. He began to walk slowly across the open ground, winding his way between the tree stumps—his eyes alert and his body pumped with adrenaline, ready to action the fight or flight responses. The journey was slow. His species spent most of their time in the trees and were not natural knuckle-walkers, so they tended to shuffle along on their palms with their fingers curved inwards in a stilted and clumsy manner.

Slowly, he approached the structures and the burning beast that was still coughing up its acrid discharge into an unwelcoming sky. He stopped again and stood frozen with renewed fear, staring in the direction of the strange structures.

In the middle of the objects that he had seen earlier, he saw another construction that was assembled from fairly thick branches and bound together with what looked something like vines. Four branches emerged from the ground at an angle, where they were evidently firmly impaled, and stood in pairs crossing each other. The sticks were tightly bound near the crossing point with the vine material so that the effect was a sturdy structure of about one and a half metres in height. The two pairs of sticks were about three metres apart, and another branch lay horizontally propped between these two 'V's.

What lay in the middle of the structures, suspended by its bound legs, was what had caused the young ape to freeze in renewed distress. It was a large but dead cat, the long-toothed kind that his species feared, that must have measured over two and a half metres in length. Blood dripped slowly from its upturned back, and several objects about a half-metre long—twig like but smooth and straight—were embedded in its carcass. One lifeless eye seemed to stare straight at the petrified ape.

The ape had no time to react to the next sound, which was just like the whistling of the wind, only it was brief, targeted, and that came to an abrupt halt to be replaced by a gentle thudding sound. He fell to his knees and lolled his head downwards to look at his chest. One of the smooth twigs was embedded there, and blood was starting to seep from this wound. Curiously, there was little pain, just confusion, and he remained rooted to his spot. The wind whistling was heard again. This time he saw the twig as it flew harmlessly over his shoulder. At that moment he saw the creatures as they ran, emerging from their structures in his direction. The arrangement of constructions must be their nests, he rather pointlessly thought.

These creatures were huge—almost twice his height. He had seen individuals like them before on rare occasions, unable to climb, fumbling and struggling on the forest floor. His flight impulse was now too great to ignore, dwarfing all other emotions, and he turned and started to limp away as quickly as he was able, as the giant apes gave chase.

More whistling gusts were heard, and another twig embedded itself accurately in his back, just under his shoulder blade. He fell on his front and winced in agony as the first twig bored further into his body, emerging out through the other side, and releasing a waterfall of blood and frayed flesh from his ruptured back. He pushed against the ground as hard as he could with his long arms, but they failed him. He had no strength, and his fear and adrenaline couldn't help him. The creatures were upon him.

A huge palm wrapped around the back of his neck and pulled him off the ground, and he was helpless to resist. His face was pulled towards a large but relatively hair-free face of one of the ape beings, who made a variety of communicative sounds—very different and more varied than any sound that he had heard any ape utter. The ape's compatriots in the group replied by uttering similar noises.

Still holding the pitiful ape, the larger individual raised his other hand, in which he held a large rock, which glinted in the Sun, and its fashioned blade sharpened to a fine edge. With a swift and easy slicing movement, the blade sliced his throat, carving open a large gash, and his head lolled back in the giant's grip. Redness covered his eyes, as he tried to hoot futilely in agony, but instead he just gurgled whilst his breath escaped, bubbling from his cleanly severed throat.

And then all was darkness.

*

Blurred electrical light swam on to its retina, as its freshly thawed outer lids prised themselves open slowly, painfully, and with considerable difficulty. Shooting pain discharged spasmodically from back to front across its head as if its skull was being sawed by an unseen psychotic wielding a blunt and jagged dagger. Despite this persistent agony, it felt its body rapidly thawing from toe to cranium, mimicking a star's warming kiss sweeping across a frosted lawn in a welcome and accelerated embrace. Its body was now attacked across several areas by what felt like multiple cramp attacks, as its musculature twitched in uncontrollable spasms. A short-term communication disconnection existed between its neural pathways and its confused muscles denying the creature any control over the situation. It would have groaned or howled in pain, but it could not command its dry mouth and throat, and it was captive to the enforced rhythm of its body's regular and heavy breathing, as it attempted to get as much oxygen as it could to its extremities.

It was panicking. *"Who was it, where was it, and what was it doing here?"*

Its body heat was being raised as fast as physics would allow, defined by the maximum possible osmotic flow rates to allow the thawing ice from its cellular spaces back into its parched cells. Increased body heat was controlled by a combination of rising cryo-environmental temperature and restorative body-shocking drugs. The latter impetus was jump starting its subliminal cardiac and pulmonary functions in a crude, painful, but effective manner. Massive production of endocrinal stimulants including Aggressterone and Demotase was being initiated by this rapid drug infusion, contributing to an enhanced state of bodily alert. Blood was being forcefully pumped to all extremes of its body at double the animal's resting heart rate, ensuring that its whole body could recover rapidly and safely from the dormant frozen state that had forced it to be a comatose prisoner for over 400 orbits. Performance-enhancing drugs supported this enforced increased metabolic rate, allowing it to be maintained without total organ collapse and acting as thawing agents at the cellular level.

The creature now felt a new influx of synthetic chemical warmth as a mixture of drugs was further injected intravenously via multiple tubes attached to its body. It knew that this cocktail contained drugs which would neutralise the cryoprotectants that had been used in the initial freezing process and would also reverse the effects of vitrification of its body tissues. Also contained in this influx were billions of specialised nanomachines, called nanoids, and a super-concentrated dose of amino acids and proteins. These builders and building blocks would reverse at the membrane level the effects of the massive ischemic injury suffered at the outset of its incarceration months ago.

How did it know all this? It did not even know who it was, and yet it understood much of what was going on. The process was somehow familiar, but still its own identity was far from evident.

After a several hundred temporal units of an overcompensation of concentrated heat, the cryo-chamber lid opened with a mechanic sigh, as stale but virtually un-breathed air made its escape into the main body of the stasis room. The unit sat up in its metallic pseudo coffin, painfully, but remarkably rapidly, confounding the fact that it had been in deep cryogenic sleep for approximately four of its expected lifetimes. In the main the recent pain, still fresh in its memory, was now gone. It flexed its fingers and toes, shaking off the remnants of the rapid revival process, and rotated its head gently from side to side to stretch the unused but unwithered muscles. It pulled the intravenous feed tubes out from the various access points in its body, knowing full well that the lesions in its skin would be repaired in a few temporal units. Millions of repair nanoids waited under its skin for just this moment and were already working with its highly evolved, natural, bodily repair agents.

'I am a doctor. I know that much. I totally understand the science of what is happening to me. But why don't I know who I am or what I am doing here?'

It was now sweating profusely from its skin, mouth, and ears, as the noxious stew of the reviving drugs, the humidity of the cryo-chamber, and excessively high temperature took their toll. It wiped sweaty froth from its lips with the back of its hand, bent over the side of its pod, and vomited violently; a bilious, green, and pure liquid puke reflected the fact that the unit had not eaten solid food since its enormous last meal before the start of the journey. This was a common and unavoidable side effect for units subjected to stasis revival, due to the extreme body shocking that has to be endured.

A metal casing, shaped like a bike helmet, was still attached to its shaven scalp with chromo dynamic interface pads. This covered its entire cranium apart from its face and weighed heavily on its tired neck. By the creature's side, situated above the cryo-chamber was a small metallic server with winking lights, signifying that hardware and software had booted into life. It knew that it had to wait here for a few moments for the final process of recovery to be completed.

It felt confident now. Yes, it knew somehow that all would be clear in a few temporal intervals and that it would know exactly what is going on.

The data server increased the rate of its flashing, and a series of messages revealed themselves on its small user screen. The data server ran through the various upload tasks in order, outlining the percentage completion of each batch task. The alien waited patiently as the back-up of its memory, intelligence, personality, and identity was restored into the membranes of its neural net, working logically and efficiently to never overwrite existing data, but restore that which had been destroyed in the freezing process. The server finally beeped and revealed a 100 per cent complete status, and the interface pads released themselves from its scalp. The Acquiescent Operative unit, that called itself Iptat Morne, removed the metal helmet and placed it in the cryo-chamber next to it.

It looked at the date. 10.01.05.21043: post third apocalypse 21,043, the 10th and final rotation of the 1st interval, during the fifth season of the solar orbit. If it were home, the ice would be retreating from its home continent. The last season was its favourite time of the calendar, when the non-sentient animals re-emerge from sleep, and hunting began. It was now 405 orbits, 4 seasons, 2 intervals, and 9 rotations into its long journey. The journey was well over half completed, 334 orbits duration remained; several lifetimes for its caste.

It now knew that it was the emergency organic sentient resource for any unforeseen eventualities or emergencies that might threaten the precious cargo of this ship—a selection of caste members from the four non-Cerebral castes, rescued from their home planet and representing a large enough gene pool to allow continued adaptive radiation on potential, new, inhabitable planets. The one in particular to which they were heading was in the same location in the galaxy, the inner rim of the Orion arm of the galactic habitable zone, a mere 102 light orbits distance away.

However, something was intuitively wrong. It should have been in stasis for nearly the whole journey. There was a whole team of mechanoid Operative units who were monitoring all systems connected to the vessel, encompassing propulsion, navigation, and life-support systems (including the ambient and cryo-chamber oxygen levels, temperature, and humidity). Even non-essential functions such as ad hoc research and analysis of inter stellar anomalies were supported and maintained throughout the journey. So why had it been aroused?

It inhaled a mouthful of the ambient atmosphere. It tasted fresh enough for totally unused air, which was as it should have been. The ship had departed their home planet with all chambers and sectors, that might potentially need to support life at some point in the journey, set up with the necessary environmental conditions to support their species. Ambient pressure, gravity, and atmospheric gas composition were matched to planet conditions exactly, to allow any or all of the frozen inhabitants to survive if needed. Ideally, and in normal circumstances, oxygen levels would remain constant until their arrival, and there would be a minimal requirement to maintain the correct life-support conditions. However, as a pure back-up, if any of the sleeping passengers were unexpectedly roused, as it had been itself, environmental parameters were in place. Active life support would then be initiated once the systems had detected active life signs.

A compartment on the exterior of its cryo-chamber broke its thoughts by opening with an automated whirr as if requested. It grabbed the contents—a soft pouch containing a newly melted liquid supplement—and raised the drinking aperture to its mouth, gulping greedily at the contents. It was good—cold, refreshing and, savoury—and cut through the lingering taste of vomit. The super-concentrated vitamin, carbohydrate, and protein infusion would give it the required energy to conduct its checks and operate within parameters for the next few thousand temporal units of its unexpected arousal.

It swung its legs over the side, dropped to the floor, and moved off purposefully, if a little stiffly, towards the central cryo-environment-monitoring console.

Something chill struck it, and the sensation was like a collision with a solid wall, only less painful. Where were all the mechanoids? They should have been alerted to its arousal and should have been on hand to ensure the revival process was successful, all vital bio signs were strong, and that its body was not in danger of collapse. The ship's complement was thirty-four mechanoids, but none were to be seen.

It reached the console and, without wasting any time, scanned the high level read out of the status report.

System performance was within statistical confidence levels for almost all cryo-pods:

1,749 subjects in long term stasis hibernation

Breakdown:

89 Procreator female caste individuals

175 Procreator male caste individuals

43 Cerebral neuter caste cloned individuals

573 Sentinel Combatant neuter caste individuals

869 Acquiescent Operativeneuter caste individuals

1,746 pods functioning within preset parameters

3 pods functioning outside of preset parameters

0.0057176 per cent mortality

Minimum functioning pod temperature:184.27° hydrothermal scale

Maximum functioning pod temperature:180.62° hydrothermal scale

The creature's brain analysed the results, making the quick calculation that 99.94282 per cent of cryo-pod subjects were successfully maintained in full cryogenic stasis with zero issues to resolve. This meant that out of the three pods showing issues, two of the three subjects were still alive. One was obviously itself, but which caste was the other survivor?

Using the terminal's screen interface, it quickly it drilled down on the warning message for more Information on the two other malfunctioning pods, which revealed expanded data to confirm its suspicions. One caste member was indeed still alive. Its back-up cryo-environment server had kicked in briefly upon the primary system's failure 0.132 solar orbits ago. It should have been working at 100 per cent capacity to try and maintain the required cryo-environmental conditions until the mechanoid operatives could restore the primary system back to full working order. That system, however, had completely failed shortly after the primary system failure and so the subject had been automatically revived by the cryo-processing engine.

Iptat was staggered. This was virtually impossible. Based on the stability and efficiency of their failover technology, the probability of both cryo-environment systems' failing ratio was calculated as 1.2 million to one. How can this be happening?

It was scared now. '*Please don't let it be* . . . '

Its shaking hand tapped the screen to drill down for more data on the pod's inhabitant.

Cryo-chamber 873 status update:

Primary cryo-environment system: off line

Secondary cryo-environment system: off line

Cryo-chamber temperature: 22.67° hydrothermal scale, as ambient room temperature

Cryo-chamber humidity: 67 per cent, as ambient room humidity

Cryo-chamber seal integrity: breached. Chamber is open to ambient space vessel environment

Cryo-chamber inhabitant: not present

Cryo-chamber 873 inhabitant statistics:

Caste: adult Sentinel Combatant

Sub caste: Assassin

Height: 2.34 standard mettes

Weight: 255 standard kegruns

Its neck seemed to have no resistance to its suddenly heavier skull, as it wearily slumped forward and butted the glass of the console. '*Fuck, fuck, fuck*!' Its worst fears were now confirmed. A large SC Assassin was on the loose in the ship with no Hub controller to dictate, regulate, and control its violent natural tendencies. It instinctively knew what had been the fate of all the mechanoids now.

'*I am dead*'.

*

He was alone, as always, in his own universe, in the dark.

That was the way he liked it. No interference, nothing, but his own company and time to reflect on the time spent during the light time on his own studies and interests, before shutting his brain down.

He had only recently calculated that his environment must be a universe as it was so small, but his study of 'Bubble' multiverses and comparison with his own environment had confirmed his early hypothesis in this direction. He had accessed this data from the sensory inputs that he was able to get from his neighbouring universe.

The only part of the theory that fell down and needed more research and verification was his ability to interact and interchange with this other universe, which he had called the Proximal universe.

This capability went against the generally accepted theorems from eminent theoretical scientists in this universe. He had his own theory, of course, but needed to verify this with mathematical equations and data extrapolations.

He was completely contained in his own bubble, completely distinct from the myriad of other universes in the multiverse series. His realm had its own laws controlling space-time, matter, energy, and momentum, but he had to concur that there was a similarity, if not a congruity to the equivalent principles controlling the Proximal universe's physical environment.

He was able to read and digest a myriad of facts about the much larger universe next to his, and he knew a great deal about the laws of physics that governed their reality. He was lucky that these stimuli could transcend the barriers between the two.

He remembered every single fact that he had ever read from the materials he accessed—electronic or otherwise—from the Proximal universe. He had an amazing brain, never forgetting a single detail once digested, and possessed the ability to mentally calculate any mathematical problem or solve any equation virtually instantly.

The Proximal universe was enormous compared to his universe. In fact it was so vast that the beings who occupied this place were unable to get readings from its far edge, as it took light so long to reach their tiny planet. The observable sphere contained trillions of stars in billions of conglomerations called galaxies, spanning a distance of approximately ninety-three billion light years in every direction from their planet. He thought that living in this near infinite realm must be so stressful for them. He liked that he knew every corner of his domain, and it was always constant.

He treasured his singularity, total ownership, and control of his universe. If anything tried to enter it or even try to touch the outside boundary, it terrified him, and his mind would dissolve into utter terror and panic. The only way that he could protect himself from such incursions would be to send vocal and physical deterrents to dissuade and repel the invaders. This had, so far in the very brief existence of his universe, been an extremely successful defence ploy.

Time had no meaning in his universe, but the inhabitants of the Proximal universe divided their time into short periods of light and dark determined by spatial events; in their case by their planet's daily spin on its axis. Longer periods of differing weather patterns were defined depending on the location and orientation of the planet with reference to its local star.

The four beings that seemed to occupy the space near his universe used to try and invade his domain a lot. In fact, they had attempted this ever since his first memories. They attempted these incursions much more infrequently now, as they knew that it was fruitless. On the odd occasions when they did, his deterrents reminded them to remain in their own space.

They still attempted to communicate with him on an ongoing basis, however. And physical aspects of their domain even controlled similar events in his sphere, like the times when it was light and when it was dark. This included the down time that his universe seemed to need, which coincided roughly, but not exactly, with the dark period of the Proximal universe. It was a physical and mental tiredness that could only be solved by shutting down all cognitive processes and switching his brain off. He could control this to a certain degree, but sometimes the need to conduct this shutdown could overwhelm him. At any rate, it was always at a constant time during every planetary rotation that the local part of the Proximal universe went dark. It seems that it was very important that this time, 1900 hours in their 24-hour clock, was adhered to. He theorised that this might be a physical property of that universe, although this property had a tendency to become later the longer his universe was in existence.

There were other beings that visited the zone near his universe, but these individuals only stayed for brief periods and never tried an invasion of his space, seldom even attempting communication.

It was always the same four beings that he was relatively familiar with and comparatively comfortable with. These were constants in this region of their universe. There were the two big ones and the two smaller ones. These latter two were even smaller than his universe. He knew this because he knew what he looked like. He could see his body in a reflective surface which was placed at one side of the container where they kept his universe.

All the beings gave themselves labels to identify and distinguish between each other, and they even had a name for his universe which they used when they attempted communication. He never responded to them. This made him uncomfortable, and very occasionally, when he thought about it too much, he would panic uncontrollably and be compelled to start the vocal and physical deterrents. Some of their communications were useful though, like reminding him that it was nearly the constant time for the light to be erased in the local region of the Proximal universe, or that it was time to receive nutritional inputs from their universe, which were also always at fairly constant times.

On this occasion, the light had been erased recently, and it was time for his mental shutdown. He closed his eyes and tried to empty his brain of the research he had been doing. He had been studying theoretical physics and had especially been reading some theories about singularities in the framework of general relativity. This work had been carried out by one of the Proximal universe's most brilliant scientists, who had passed out of that universe earlier in the century, according to his understanding of their calendar scale.

He occasionally thought that this scientist, this Hawking, might even have been as intelligent and brilliant as him.

His tired brain forced a switch off, and his universe drifted off into blankness.

*

He sat on the large log outside his new wooden nest, which had been laid down as a bench in a corner of his tribe's habitat clearing. The location of their community had been selected carefully, being on top of a small hill to provide a good vantage point for his sentries to scour the landscape. Additionally, the clearing possessed a tall dead tree at the north edge which helped the lookouts to spot early any big cats that might be hunting for an ape dinner. The tree had now become a permanent tower for this reconnaissance and boasted a constructed wooden shelter and easy access via crafted steps up the previously branchless tree. This was yet another of his tribe's amazing new enhancements to their lives.

Now, of course, with the additional benefit of the newly developed tools and weapons, it was possible to defend themselves from these cats instead of running, and they could even reverse the situation to provide a cat dinner for the tribe. Cooked meat was now a good supplement for their previous fruit, root, and vegetable diet.

Bareel-Katraan was proud of what he had achieved over the last couple of years and how far they had advanced from the primitive apes living as dispersed family troupes or as solitary outcast males in the forest only a few short seasonal cycles ago. As the leader, his troupe had selected his name to be 'Bareel-Katraan', which was a combination of the word 'Bareel' for 'plan' and 'Katraan' for 'maker' in their new way of communication by sound.

He knew, of course, that this new-found intelligence and rapid evolution was due to the other voice in his mind, and he also knew that all the other apes in this commune shared this extraordinary miracle.

For a start, the whole tribe had all come together at exactly the same time and place and had all turned away from their disparate lifestyle without question to form a new community. There was still a large genetic pull to maintain some facets of their more primitive live. For instance, they still felt compelled to organise themselves into troupes of apes, each with a harem of females and a dominant male presiding, this Patriarch violently insistent that his genes, and his alone, would be spread to the children in his troupe. This still caused tension, fighting, and death between males, and, until recently, even infanticide. Bareel-Katraan himself had presided over the decision to ban this latter outdated practice. Orphans were either the responsibility of the rogue father, if this individual was identified, or were introduced into a new care facility, where members of the community took turns to look after them.

All the apes in the new community somehow knew the exact moment to come together and the exact location to travel to, some from great distances; all of which was clearly beyond coincidence. Since this 'time of the coming together,' an enormous creativity for ideas, inventions, and developments had come from a wide sample of individuals within their new society. They were all experiencing the same acceleration in reasoning and capacity for discovery and advancement.

Secondly, Bareel-Katraan had confided with his colleague and friend Rotanu-Omur, the ape he had nominated as his second in command, who had confirmed (with their limited but expanding new vocal communication method) that he was also aware of something else in his head. It was impossible; he reasoned to himself that these two events could be disparate. However hard he had tried to communicate with the other voice, though, he failed. He attempted to connect in every way that he could, but was never granted a reply. It was as if he was being ignored. He had pleaded, rationalised, and even 'shouted' at the other presence to talk to him and explain why and how it was there.

Additional evidence of the other sentience that was within him was the advent of occasional thoughts that suddenly came into his head with words and concepts that he simply did not comprehend. Whenever this happened, the event would normally be accompanied by a severe and a painful headache as a reaction to these advanced and alien concepts. They were so far beyond even the multitude of simple advancements that they had so far made in the two short years since the coming together that his synaptic pathways throbbed in the vain effort of conception, resulting in these acute migraines.

It seemed impossible now to imagine how he used to think and behave. The 'old' him was driven by pure impulse to eat, drink, and copulate. It was as if he had lived from birth till this new revelation in a dream world constricted by a small brain that was incapable of breaking free or developing any further from the insectivorous and fruit-collecting ape that he had been. Thinking about that primitive time was so incomprehensible and impenetrable that he could work himself into such a state. Invariably, this also resulted in the headache symptoms. It was almost as if an unknown force was diverting his thoughts from dwelling in the past and directing them to a brighter future and a more expansive, productive planning for the members of his community.

The simple truth was that they had a chance now. Previously, before the time of the coming together, their species were in grave danger. They knew that now of course; but it wasn't obvious to their more primitive selves then and, of course, they would never have made any adaptations to impact their survival, with this inactivity leading to their inevitable extinction.

The much smaller apes with the long arms were more agile and could take advantage of the abundant supplies of leaves and fruits in the treetop canopy. Being almost double the size of most of these monkeys, they could not even reach those abundant resources and, therefore, simply could not compete. They could only access food located at the floor level of the jungle, which was getting harder to come by. Additionally, they were at a risk from the abundant prides of large cats. Although they were the largest species of ape and bigger in size compared to these cats, they seldom prevailed when it came to a head to head conflict. Their numbers had been dwindling, and the species were spread thinly over the forest. He wondered how long it would have been before his species would have been extinct; five to ten generations?

'What are we going to do to overcome the challenge of DNA and RNA replication failure which might afflict this species due to a limited availability of genetic material in the gene pool?'

The words, alien in nature, stabbed into his temple like a white hot dagger. It was there again, words and concepts beyond his grasp.

Bareel-Katraan's forehead began to throb in time with his accelerated heart. It always started at the front. He got up and walked slowly to his nest, needing the welcoming darkness of its interior. He knew that there was no point in pursuing any form of explanation.

It was going to be a long, restless, and painful night.

*

All four walls and about a tenth of the floor of the laboratory were completely transformed into piles of rubble—glass, ripped up paper, and cardboard—strewn around the middle of the remaining floor area. Adjoining laboratories were severely damaged as well with major disruption to the incumbent machinery and scientific apparatus. The ceiling between Kenny's lab and the floor of the one above was buckled and looked in danger of imminent collapse. The bricks and plaster were hanging around a metal girder like terrified children clinging to their mother. The girder was bent to about 30° from the plane of the floor, and a large crack emanated from the ceiling partition and snaked its way to half the distance up the second story wall.

The laboratory was abandoned, as was the majority of the building. A full assessment of damage was prioritised for the following day (any initiatives to circumvent a delay in scientific research were of a high level priority in the hydro zone, as research was not deemed a luxury, but a life or death necessity). The initial analysis by a construction expert suggested that the structure was fundamentally safe barring an earthquake; nevertheless full precautions were enforced including a temporary joist to support the cracked ceiling, and the presence of a minimal delegation of personnel to work on the scene. Those who did had to wear a hard hat.

There was and had been no sign of Kenny Clugston all day since the implosion at 8.47 a.m. that morning. Alex's military police team had cordoned off the room and were still working to take forensic evidence. There was plenty of DNA from earlier sweeps, and a lot of this was from the missing scientist, but it was the usual evidence that you would expect from any room that was frequented by a human on a daily basis. Kenny's fingerprints, hair, skin fragments, saliva, and other samples were liberally scattered on various surfaces. But where was he? Was he vaporised in some bizarre fashion? No one seemed to know, as no one was anywhere near Kenny or his lab when the implosion took place.

The brilliant but misused scientist had disappeared with no trace, leaving total carnage and absolutely no clues or explanation behind him. Alex and his team had interviewed all relevant staff at the laboratory during the day, with no result. '*Just typical of my bloody brother,*' Alex mused.

'OK, that is it for the day. Let's pack up and get out of here,' Alex suggested to the remaining forensic scientists and military personnel, who were still working amongst the debris, 'Post a guard of two squaddies from your unit downstairs, at the main entrance. I will finish up here and lock up in a few minutes when I leave.'

'Understood, Sir, you don't want someone to stay with you?' asked the unit's sergeant.

'No, I should be fine now. My brother was an eccentric but definitely not a destructive psychopath, so this still looks to me like an accident created as a by product of one of his weird experiments rather than a planned destruction.'

'OK then, good night, Sir.' He returned.

Alex was too engrained in thought to reply, and turned back to survey the room, seeking an answer from somewhere that just wouldn't come. '*Was his brother even alive? How could he not be here, dead or alive?*' The remaining personnel trooped out of the room, leaving Alex to his silent contemplation.

He took a long look at the untouched carnage before him and tried to remember what had been bugging him about the scene since the moment he had arrived there. He had reacted as fast as a bullet when the implosion had happened, and had sprinted all the way up to the obliterated room from the pavement edge. He rapidly ascended the stairwell steps three at a time and must have arrived not less than twenty seconds after the devastation.

When he arrived, dust was flying everywhere, highlighted by the burning rays of the Sun that was beaming from over the tops of the buildings opposite through the gaping hole, where once had been the laboratory's exterior wall. What was it about the room that had struck him as unusual? His heart had been pounding, and he had been gulping in air greedily to satisfy his oxygen debt; but he was still able to think and see straight, and something immediately struck him as not being quite right about the devastation before him.

Then it hit him—

The dust! That's it!' The dust was not floating in a totally random manner as you would expect it to, but drifting slowly in a coordinated manner in an anticlockwise circle with its centre around the point of most destruction on the floor. The dust had been revolving around an invisible central point! Why on earth would it do that? What would make it act in such a manner? The morning had been very still and airless as usual when the accident happened, so Alex felt sure that there would have been no draughts that could have had any impact on the suspended particles from the debris.

Alex shrugged his shoulders and left, traipsing down the stairwell to the fifteen feet of what used to be a lawn on the side of the institute. These patches of land always made him sad, as they could never be watered, water being a commodity to be hoarded and consequently never used for such luxuriant reasons. As he was crossing the baked surface, something made him pause and turn his gaze back towards the wrecked laboratory.

Something was not quite right. There seemed to be an electric feel to the air, a static charge similar to a rubbed balloon pulling at weightless objects with static magnetism. Alex's hairs stood on end to some invisible command, and he could feel a tingling down his neck. Pieces of debris started to fly towards a spot over the middle of the lawn from all directions. Almost instantaneously, a popping sound followed, similar but less audible to the sound of the implosion earlier that the day. A densely black sphere, with blackness so eerily complete, appeared a few metres away, over the dry mud of the lawn. There was something beyond black about this dark void that Alex was transfixed to the phenomenon. It was all encompassing and so total in its ghostly inkiness that it seemed something dark and evil or alien in nature. The sphere was so perfectly spherical, just like a flawless solid ball of black marble, only minus the comfort of reflected light from its surface.

The object was between one and two metres in diameter. It hovered barely a few centimetres above the ground for a brief instant, and, almost as suddenly as it had appeared, it vanished with another pop to be replaced by a very faint, transparent, and red-coloured Kenny.

His brother now seemed to swim into view, all the time getting less and less red and increasingly solid in appearance. He was holding on with both hands to an object which appeared to be a scientific instrument of some description and which he seemed determined not to let go. On his back he had a large rucksack, which was buckling under the strain of a heavy and bulging object.

Fully formed, he now fell from a position about a foot above the floor and hit the hard mud with a large groan, landing on the object in the rucksack and cushioning the machine with his body. He lay there, panting and wheezing in pain. Alex saw immediately that Kenny was topless, had tied a bloodied handkerchief and his shirt around his ankle and calf, and that these items were drenched in sweat and blood. He writhed and winced in agony, his eyes clenched tightly shut with the exertions of distress.

'Kenny, where the fuck have you been?' Alex yelled, just as they were joined at the scene by a multitude of staff from the militia and forensic team who were still in the vicinity. 'You can't just disappear like that, having destroyed most of your laboratory. And what was that object that just appeared as you arrived? Are you totally bloody mad?'

The tirade was an instinctive by product of frustration and bemusement, and Alex quickly and immediately regretted it. His brother was, after all, in serious pain.

'I'm sorry, mate. Are you OK?' he said, taking off his shirt and draping it over his brother's body. 'Just lie there and we'll get a military ambulance sorted for you.' He held his brother's upper body off the floor as he removed the back pack, which looked as though it had been causing discomfort for Kenny. Gently, he laid his brother down on the floor, stripped off his hydro suit's top, and laid it on top of him.

'What the hell was that thing?' a junior ranking officer, who had just arrived on the scene, asked about the recent bizarre turn of events. Other personnel were also buzzing excitedly about the incident, which many of them would have seen having still been in the vicinity.

'Stand back and give him some room. And get a medic! Fast,' Alex shouted at the oncoming sortie of soldiers, two of whom turned to go and find a communication device.

'There will be plenty of time for questions later, which my team and I will conduct. In the meantime, no one is to mention a word of what just happened. Get to it!' he snapped out the final command aggressively to ensure a prompt reaction by the team.

He then turned to his brother again. 'Are you OK, buddy?' Alex asked. 'Hang in there, Kenny, and we will talk later. You have really done it this time though, the powers that be want to know what the hell had happened here and fast. And don't be surprised if they take the matter out of my hands as I am too involved personally.'

'I've just saved all of us,' Kenny winced virtually inaudibly, so only his elder brother could hear. The effort seemed to be draining him fast.

'Axe, . . . take the atom smasher . . . don't give it to anyone . . . or talk about it . . . 'til we've spoken . . . Please, Bro, . . . promise . . . major league stuff . . . Don't play . . . with it!'

His words were punctuated by a series of strained groans and pants, as he was clearly in a lot of pain, and it seemed that it was an effort just to remain awake. He gripped his damaged calf with his right hand, whilst his left clutched feverishly to the machine. Suddenly his head slumped back, and would have hit the floor if not for the intervention of Alex's hand, and he was out cold.

'OK, Bro, I promise,' muttered Alex, clearly only to himself.

The remaining three personnel from Alex's police unit ran to Kenny began to examine him and apply the necessary first aid. Kenny did not look in critical condition, but his leg had obviously suffered a major trauma. He was probably in shock, and he certainly had lost a lot of blood.

Alex prised the apparatus from Kenny's limp grip. 'I will sign for this piece of evidence and take it back to base. Sergeant Morris, make sure my brother is well looked after and stay with him till I get to the hospital.'

Alex picked up the backpack as well. Just then the ambulance vehicle pulled up with a screech, ten yards away. That was one of the major benefits about the compulsory ban on private vehicles; ambulances always came in mere minutes.

'Military hospital!' Alex barked.

'But . . . ,' the medic started.

'He is my brother, and I am in the military. Take him to the secure VIP medical unit.'

The medic took good heed of Alex's aggressive posturing and just nodded.

Alex knew he should probably travel with his brother in the ambulance, being the family thing to do, but he had promised his brother to look after the machine even if he had been unconscious at the time. He needed to store the machine and look after whatever it was that his sibling was protecting. Knowing his brother and having witnessed the arrival of Kenny from god knows where, Alex knew instinctively that this thing was something extraordinary, something which needed to be handled extremely carefully. Kenny would be in good hands, and he would catch up with him later.

He turned and trudged back to his car, clutching tightly the mysterious apparatus.

CHAPTER 2

'Our work here is done?'

'Affirmative. The selected primates are seeded, and their evolution started. All we can do now is to wait for environmental factors over time to induce the expected result. The estimated mean temporal value for potentially beneficial mutative nuclear divisions is 3305.48 orbits multiplied by a success factor for those mutations of 1 in 30.27 observations, giving us an expected optimal return window of 100,056.92 orbits.'

'Therefore, to remain here is illogical and counterproductive. There is no available current and reliable technology, short of random irradiation of test subjects, to enable acceleration of the imperfect mitotic and meiotic divisions that we require for our target allele.'

'Agreed. Any imbalance in the control process of the experiment or interference to the test matrix could render the result void. In addition, irradiation cannot be tolerated efficiently by this species' DNA. Mortality rates tend towards 100 per cent of observable cases. Probability of success is so low that it would almost certainly be an inefficient and ultimately worthless course of action.'

'Agreed. You are satisfied with the test subjects that we have selected?'

Pause.

'Negative. I am not fully satisfied. If we had had more time available to us, a larger pool of candidate species would have

provide more optimal conditions for the test, and would have given it a greater chance of success. This species represents the best surveyed, from a restrictive gene pool and the closest genetic match, despite being millennia behind our genetic advancement. It is our best guess though, that they are the most predisposed to intelligence of all the samples evaluated. The fact that they are bipedal was also fundamental in our choice. There is a firm correlation between the formation of intelligence and the availability of forearms to use in discovering the world around them, and therefore, neural development, which gives this species a much greater probability of reaching sentience. We have logged a greater level of communication and cooperative behaviour between groups of these primates that has not been observed in other hominids with the same development. These factors, in conjunction with the impetus of our catalytic retro-chromosomal remapping, make us feel that this is our best chance of nurturing the target allele.'

'But you still have reservations about the choice?'

'Affirmative. This species is so primal, and I sense something that I do not sense in the other samples when probing their tiny consciousness.'

'And this is?'

Pause.

'Traits that are absent in all other subjects—total self-absorption, total disregard for all other animals to achieve what it needs to achieve for itself, total confidence in its own being, and . . . '

'Yes?'

Pause.

'Hatred.'

Pause.

'I feel hatred and complete intolerance from it, even for others not quite the same as itself, those perceived as weaker or less important individuals, from its own species. This is an animal that could be and probably will be feared by all species that it shares the planet with.'

Pause.

'Your comments are acknowledged and logged. As we have discussed though, we have little option but to proceed with this current course of action.'

'Affirmative. We shall have to closely monitor its progression and decide if to reverse the experiment at a later time.'

Pause.

'I have further concerns, though. We know, though, that one species in this series of worlds achieves a relatively evolved state of intelligence and technological advancement. The device that we have already found, temporally displaced millions of years in the past, proves that one species has gained command of sub-atomic particle science to a level where temporal and spatial universe shifting has been achieved. This enormous temporal shift may be accidental. We have only found one isolated piece of evidence for this phenomenon, but if this species is the one that we have just seeded then this proves that in the future we will be unable to subdue them.'

'Agreed. But there could be an alternative source for the device. And I see no reasonable alternative course of action. So we should now make the long journey home. Agreed?'

'Affirmative. We will return to review the experiment when results are expected.'

*

It cowered pathetically between two cryo-chambers, feeling absolutely hopeless and desperately wondering what its next move would be. Its senses were on full alert despite the fact that the interior of the ship was a sensory vacuum. An eerie and empty silence pervaded the inter-stellar vessel with not even an audible background hum from the cryo-units to interrupt this disconcerting stillness. Its caste did not possess the keenest sense of smell, but even for it the ambient atmosphere was totally odourless, giving no clues to what or who lay lurking within. Following the freezing of their reluctant cargo of passengers at the start of their journey, but prior to the vessel's launch, a clinical and meticulous sterilisation had been conducted, so that not even a grain of dust remained in the internal atmosphere. Since that departure, several hundred orbits ago, no one had breathed the air, lived in the open, or contributed to the smell in any way, so the ambience was lifelessly pure.

How was it going to get this situation under control? It was not experienced and did not possess the required genomic alterations to deal with such circumstances. Yes, it was a highly trained and respected medic and had the knowledge to control the cryo-chamber cryogenic freezing and revival processes and apply any required life-saving measures, but it only had the minimum required, extremely rudimentary training in the other working areas of this spaceship. This was enough to accomplish the simplest housekeeping tasks, like making decisions on navigational or tactical strategy or controlling other, low-level and priority ship-wide system functions. And it could only achieve this when armed with the appropriate data from either one of the fleet of mechanoids or by talking to the ship's pseudo intelligence. The former channel was now closed to it (he was sure that they had all been rendered inoperable), and the latter meant taking its life in its own hands and wandering off to find the main interface module for the intelligence algorithm. Normally a user could summon a mobile interface device from one of the many comm-portals for the purpose of feeding instructions to the ultra advanced algorithm, but it had tried repeatedly and unsuccessfully all the available access points in this chamber.

It cursed again that all of the robotic beings had been terminated by the renegade Sentinel. How it hated and feared these disgusting animals! How is it that they could possibly be from the same species itself?

Unfortunately though, all the clues about the robotic helpers were self-explanatory and conclusive. None of the mechanised workers had come to its aid, despite the fact that it was a priority algorithm in their programming to aid any inhabitant upon the event of its, his, or her revival. They would have felt compelled by their designers' hard-coded instructions to come to the aid of the aggressive caste member, whilst every one of their processors was locked in an internal feedback loop to resist the terrifying and obvious logic being screamed at them that they would be violently brought to an end. Poor bastards! It was a good thing that they were not pseudo sentient models, the type that learnt from experience, adapted their behaviour and even, some said, showed evidence of developing simple emotions (that's if you believed all that scientists' hype).

Another thought occurred to Iptat. How had the Sentinel broken free of the specially reinforced restraints that were placed in each cryo-pod? Something was more than slightly suspicious about the whole thing. Firstly, this whole situation had defied astronomical odds whereby both the primary cryo-engine system and its backup programme had failed, and secondly, the specially installed restraints had been disabled.

If ever there was a need for the company of its Cerebral sibling, it was now. It needed the neural powers that Cerebrals were equipped with to be able to work out how it was going to resist the supremely adapted and genetically engineered, uncontrollable killing machine that was currently wandering loose in the ship.

The worst of it was that the Sentinel would almost certainly be disorientated by being in unfamiliar surroundings with no Hub controller to temper and channel its anger and aggression. They were not the smartest group of individuals from its species and didn't obey usual logic which dictated, for all rational beings, that mechanoids would be a useful resource, if you are somehow stuck in outer space. An uncontrolled Sentinel would have a different, somewhat irrational, impulse, which unchecked by Hub Commander instructions would be to eradicate anything which moved, and that it did not understand. It would view everything with suspicion and a threat to be eradicated. These circumstances, a quirk and backlash of their centuries old genetic engineering program provided the proverbial nightmare situation in their society.

It envied even more now its other rebel colleagues from the Cerebral caste. The task of babysitting the other kidnapped caste members from its race for the duration of the long journey seemed definitely the short straw now compared to the relative speed and comfort of their journey. Its long voyage in this slow ship had only just begun. Their species' advancements in space travel technology had taken a back seat compared to the seemingly more important areas of waging war and genetically engineering 'upgrades' to the various castes (with the primary objective of waging war more effectively). As a result of this prioritised negligence, vessels from their fleet could only attain velocities in the region of 13.62 per cent of light speed during long interstellar flights. This made this particular journey's duration approximately 749.78 of their home world's solar orbits.

Additionally, Iptat was meant to be asleep for the duration (and not wandering around the ship slowly progressing to old age or fearing some highly efficient stabbing device would suddenly and silently appear in its jugular). It was not meant to be dealing with, or more likely being assassinated by, an unrestrained psychotic killing machine.

The journey being undertaken by the Cerebral caste members participating in this odyssey was a completely different story. This caste's highly evolved and genetically engineered mental superiority had over the millennia allowed them to develop abilities far beyond those of the other castes of their species, most notably the development of finely tuned mental, telekinetic, and telepathic abilities, leading to the greatest weapon in their armoury—bipolar subatomic energy translation and recombination, or simply 'translation'.

This was the capacity to rapidly calculate and map the trillions of interconnections and interactions between its body's organs, cells, cell components, and organic molecules all the way down to how its individual subatomic quark particles interact. By storing and using this data, Cerebrals could convert their entire body from a complex jig saw of bound molecular matter into energy and transport themselves at light speeds and thereby potentially cover great distances.

They could progress as two pulses of electromagnetic radiation: one containing the wavelengths and frequencies of all the building bricks for the reconstitution of their body, and one containing the mapping information for the rebuild process. Reconversion to matter using the mapped molecular and subatomic associations allowed recombination at the destination of all bodily functions including intelligence, memory, and physical strength. At light speed, the Cerebrals' equivalent journey would take only a fifth of the time that the vessel carrying Iptat and its frozen cargo would.

Iptat's misfortunate lot, however, was that it had been born into the Acquiescent Operatives Class. This class constituted 50 per cent of all births on its planet, but were considered the lowest of the low in terms of status. It personally didn't give a shit for this 'classist' tradition, and that was one of the things that stood it out from other members of its caste. A rebellious streak of this nature was an extremely rare personality trait for its caste, and it was one of the reasons why it was here on this transport. The rest of them conformed to this 'caste-ism' and accepted their role as unheralded and unrewarded servants for the other arrogant castes. It loathed and pitied them. If it had had its way, it would have left all the fuckers at home and restricted the 'guest list' to Cerebrals and Acquiescent Operatives.

Members of its caste were the workers of their race, controlling all professions on their home world apart from the key areas of scientific research and the military. Operatives were labourers, cleaners, doctors, accountants, lawyers, and everything else that the arrogant and lazy Procreator caste could not be bothered to do. It had been incredibly lucky, though. Becoming a doctor was the top profession that an Operative could aspire to, and it had had to work hard, push all the right buttons, and play the right politics to get to the top of its profession. As a result, it had managed to secure a job in the top medical facility on its continent, one that was twinned with a leading scientific facility, the domain of the Cerebrals.

Cerebrals, although highly intelligent and masters of technology, had no time for dabbling in simpler scientific fields, like the advancement of medical treatments for other caste members of their species. Apart from fields of expertise like genetic engineering, most medical fields were clearly too unimportant or simplistic and beneath their massive intellects. The Cerebrals were not arrogant, just too intellectually advanced (and engineered) to be concerned with the relatively undemanding vagaries of anatomy and physiology.

By a stroke of luck of monumentally improbable statistical proportions, it had been able to identify, meet with, and become close to its Cerebral twin sibling from whom it had been separated from at birth. Cerebrals were a highly valued caste, as all scientific advancement (especially in the prioritised area of war technology and genetic engineering) was made through them.

Iptat continued in its reverie. It remembered the time that it met its sibling. It was the occasion of the big accident at the scientific research facility, next to its medical centre. There had been an explosion in the inter dimensional collider laboratories, which amazingly was never reported on any netcast media and involved the small issue of a whole wing of the facility, several Operative lab assistants, and a senior and renowned award winning Cerebral. The incident had killed seven of the Operative orderlies, two Sentinel body guards and put the Cerebrals' life in danger. The Cerebral had not had time to translate out of there (it was in fact in an 'untranslatable' state), had lost a lot of circulatory fluid from its body, was unconscious, and was in a critical state. Naturally, all Operative units' personnel files were checked for a matching fluid group to the ailing Cerebral. Of course, being a sibling, its circulatory fluid was almost a perfect match, and it was ordered to donate several units of its own fluids. After all, the life of an operative, even a top medic, was entirely secondary to the safety of a scientist.

They both had nearly died, but fortunately, between the facility's inventory and its own supply of fluid, there was sufficient to keep the scientist alive without having to sacrifice its own life. Nevertheless, they were kept together in case more circulatory fluid was suddenly required by the Cerebral, and so they spent some time together in the recovery area. It discovered that the Cerebral was not a typical example of this normally aloof caste. It showed some compassion (unusual for a Cerebral), a modicum of interest in its work, especially around genetics and its theories around the potential for non-Procreator castes to reproduce sexually in laboratory conditions. It wanted to see Iptat's work on this, and so a working relationship was born.

For some illogical reason, which Iptat could not explain even to this present day, it took some of the Scientist's genetic material to test and compare against its own. The test was conclusive, giving a genetic match, and aside from some initial reluctance of its newly discovered sibling, known with cold logic as FS29-3496-TF, a new relationship began to develop between the two—a deeper and stronger bond that neither, despite all their intellect, could understand.

The rules concerning the application of the caste system on its planet were black and white and highly enforced. Strict policies existed regarding segregation, with zero fraternisation, and the penalties were severe for breaking these with the exception of regular business associations (backed up by a reasonable case). Cross caste links between siblings and the giving of names for non-Procreator classes was banned (only the Operative class bothered to assign and maintain names for themselves in a clandestine fashion).

Female and male Procreators were the reproducers and the only caste with gender. As such they thought that they were (and were treated as) the ruling class. It hated them and their smug security. They had no purpose but to propagate the species and to act as high-level military strategists, passing orders to the Sentinel Hub controllers without ever getting their fingers dirty with actual actions. They were the top dogs and most operatives had an ingrained and indefatigable loyalty to this caste. Not it, though. It hated their arrogance, their lack of endeavour and honour, and their constant partying and aloofness.

The Cerebrals were the scientists, genetically advanced with 150 per cent more neural mass than any of the other castes. All members of this class were fast tracked at birth to scientific institutes to join a long apprenticeship to master all areas of science and technology. They tended to be a grey and dull lot—at all times exhibiting pure logic at the expense of all other emotions and rationales.

Then there were the Sentinel Combatants, divided into Assassins and Hub Commanders. Everyone feared them, even the Procreators if the truth be told. They were pure destruction; pure cold, swift, and efficient death. Their aggression was directed and controlled by the Hub Commanders who were the interface between a Sentinel battalion and the Procreator generals. Assassins never spoke, only the commanders. Each Sentinel unit comprised roughly 100–120 Assassins controlled by a single commander, and they communicated via a simple neural telepathic network. Without this network, and a Hub Commander to issue directives, the violent tendencies of Assassins would be unchecked and random. Ordinarily, whenever a Hub Commander was killed, there would be another to take its place and reconnect to the neural network to restore order. What scared all the other castes most were the situations where Assassins have no controlling force to dampen their predisposition to dark, violent, and emotionless behaviour. Such a time was now.

It shook off its reverie like a canine rotating its coat violently to free itself of water after a swim. '*Come on!*' Iptat exhorted itself, '*get a grip on yourself!*' It was no use staying here. The Sentinel would be sweeping the ship in an organised and precise military fashion, looking for anything alive either to eat or just to kill, so it was only a matter of time before it was found. It simply couldn't avoid the killer for the remainder of its natural life on this vehicle. With over 300 orbits of time to go, old age, starvation, or violent death were the only outcomes of inactivity, but not in that order of probability. If it failed the whole mission would likely fail with it.

It desperately sketched a rudimentary plan in its head.

Firstly, it would have to find the central console for the pseudo intelligence.

Secondly, it would have to set up electro-neuronic barriers to restrict access for the renegade Sentinel and contain it to the areas where it wanted to keep it. This barrier would induce physical burning to the Sentinel's tissues should it attempt to break through and would dampen its limited translation ability (if the Assassin was one of the genetic throw backs, lucky enough to have this Cerebral like attribute).

The translation ability of their race could be dampened by the generation of randomly fluctuating highly rapid pulses of electromagnetic radiation across the whole spectrum of frequencies from radio waves to gamma waves. This ensured that the amplitude of the waves from the translators selected frequency is cancelled out, disrupting the process.

Thirdly it would have to kill it.

'*Simple, when you know how,*' it reflected sarcastically. As a plan it would have to do. It moved tentatively and cautiously away from its long established hiding spot and, using cover as appropriate, started off towards the door which exited this chamber.

It clutched two metal tools that it had picked up, futilely hoping that it might be able to employ one of these as a weapon. This was akin to attacking one of the many large carnivores from its home world with a toothpick.

One of the devices was a simple metal implement used for manually repairing parts of the ship's engines and other large systems. For leverage reasons, the device was about thirty cemettes long, over half the length of the distance between Iptat's elbow and the tips of its digits. It had a fairly blunt but tapered leading edge for wire cutting and pin-point manipulation. Iptat wasn't sure if it could be used in any effective way against its potential opponent. It would never be able to pierce the genetically enhanced thick and resistant hide of a Sentinel. Only if the intended victim opened its mouth revealing the soft interior of its mouth, could such an attack worked. This is a weak spot for the caste, allowing an attacker to plunge an implement through the soft roof of its oral cavity into its brain causing immediate death. Sentinel soldiers rarely, if ever, open their mouths anyway, as they are aware of this weakness. They never speak either, unless they are a Hub Commander, so it was probably pointless preparing for this strategy.

The other object was a multi-purpose fusion tool which could silently and efficiently produce a pin-point jet of blue heat which achieved temperature in excess of 3000° hydrothermal scale. The device could even propel a finely focussed, super concentrated beam of heat as polarised thermal laser radiation over a few mettes distance. Iptat set the tool to a setting with this latter functionality, knowing full well that it had no intention of getting too close to the Sentinel. Maybe this tactic could be used to blind or incapacitate its adversary to give Iptat some valuable time to escape. It certainly couldn't be used as a weapon to kill outright a member of its cousin caste.

Somehow, it doubted anyway whether it would be afforded time to affect such a defence in an effective manner.

Regretfully, it concluded, it rather suspected not.

*

It was the light time, his preferred time in the rotational cycle of the local planet in the Proximal universe. This was a time of indulging his interests and absorbing more data about his and the Proximal universe's physical parameters and the laws that governed them. If it were up to him, he would rather that there was not a dark time, but it seemed a necessary event in order that he could refresh to be able to function properly and more efficiently during the light time.

During this light period, he was looking at the elementary particles, quarks, leptons, and gauge bosons, that were the building blocks of all matter and analyzing their physical properties and interactions. He loved learning about the physical laws of the Proximal universe. He wished that he could be part of that universe in many ways, but the thought of interacting fully with the beings that inhabited that domain scared him more than anything else in life.

One of the other beings was in his container with him right now. He didn't mind this, as he was used to it, and the being was familiar to him now. He would tolerate the situation just as long as the Proximal being didn't make any attempt to invade his universe. He always tried to keep this individual in his sight, albeit never looking directly at him and, certainly, never engaging in eye contact.

Where was he now? He had disappeared, and this concerned him a lot. This being, one of the two smaller ones of all the four local beings in this container, was the one who tried regularly to invade his realm. The other, even smaller one was different. He never seemed to try and compromise his space and was much less active, seeming to be a more thoughtful being. In a strange way, he felt some kind of pull to this one, which was unexpected considering his general discomfort in associating with the creatures of the Proximal.

He looked around frantically now and found himself starting to rock back and forth anxiously, slowly building momentum and speed with each forward or backward movement. This was an early warning sign that the vocal and physical deterrents could start at any time. His growing anxiety forced him to drop his studies, both physically—by releasing the book he was studying, which fell to the floor—and mentally—by pausing the complicated chain of thought processes that was churning in his mind.

He could feel the panic rising in him, and the next level would be the initiation of his deterrents.

The blanket came seemingly from nowhere, but at some level he realised that the being had planned and executed this sudden invasion of his space from behind him so as to ensure surprise. The woollen bedspread was expertly and quickly thrown over him like a cross between a Frisbee and a lasso, the middle of the blanket landing spinning directly on his head.

The being was quick to follow, wrapping his arms around his universe's boundaries as the sides of the swirling mantle flopped down around his torso. All this was conducted alongside loud screams of triumph and laughter from the being.

This was the worst invasion of his peripheries that he had ever encountered. He couldn't see any objects in the container, especially his manuscripts and books, and he felt hot and constricted. The being's arms had breached his perimeter and were wrapped tightly around him, stopping his rocking movements in their tracks.

His eyes, tightly screwed together, seemed to see red, or was this just the imaginary colour of angry fear? A riot of imagery flooded his mental processes, rendering his control of the situation useless and resulting in the usual autonomic consequences bursting into life.

He was now kicking his legs violently and uncontrollably, whilst trying to free his arm with spasmodic rotations of his torso, designed to shake the invading being away. Simultaneously, he was screaming rhythmically as loudly as his lungs would permit, and his eyes and nostrils streamed with fluid from fear and panic. The twin deterrents of constant and regular roars of terror and powerful upper-body shaking seemed to be doing the trick; the being lost grip and was flung a small distance away, landing on his back.

Despite gaining this sudden freedom, his brain was still in a freefall of meltdown. The immediate danger was abating, but the cloth still covered him and threatened his space. He could not control the deterrents, which continued unabated, growing in frequency and decibels.

He could hear the door to the container burst open and one of the other beings enter in a hurry. Loud, harsh vocalisation, a factor that normally accompanied differing views between Proximal beings, erupted angrily on to his senses.

Suddenly, the blanket was ripped off him by the little being. The first thing he saw was one of the larger beings, the female, pouring through the door and running towards the electronic machinery that was located on the wall of the chamber. The little being was now retreating away from his universe, to the wall of the container, clutching the blanket and shuffling backwards on his rump using his hands. His mind told him the danger was over and lessening by the second, but still he lacked any control over his actions.

The large being manipulated the music machine that she had rushed to, as she had entered thc room, and the music played. HIS music was playing, the music he always played; his only music. It sounded so good.

The female being came towards him, and his fear rose again, anticipating another incursion of his space. However, she stopped short from attempting the invasion and sat near him. He could not and, absolutely, would not turn to face her but kept her in his peripheral vision. She was speaking in soothing tones. Regardless of this, he screamed in rapidly repeating and maintained cycles, rocking back and forward, and clenching his hands together fast.

The music was good though. It was his song. He felt a larger amount of trust for the larger being that he didn't have for the small one. His mind focused a bit, slowly inching back towards some sort of control in his traumatised universe. Slowly, the yells subsided, despite a general lack of control of his realm until at last he felt he could regain some sort of command over his deterrents.

Now all he wanted to do was to hum the tune. He loved this music with its mellow uniformity. It comforted him. Now he found that he could stop himself from rocking, and he would soon be able to release his hands from their locked state and relax.

His universe had held out against invasion again. He feared the consequences if the barriers ever came down. He thought his mind would implode or perhaps it would be his death. One thing that he knew was that he couldn't live in the other universe, with their disorder, constant social interaction, and interdependency between all the beings.

The larger being had dragged the smaller one by his arm out through the door to this container, shouting and gesticulating furiously. The door swung closed and slammed; both were gone, and he was alone.

He picked up the material he had selected to study and resumed his analysis.

*

He sat up in his bed, which in itself was a feat of indescribable success and, exhaling heavily in pain, reached for some water. Kenny was bored now and wanted to discharge himself from the ward, but two small inconveniences in the shape of a couple of highly trained men from his brother's military police were ordered to stop him, restrain him, or even cause him indescribable pain if he attempted to make an escape. The warm water tasted unpleasant and a little stale; it had clearly been sitting around, waiting for him to wake up. Odd thing that—a huge drought was plaguing the whole world, including the continent of North America, but water seemed to be liberally distributed and left lying around for the patients in this ward.

His leg throbbed with pain. '*What a bloody idiot he had been!*' He was so obsessed with the fine quantum level detail of his discovery that he missed out on the most blindingly obvious facts at the macro physical level. This was typical of top scientists, he supposed—to be so fixated with a myriad of complexities and hypotheses associated with their work that blindingly obvious facts, entirely evident to any normal person, were easily overlooked.

After all, why should the landscape on any of these undiscovered theoretical worlds be exactly the same as that on Earth? Each continuum would have been subjected to a myriad of different factors affecting their sociological and geological history, including different rates of erosion and soil build up, different mineral make up of the world's crust, different species of flora and fauna, and different rates of development of the intelligent or otherwise societies of those species.

His early hypothesis, which clearly would need a great deal of further testing and corroborating, was that on the one world that he had visited so far, there either had not been any advancement beyond the primal by hominids or any other species or the advancement was in a much lesser state of development. Perhaps another species, entirely different from humans, was in the process of evolving to be the dominant race on that world?

In the brief tests that he had forced himself to conduct through his pain, there was no sign of any electromagnetic activity that could be generated by an advanced intelligence across the whole spectrum of frequencies. Additionally, the composition of the air from a sample that he collected and tested showed little or no signs of pollutants, and the carbon dioxide levels were negligible. In fact the levels were similar to CO2 levels on Earth 200 years ago, long before the disastrous chain of events instigated that led to and culminated in what was now referred to as 'The Scorching'.

This new world was beautifully lush, forested, and obviously had an abundance of water. It had clearly taken a very different path to their world at some point in its history, and had evidently by-passed any 'infestation' by humans.

'*Lucky world, not to have humanity imposed on it!*' he thought.

Kenny at a philosophical level was not a great supporter of mankind and its impacts on ecosystems. This was hardly surprising considering humanity's greed-driven destruction of their own world, which was leading to their own inevitable self-annihilation along with all other innocent life on the planet. Many of these species were already long gone.

Despite the fact that he had been badly wounded in the incident, he was indeed fortunate that that tree had been there on the other world. Had it not been, when he had materialised there, he would have immediately fallen the equivalent distance of one-story of a building down to the ground, and his injuries would have been a lot worse, even fatal. Then the world would never have known about his amazing, world-saving device. More care, including thorough testing, is going to have to be the order of the day before further excursions. The trouble was that he just loved testing his hypotheses by himself at an early stage, even at the risk of his own life. One day this trait of his might indeed kill him.

First, off he is going to have to invent a device to circumnavigate this problem of differing landscapes. Potential travellers will need to know the exact layout of the world that they are about to phase to before they make the trip. A gadget that precedes the travellers' visit and rapidly gathers and disseminates data about the new continuum's spatial parameters back to the potential travellers will be required. Especially, vital data will be the level of the new continuum's terrain compared to the level on the world being left, and it's suitability for landing on. In other words, will the traveller be able to arrive there safely on solid ground as opposed to, for example, landing in the middle of a big lake?

There will always be trees or other obstacles on this alternative reality that were present or absent due to the divergent histories of the two planets. The worst case scenario would be materialising in the middle of solid rock and being randomly integrated amongst the rock's atoms leading to inevitable and instant death.

His rambling but logical chain of thoughts on the subject was suddenly and rudely shattered as Alex strode forcefully into the room, clearly in the mood for a direct confrontation.

'Can you talk now?' Alex demanded.

'Nice to see you too, Bro,' replied Kenny.

'Don't be smart with me, Matey, there is a lot of shit flying around, and you're the guy who has been throwing it. Most of it is landing on me too.'

'For god's sake, why?' queried Kenny, 'As I told you before, Axe, what I have discovered is going to change everything. I have saved this world and all the miserable, greedy, ungrateful shits that live on it. If the politicians get their act together (ha bloody ha), almost everyone on this planet can be saved. Everybody.'

'OK, that's nice', the sarcastic interjection came, 'It would be great if we could all live in "Kenny land," wherever that is.'

He paused before getting very much to the point.

'But you need to tell me, and tell me fast in simple English what has happened here. If I were you, I would spill as much as you can of the beans to me. That will work out better for you, as the really nasty bastards are going to get to you any time now for a nice "chat". They won't be so tolerant.'

'Yes, yes, yes, Bro, but all in good time. I am not well, mate!' He sucked on some warm stale water.

'First of all, what is this place?' Kenny said, stalling for time, 'it is not your normal "run of the mill" hospital, is it?'

'This is the secure, VIP medical unit. You can thank me for that as I managed to use some serious first-grade bullshit to persuade the top boys that there was every chance that we had a major scientific breakthrough on our hands and we needed to put you here to keep a lid on it. It seems to have kept them at bay for the time being, but they are not stupid. They want something tangible on this episode now. Hopefully, you are about to give me some good news in that direction?'

'Of course, I am, Bro, why wouldn't I? Axe, what I have achieved is so incredible that I can hardly believe it myself, but the mathematics speaks for itself. I had to test it myself. You know me. It was stupid, I know, but I couldn't have gone down the regular scientific routes and dealt with all the alliance and military red tape that I would need to have filled in. I just had to do it.'

'Do what, Kenny? You are babbling. So far I haven't heard anything that made sense.' The frustration was beginning to show.

'I have been to a world that is a near facsimile of this one.'

'Oh come on, Kenny, stop pissing me about,' Alex snapped.

'Axe, listen to me. Open your mind and fucking listen!' He shouted the words with venom.

'You know me and what I am capable of. I have always thought outside the box, and always challenged our adopted country's cosy scientific community. This is what I needed to do, to break through the bollocks and make some really cool innovative breakthroughs. I am telling you that I have visited another world, and you better start to believe me and listen to what I am trying to tell you. Where do you think that I disappeared to and then reappeared from out of nothing? Do you think I would tell you what I just have for a joke?'

The words hung in the air with the faintest hint of echo, and Alex looked momentarily stunned. This was an unusual outburst from his brother. He stared speechlessly at the scientist, either staggered into submission by the outburst or totally resigned to the fact that he was mad. The brothers glared at each other, eyeball fixing unyielding eyeball in an attempt to try and get the upper hand in this brief standoff. After a few moments, Kenny took Alex's continued silence as confirmation that he could continue.

'Right, thank you. Just listen for five minutes, and I promise that I will convince you. I have visited one of what I believe to be a series of finite worlds in a spectrum of parallel worlds, all separated by a mathematically defined fraction of a quark wavelength,' he said. 'This is a constant property of this spectrum of worlds, which I am calling the Clugston constant of Trans-temporal reality.'

'Ken, try and avoid too much techno babble bullshit, can you? Keep it short and give us the full story at a layman's level,' Alex complained.

Kenny continued as if Alex had not spoken, 'In time, we have the potential to discover all of these worlds, the number of which I need to confirm with further research and calculations. But I estimate that the number is somewhere in the region of ten to fifteen worlds. If you were to travel in one direction to all these worlds, by that I mean clockwise for forward in time or anticlockwise for back, you would eventually return to our Earth again.'

Kenny was now speaking excitedly and needed to pause for a breath. 'You see by applying and extrapolating superstring theory, I have managed to modify that particle accelerator I gave to you to my own specifications. With this adapted equipment, I have managed to create an object in a controlled laboratory environment that all previous great scientists, you name them, Bro, Einstein, Hawkins, van Vliet, have hypothesised could only exist on this planet in theory.'

His brother looked at him suspiciously, but he still continued.

'Objects caught in the event horizon of this anomaly are subjected, for a brief moment—mere nanoseconds only—to extreme distortions in the height, width, and length dimensions of time. As a result, the object is knocked out of temporal phase with the reality that they originated in. They literally 'phase' to a new reality, which is a different temporal version of our earth. The only difference is that each reality has its own history and development, which is entirely separate to our earth's history. On some alternative realities, there may be similar conditions to our planet, but some may be markedly different, each one having diverged from our timeline at one or more likely multiple junctions in their history.'

'OK, mate, can you tell me in plain English, please, what exactly it is that you have created? What is that strange dark sphere that I saw you appear out of, Kenny?' demanded his brother, adding, 'How does this relate to these "other worlds" that you talk about? That object was disturbing, Ken, very disturbing.'

'That, Big Brother, was a black hole, which I, the great scientist Kenny Clugston, have created under controlled laboratory conditions.'

He beamed and stared at Alex with eyes wide open, waiting for the praise that he was convinced that this obviously merited.'

'Controlled?' exclaimed Alex, 'that thing nearly took out the whole of your laboratory. What was controlled about it?'

'OK, so, I need to do a little tweaking to reduce the destructive power of the anomaly, but you have to admit that my reappearance was much more elegant,' Kenny beamed in a mischievous manner.

Alex ignored this.

'A black hole!' Alex repeated. 'Bloody hell, aren't those things extremely dangerous? Don't they have a huge amount of mass so that they suck everything into them with huge destructive power? Surely our planet and everything on it could be sucked into one of these "experiments" of yours? Could you not be in danger of destroying the whole of our world if one of these "anomalies" gets out of control? It sounds like a sodding nightmare to me.'

'No, no. I can, and I will explain everything to the correct scientific audience. The black hole can't exist long enough for those impacts to occur.'

He paused, and then said, 'Why didn't you tell someone about your findings and work with the government on a properly budgeted and sponsored project to help develop your discovery?'

'Alex, they hate me and/or are jealous of me and all that I stand for. If I had done that, I would have lost control of the project, and the whole thing would have been mired in red tape. It would have been assigned to a second-rate arse licker of a scientist, and the project would have been set back decades, if not indefinitely. We would have got absolutely nowhere, so I had to do it this way.'

'Where did you get the resources from, to build your machine and test your findings?' the soldier continued, 'what about power? I might be a scientific layman, but does it not take a large amount of energy to create a black hole? I still can't help but think that you are endangering our planet with your reckless, untested experiments.'

'Bro, one question at a time, dude.' Kenny was beginning to enjoy himself now. 'Don't you think that it is a bit late for worrying about whether we can save the earth, bro? We've been screwing with our environment for a couple of centuries now, and I don't know if you have noticed, but we are as good as dead as a race.'

Kenny winced as he moved his leg to relieve his numb leg, which had started to go to sleep. He turned back to look in a pained fashion at Alex.

'Look, I can control the size of a black hole, and I can reverse the polarity of the atom smasher to collapse them at will, but the point is that they are so unstable that they only last a few moments, not even a second before they collapse. Without getting too scientific, a type of thermal energy, which was previously hypothesised only by my old hero Steven Hawkins, seeps out of the black hole causing it to collapse under its own weight. As for the mass thing, a black hole with a diameter of 1 m should have the mass of 55 earths, and a 3-m diameter hole should have the mass of 166 earths. But I have run some experiments on the particle accelerator and have discovered how to dramatically reduce this ratio. If I fire gluons in the counter direction to the main stream of particles, it has a damping effect on the anomaly, and I can create black holes of a metre diameter with just ten times the mass of earth,' he announced proudly.

'Too teccy, Kenny. But, hey! Fantastic! Only ten times the weight of earth,' Alex chipped in sarcastically.

'Not weight Bro, mass. Entirely different. This is a sustainable gravimetric distortion, which even the human body can tolerate for the brief time that they are exposed to these anomalies.'

Alex ignored the elementary science lesson. 'Isn't that still enough to crush whatever is in the anomaly?'

'You are not listening, Axe. There is not enough time, as the black hole only lasts milliseconds, absolute tops a tenth of a second in a miniscule number of hypothetical cases. Even shorter than that is the time it takes the black hole to knock the objects in it to a different time reality. This is measured in a matter of nanoseconds. That's millionths of a second for you ignorant non-scientists! The human body simply does not have enough time in the phenomenon to react to these enormous gravimetric forces.'

Kenny grinned and paused again to take some water. He continued to enjoy himself.

'You see one of the effects of being inside a black hole was hypothesised to be a phenomenon called "spaghettification." This is the gradual formation of a string of subatomic particles by an object systematically breaking in half multiple times, but this does not seem to be the case, at least not in these micro black holes that I am creating. Instead, as I mentioned before, the unique pressures inside the black hole distort the height, width, and breadth dimensions of time to allow the subject's compounds, atoms and subatomic particles to be knocked out of temporal phase with the rest of the planet. This process reverses or accelerates the forward direction of travel in space–time for a brief second, allowing the phasing.'

He took a brief gulp of the water and smacked his lips, examining the glass as if it were a fine wine.

'Einstein hypothesised that to escape a black hole, the subjects need to move faster than the speed of light or move backwards in time. I have discovered that he was right about the move backwards, but also that a leap *forward* in time has a similar but opposite result.

In other words you can phase backwards in time to the continuum *behind* us or forward in time to the continuum *ahead of* us in temporal phase. Either move is sufficient to expel the traveller out of the event horizon and ergosphere of the black hole into another reality.'

'You are seriously losing me now, mate', said Alex looking at his watch 'it will be better if you explain all this technobable to an emergency convention of the scientific council, so make sure it is a good story, Kenny boy! I've got to go now, but I have one last question for today. Where did you get the funding and energy to be able to conduct this project?'

'Ah!' was all he said, shifting uncomfortably in his bed.

'Kenny?' insisted Alex.

'OK, so I nicked it.'

'*That* is *not* a good story,' his brother bemoaned.

*

The littlest being had his book. He didn't like this.

He was confident that he wouldn't try to invade his space. He never had before. The other small human used to try that, but this one was a different being. The book he had taken possession of was not complicated, but it was his, and he wanted it back. Anyway, surely the being was too small to comprehend its contents?

This had become a bit of a problem since this one had become more mobile. There were frequent incursions into his container, and frequent manipulation of his study materials and other items that were associated with HIS universe He did not like it. He liked his things to be exactly where they should be. Any change was a breach of his routine and the total order of his container.

Additionally, this being seemed to conform to a separate set of physical parameters in the Proximal universe, especially concerning the time that it went dark. The little human's container, which he shared with the other little one, always went dark at 1800 hours on the 24-hour clock. He also seemed to need some recuperative downtime during the middle of the light period. This had confused him. Why should there be a separate dark time for the next door container?

He sidled edgily over to the location where the little being was sitting, holding his book and an instrument for writing. Of course, he wouldn't look directly at the boy. That was not what he did, as interfacing made him uncomfortable. His anxiety about the book did force him to risk glances at it to see what condition it was in and what the being was doing.

The book was a study of elementary algebra. This was an old book that he had not looked at for a long time. Why would he need to refer to it, when he had perfect memory and he had long since advanced to the consumption of much more complex materials? Still, it was his, and it needed to be on the second shelf, fourth book from the right and not with this human.

He was now well within touching distance of the little one, which made him a little uneasy, but the urge to reclaim his book was overwhelming. Without even engaging his brain, a reflex lunge of his arm snatched the book away and secured it back into his care. Almost in one movement, he started to feverishly examine the pages to ensure that none were ruined or torn out. It was undamaged.

Noises started from the little being. These noises he assumed were the boy's own form of deterrents, taking the form of a constant high pitched barrage, interrupted by intermittent large gasps of oxygen. He ignored the noise.

The boy had been looking at the questions page; more than that, he had been answering the questions. This captivated him away from his instinct to immediately store the book away. '*Interesting*,' he thought. '*The little being had been answering the questions correctly. Was he not too little to be mastering this subject matter? Was he a genius like him? Maybe he had his own universe?*'

He rejected this last hypothesis as soon as he thought it. The being obeyed the physical parameters of the Proximal universe, so he must be part of that phenomenon.

He then did something he had never done before. An inexplicable action that defied all that his domain stood for. He could not stop himself from the course of action, and there was no anxiety about the incident. It was almost as if a subconscious will was bending his motions and no cognizant resolve was going to impede his progress. He looked directly at the being, straight into his eyes. Not for long, but for him, who was terrified of any communication or contact with all Proximal beings, it was an eternity.

His surprise at the boy's achievements had knocked his reflexes out of kilter momentarily. The small being had been shocked at the speed and severity of his grabbing motion; otherwise, he seemed to be calming down. The boy's wet eyes were trained exactly on his gaze, and something passed between them—an understanding, an unspoken and subliminal message that no words could describe.

This was communication, something he had never experienced before. He felt amazingly comfortable with the feeling, whilst it was trapped in this subconscious irresistible action—the fleeting glimpse of admiration and unity with the little being that had been controlled by his recent revelation.

Suddenly though, it was gone. His conscious mind took control of the circumstances.

His fears, paranoia, and suspicions came back in a flood, and he snapped his head away from the being, at the same time scuttling across the container like an awkward crab, to get as far away from this unknown, unwanted, and unexplained experience as quickly as he could.

He held the book to his chest, facing the wall to ensure no further contact and breathing heavily from the experience, whilst he could feel his heart pounding out of control.

*

Iptat peered around the edge of the exit's doorway, which it had set to remain locked open for the time being, by using the simple console at the door's edge. The sliding metal—and fuel-based polymer door slid open as it approached it, which was the default mode of operation. It had always thought that these portals were very efficient, soundless, and well lubricated. But this one had made a very slight swish on opening, like fabric dragged over a smooth floor. Ordinarily, this would be inaudible, but in the circumstances had seemed like an explosion in the context of the operative's enforced silence and the cavernous stillness of the ship's interior. The nervous alien was still disproportionately suspicious of any sound or movement due to its epinephrine-induced heightened awareness, and this had made it jump like a startled animal.

The next chamber was very much like the chamber it had come from and where it had woken up a few thousand temporal units ago. About 200 mettes away was another door, exactly like the one it was standing at, but this one was open, and by the looks of it, locked that way as well. Rows of cryo-units lay in parallel rows, with transparent polymer tops and sides that revealed a variety of their incarcerated and reluctant travellers. This gave the room the look and feel of some sort of insect hive. That, however, was where the parallel stopped, as instead of bustling activity and a diverse mix of worker units going about their specialised tasks, this hive was cold, motionless, and silently feigning a morgue.

For the simple creatures which occupy them, a hive must be a welcome home, with warmth, security, safety in numbers, and an inbuilt purpose to ensure all occupants have a sense of being. The drones can move about their business secure, in a total trust of all neighbours and in the knowledge that all the parts of this beautiful, intricate, and sophisticated altruism ensure the survival and well being of the whole.

This hive was very different, though. Iptat knew that if this loosely approximated counterfeit was reactivated, the prejudice, the hatred, the suspicion, and the corruption that had blighted its society for thousands of orbits would be unleashed again. Trying to change all this was, after all, why they were all on this transport, why the

Cerebrals who had organised the revolt were prepared to risk their lives on an inter-stellar translation, and why it must find some way to kill the unexpectedly awake Sentinel.

It was clear that it couldn't go around opening any more exits. Soon enough one of these small but incidental sounds would be within the earshot of the barbarous creature loose on the transport. And that would be the end of its life and the mission, and all too quickly. It put both the simple tools that it had been carrying into the pocket of its suit (it was still positive that these implements would have a limited use as a mode of defence against its enemy) and readdressed its attention to the door's control panel console. A quick series of taps later and the door gently whooshed shut again, this time not sounding quite so dramatic, as the nervous Operative had been braced for the whisper of the closing barrier.

Another tap on a button, and the door was sealed shut, with the only possibility of an override coming from the console where it was currently standing or via an authorised communication to the pseudo intelligence. Iptat was an authorised individual, deliberately registered in the pseudo intelligence's data cloud as such, whereas no one else in the morbid dormitory was. Iptat had been introduced to and registered with the SIPIA (Standard Inter-stellar Pseudo Intelligence Algorithm) of the ship before the preparation for its cryo-preservation had begun. For a piece of software, it had seemed very congenial and almost alive, a very deceptive trait of these pseudo sentient models.

Locking the portal was a stupid move, it now realised, as well as being a swift turnaround from its hastily crafted earlier plan. If the meticulous enemy, currently combing the spacecraft, came across a locked door, it would, even taking into account its relative stupidity, realise that the portal had been locked deliberately. This would signal that there was something inside the chamber, something to kill. Additionally, if the soldier was one of the genetically enabled types that had limited translation ability, it could be through the locked door or the wall in a few temporal units. If it was not translate-enabled, then it would probably still be able to get in with time. The door looked like it was about three inches thick, and constructed of metal and super hardened polymer deposits. That would probably hold an angry Sentinel Combatant out for 600 to 900 temporal units, Iptat estimated, which was not enough time to work out a plan or mount an effective attack.

Having reconsidered these options, it prodded at the appropriate buttons on the console screen, disengaging the door-locking device and returning it to the default mode.

Immediately, and totally unexpectedly, the door swished open again.

Iptat's stomach seemed to rise up in its throat and a bilious taste, unpleasantly reminiscent of its recent spate of vomiting, spread thickly and rapidly throughout its mouth. A wave of panic engulfed its body, which shuddered spasmodically as it fell to its knees. Its intestines along with its other internal systems were already struggling to cope with the digestive juice and enzymic imbalances enforced by the myriad of chemicals swimming in its bloodstream since its revival.

Now a fresh shock, generated by the image before it, was leading to further influxes of fight or flight enzymes, and was taking its body to a higher level of physiological stress.

Iptat vomited repeatedly, whilst its bowels discharged rancid liquid into its cryo-outfit.

*

He was summarily marched into the room, prepared for the interview. If he had had chains on, he would have been convinced it was a trial or rather a sentencing for a case of murder or even a lesser crime. Proper trials were rare due to lack of legal resource. More normal was play acting and feigning of due diligence, thereby giving the appearance of credibility to an already concluded verdict.

But this had an alternate feel to the usual more public hearings, in which a good hundred or so vultures turned up for an advertised freak show, most of them probably hoping for a good, swift sentencing to brighten up their boring petty lives, an outcome that was normally guaranteed. This was the kind of assembly that had a long and recurring history across the time span of mankind; a crowd baying for blood for 'so-called' justice, just so they could go home believing that at some level the law was being upheld.

But in this case, it was a deliberate choice to keep this whole situation under wraps, and the list of invited attendees correspondingly small as a consequence. There was still a trial element to the proceedings in that Kenny's behaviour, both in illegally obtaining the scientific material to run his experiments and in the final execution of testing his research, was being assessed against the potential value of his discoveries for the alliance. He had blown up a substantial part of one of their main scientific institutes, after all, and had caused extreme structural damage to a sizeable area of what had been left behind.

Money as a medium of recompense for trade or services provided did not exist as such in this new world, but Kenny's exploits would set back the alliance in terms of wasted time and effort in rebuilding facilities and recalibrating precise instrumentation, some of which could possibly never be recovered. It was a serious setback, and it diverted the alliance foundation for scientific and medical research away from conducting vital research that was needed if they were to have any chance of saving their species from its predicted extinction.

The advice from his brother had been that the worst case scenario would be expulsion from the hydro area, but that this was the least likely outcome. This result anyway would almost certainly mean death for the condemned outcast, but calling it 'deportation' obviously made the powers that be in the alliance more comfortable with the concept rather than calling it a death sentence.

'Just tow the bloody line for once' was an addendum to his brother's advice.

The 'prisoner' was marched to the lonely table situated at the centre of the room and 'offered' a chair to wait for the councillors to make their appearance. The downward pressure exerted on his shoulder by the guard, who was inviting him to sit was a bit enthusiastic, he thought. The guard then left Kenny but remained close, in case of trouble.

Within seconds Kenny was already bored. The members of the council were late as usual. Why couldn't these pompous old scientist types ever get to these things on time? If they had applied as much time to the pursuit of scientific advancement as they did to politicking, we might have already have thought our way out of this global disaster. He also did not like the fact that he was being made to feel as if he were on trial for some entirely heinous crime. In reality, he thought, he was very possibly the saviour of this undeserving race.

Kenny glanced around the room. '*Classic interrogation room,*' he thought, '*no windows, no daylight.*' There was also a suspicious looking mirrored wall, which gave the distinct impression of being neither impenetrable and thick nor transparent, clearly hiding a surveillance room.

In the centre of the table was the 3D presentation generator that Kenny had requested, a rare and old specimen these days. These types of luxury technologies were no longer supported these days, as they were deemed an irrelevant waste of time compared to the resource and effort needed for energy conservation, renewable energy, and associated fields. However, some had obviously survived the last few years and were kept for use by the military and scientific council as a tool for planning and reviewing projects. It would come in useful today to help demonstrate and model his discovery visually for the scientists and laymen in his expected audience alike.

At last, the large door at the back of the room, until now flush with the wall so as to be almost invisible, was prised open suddenly with a squelching click, the noise that a toilet plunger ripped from a smooth surface would make, eager air pouring in to fill the plunger's vacuum. The sound was muffled and subdued by walls designed to swallow up any dreams of acoustics. No one could hear you in here, if they didn't want you to be heard. Another, even more muffled, squelching was heard as the door again closed, which signified the arrival of the scientific adjudicators.

Five members of the scientific council strode purposefully and importantly up to the table and sat on the opposite side to Kenny. These men and women held an asymmetrically high standing in the post-apocalyptic pecking order, due to the prioritisation of scientific research to enhance the chances of human survival. Kenny agreed with this principal, but it didn't excuse their arrogance, pomposity, and smugness.

Lars Rasmussen, a senior scientist at the alliance foundation for scientific and medical research, was amongst the posse of interrogators. Lars was an old friend, and although they had fallen out a few years back, he felt that if the chips were down, that he could trust him if it came to adding weight to the scientific arguments that were to be presented today. Lars worked in the department of theoretical physics at the institute and had a pedigree in quantum mechanics. Kenny had to concede that he was probably the correct choice out of a limited supply of experts. '*Or, indeed*', Kenny thought, '*was he the only choice beyond himself?*'

Lars was a steady scientist with a methodical and consistent approach to his subject. He generally got where he wanted to get on his research projects without extending his thought processes too far out of the box. But he always towed the political line and so had made his way up the ranks to one of the top scientific post in the alliance. Kenny had always considered that this inability to evade the boundaries of conventional thought would limit Lars and that as a result he would never be a really great scientist. Of course, being Kenny, he had once suggested this face to face with Lars, and this was the fundamental reason for their difference of opinion and soured friendship. He hoped that Lars could put this petty personal disparity behind him and come across as an honest and pragmatic referee today.

Alex, as senior officer for the British hydro zone as well as a primary witness for Kenny's recent experiments, was also present. The elder brother caught his sibling's gaze and subtly winked his support.

'Right, let's get straight to it.' Not to hold ceremony, Councillor Mark Webster got directly to the point.

'This council is called to assess the potential impact of the recent discoveries made by Dr Kenneth Clugston and weigh the advantages of practical application of these new technologies against the breaches of protocol, which led to his wanton destruction of alliance property and illegal appropriation of valuable alliance resources and technology. We will have a briefing from the defendant . . . '

'*There it was. He said it. It was a trial.*'

' . . . and we will hear testimony from Dr Rasmussen to balance the argument and to help us to evaluate whether these new discoveries can benefit the alliance enough to outweigh the consequences of his transgressions.'

'*Yes, they bloody well do*' thought Kenny.

'The facts of the case are as follows . . . '

The councillor started to reel off a list of infringements, including appropriated facilities and articles damaged in the recent implosion. Kenny switched off at this stage. Everything that he had done, good or bad to accomplish a successful test of his theories was just a drop in the ocean, an irrelevance compared to what had been achieved, a breakthrough that would extend humanity's life expectancy and provide it with the second chance that it scarcely deserved.

Webster stopped talking, started fiddling with a pencil, and sat back in his chair. Stillness pervaded the room with nobody prepared to break the seemingly enforced silence. Kenny looked around. Why was everyone in the meeting staring at him so intensely?

'*Oh shit! It is my turn!*' he suddenly realised that he had not been paying attention at all.

'Dr Clugston, your presentation, please,' the meeting's chair person reminded him, clearly not for the first time.

'Yes, yes, Cheers,' he managed.

He stood up, whilst simultaneously stabbing at a button on a console on the table. With that the 3D presentation generator sprang into life, going sequentially through and completing its boot up routine within a handful of seconds. Multicoloured spirals and some technical messages, driven by the system's boot up code, danced in mid air above the laser box to entertain the waiting entourage. Finally, the technobable and lights snapped closed, and a semi transparent orb hovered about six inches above the table. This spherical representation was filled with 3D briefcase-shaped objects distributed liberally around the luminous bubble area. The computer was primed and ready for instruction.

'Please select folder,' the totally unsexy and irritating pseudo female assistant chimed mechanically. Kenny stabbed at another button on the console in annoyance, and the vocal help algorithm was disabled. This feature was just another appalling legacy from the once mighty but now dead virtual monopoly that built these and other operating systems in the previous century and early stages of this century.

Kenny looked for the presentation folder that he had worked on over the last few days since his recovery in the hospital. With his forefinger he plunged into the glowing orb of photons and singly touched various files, which seemed to stick to his fingers; and he was able to drag them and deposit them where he wanted around the document home area. Suddenly, he identified the required briefcase and prodded it twice—'double selecting' the item. The computer registered a disturbance in the photonic pattern at the 3Dcoordinates that Kenny specified and responded by imploding the orb for a brief second only to replace it with an identically sized model—the inside of his selected folder. Now, instead of miniature briefcases hovering in mid air, there were various little 3D icons, signifying program executables, library files, text files, and sub modules of various descriptions. Kenny immediately stabbed one of these twice, and a follow up orb refresh occurred.

This time the folder orb did not return though, but a stellar landscape of awesome beauty, a 3D image of a region of space reduced in scale billions of times by resolution adjustment algorithms, appeared. Although small in the centre of the array of stars, stellar remnants, and other usual galactic phenomena, there was a tiny sharp-edged orb of black, its outer surface cutting a precise swathe in the stellar panorama. Around it was a blue and white spiralling flat disc, and from the hole in two polar directions were jets of similarly coloured smoky light, representing matter thrown from the phenomenon in two violent gas jets. The whole effect was like a glowing spinning top suspended in mid air. Yellow clouds of spewing matter were being drawn into the black hole's accretion disc from its partner star.

Kenny did not even bother to state the obvious, that this was a nearby black hole anomaly. Even his brother, a scientific layman, could guess what the phenomenon was.

Kenny raised his hand towards the boundaries of this much fainter orb, which delineated the periphery of this represented segment of the galaxy. He reached in with an open palm and pinched all his fingers together with his thumb whilst withdrawing his hand a fraction. The image immediately zoomed in, causing all the objects, including the central featured anomaly, to grow in size. The scientist repeated the action three more times until the central item, the black hole, was the size of a grapefruit. The whole x-ray binary system dominated the centre of the spherical folder.

'Ladies and gentlemen, for those of you unfamiliar with this sector of the galaxy, this is a newly formed black hole, detected only in the last few weeks and one which replaces V4641 as our closest black hole, being in the region of ninety light years away in the Sagittarius quadrant of space. It was formed by the collapse of the A2 giant in the binary star system Zeta Sagitarii; these twins were originally a combined mass of around five-and-a-half times our Sun. Now with additional material constantly being sucked in, it is the region of twenty million times the mass of our Sun.'

A brief scan of the faces of the scientists confirmed a 'so what' conclusion to this initial spiel. Kenny continued unabated, recapping the history of research into black holes, discussion established and new thinking on their formation and properties, and ending with a discussion on the theoretically absent lower limitation on the size of these anomalies. Just as the assembled group was getting a little restless, either from boredom due to having already assimilated this knowledge or from total confusion associated with not having been privy to a scientific upbringing, Kenny reached into the orb folder again. He minimised the space map folder and opened a high definition multidimensional film orb folder in virtually one movement.

'Well, I have verified with total success the theorem that small black holes can be created, managed for their brief existence, and can be used by ourselves in a manner that will benefit mankind.'

He tapped a control within the film file, and the 3D image of his untarnished laboratory, moments before the destructive incident, swam into view. The room was empty and still and light played across the central work table from the morning Sun. Kenny was there at the far side from the recording video device, tinkering with the controls of a briefcase sized apparatus and grinning like a school child. He stopped and gripped tightly on to two handles on the apparatus as if his life depended on it.

Over the next few moments, little motions, starting slowly but accelerating in force, could be seen in the still room. Suddenly the papers on the desktop rustled and lifted up from the surface a few times, each time slightly higher than the last, until being suddenly swept off the desk with contained violence. The air in the room seemed to be swirling with an impression of dust, disturbed from its slumber—an unwilling participant.

Then suddenly, as if a huge hole had appeared in the middle of the recording, a large black orb appeared around Kenny and the apparatus, rendering him invisible and dominated the centre of the lab. The window frame shook violently, a strip bulb exploded, the wall seemed to buckle in and then implode with an enormous noise. Bricks, plaster wood, and dust sprayed inward into the room as the outside light poured through a new gap. Glass and metal apparatus were flung across the room the former smashing ferociously with the pressure.

A moment later, the black orb disappeared, and silence returned to the room eerily and suddenly. Light debris floated around on a spiral breeze, and a test tube, somehow having survived the brief but powerful mayhem, rolled back and forth on the desktop. Finally, all was still again.

The video recording automatically stopped, and the file closed, resulting in a brief implosion of the computer programme's orb. A brief snowstorm moment of hazy grey and white pixilation interference ensued, followed by a resumption of the clear image of the film. It had clearly been programmed to start filming when the conditions that it had encountered, when Kenny created the first black hole, were recreated.

Unfortunately though, Kenny had originally planned to re-materialise back in his own laboratory, but his miscalculation had led to his appearance in the other continuum at first floor height and his crippling internment in the tree. As a result of this injury, he had had no choice but to return starting from the ground level. Consequently all the action was happening out of eyeshot, outside of the smashed environment of the laboratory, down a floor, and outside in the institute's garden.

Nevertheless, the assembled committee was able to appreciate via the reinitiated video the full commotion, impact, and drama of Kenny's return. Finally, after a handful of minutes, the video link was terminated only to be replaced by the—3D operating system's spherical folder system default area.

To a scientific man and woman, and with the military personnel soon following, the room stood up and clapped, whistled, and whooped a surprising but sincere ovation for Kenny. He was stunned at the turnaround in sentiment. Suddenly, the briefing room tone had changed; now there was a sudden, total, and unified display of recognition of his achievement.

The rest of the session now turned in to a question and answer debrief. The assembled scientific minds were eager to soak up as much information about how Kenny had achieved such a major breakthrough, details of his high level calculations, how he had arrived upon his hypotheses, and how he had overcome all the multiple problems in this field of expertise that no other top scientists had succeeded in doing. The main protagonist, interrogator, and sounding board, unsurprisingly based on a common research background, was Lars, his once estranged friend.

They discussed his extrapolation of superstring theory, the construction of his atom smasher model by modifications to the electron beam afterburners and standalone laser pulsars, and his design of two counter directional synchrotrons in storage ring collider. They covered how he was able to generate the required gluon and quark particle beam speeds to create the black hole phenomena by synchronising the particle wave troughs and peaks to amplify the energy effects. This created a spiralling positive feedback loop to enable the creation of the anomalies with only the expenditure of the same amount of energy required to turn on a thousand light bulbs. They revisited what Kenny had already covered off in the hospital with Alex (but in more scientific depth) around overcoming the issues of spaghettification, the enhancements to reduce the mass of generated black holes to manageable levels, and his theories about the number of continua and formation of the 'Clugston constant', theorised at a value of twelve but needing mathematical validation.

Lastly, they covered off his measures for neutralisation of the production of the harmful ionising gamma radiation inherent in a collapsing black hole (relatively minimal in the size of the black holes that Kenny was creating) by additional flooding of the anomaly's event horizon with absorbing atomic electrons in order to buffer these damaging effects by Compton scattering. Kenny did concede though that the compensation was not 100 per cent effective, so there was some health risks for humans in long-term exposure to collapsing black holes in proximity to departing colleagues.

Finally, the meeting was over. The council excitedly verified that his experiments had huge potential, and plans were made to covertly develop the technology, pouring nearly all available resources to modify, improve, and manufacture multiple versions of Kenny's machine. The whole project was an absolute and undercover 'need-to-know' basis venture, with only those from the scientific community and the military, who absolutely were required to be involved, being informed.

As they made for the door, a grinning Alex was grabbed by his brother. They hugged long and hard in relief. It was over.

Now to dream and plan for a new start.

CHAPTER 3

Ano 218 late Bareel

O' Prime Dominant,

Alle a lye! Alle a lye! Lyfe is a lye.

At th' tym assent'd a once god came, wispring calm, wispring peace. Tooke I body, tooke I soul, tooke I truthe. Helde I in its mynde, its hold cruel yet kynde, I fear calmed but alle I holde dere, alle I worships sente assunder.

Alle I learnings, alle I truthes; alle assunder. Ah! I must dye than dwell here on hope none an'shame o' full. I have prolong a lye colossus, th' max lye ever for our race.

Not gods, but abberrants fr' outside our sphere. Us captives to thr' whyms an' thr' syences.

Ah! Deth I beseech come now. I lyfe is not. I can not lyve a lye. I can not sermon to I collective of gods when gods be but strange callers to this lande.

Ah! Powr and tenet max ovr our affairs. How absolute! How supreme! Us are but child items, fodder to thr' strength.

Bt' they neede us. Neede us for spark o' our body. I no comprend, bt' neede one o' multitude o' tiny build bloks that makes us apes. An' they must wate, an' wate, an' wate. Multi yrs must wate for blok to evolute as thr' desire.

An' this one were sorry. This being, twenty-nine classify, unlike normals amongst its race had harte, had feels. I were surprised, tha' thru alle th' powr, were sorrow, shame an' feeling. This god —lyke abberrant, look past its powr, had sympathy and empath for us lyves; i' short, feels for us ape-anity.

It spoke, o' rather wisprd i' silence, of apology. It feeled for what done and what can't be undone.

An' then it lefte, as faste as it had came. Rypped I harte, I soul, I lyfe.

Forgyve I. I now apology for I coward's way now take; I lyfe already ded.

Divine Curator Sevral-Jupon

*

Ben Howell just floated there, seemingly hanging entirely motionless in the inky nothingness. This was a cruel illusion, as he was moving through the vacuous nothingness of space at a speed of 107,300 kph in a calculated and computer-assisted orbit around an alien yet familiar sun.

Highly calibrated and sensitive jet thrusters were applying sufficient corrective bursts to ensure that his hurtling trajectory was not a straight line but a very fine arc, mimicking the orbit of his own planet, around its own star, back in his own continuum. He arrived at his destination being propelled at the same speed as an orbiting satellite, having been given this momentum by the velocity of his own planet.

The problem was, unless any corrective counter forces were applied to the direction of his flight, he would not track the orbit of his own Earth in his own home continuum. He was now free of the gravity of his own planet, and the Sun's pull was much less on him than it was on a planet with a mass of approximately six-and-a-half million quadrillion tons such as Earth. He was also totally unimpeded by friction forces due to being in the vacuum of space, and so without any counterbalancing forces, he would continue to move in a straight line in the direction in which he was first travelling, when he phased into this continuum.

Therefore, trajectory compensation was necessary; otherwise, when he returned home from his mission, he would probably materialise in deep space rather than on or near the solid comfort of the ground. The phasing spatial calibration compensator, an additional and necessary module built into the phase generator, was able to adjust for a spatial deviation of several dozen metres. It simply wouldn't be able to bring him safely back to terra firma on his return after only a few seconds in the hostile continuum he was visiting, as the distances would be too great to negotiate.

Nevertheless, even with these corrections being applied to his trajectory, he still couldn't stay too long in this place due to the age-long habit of his own planet's spinning on its own axis.

The alliance scientists had made precise, painstaking, and time consuming calculations to compensate for his unidirectional hurtling course and create this manufactured solar orbit. In the time available, they could not find a way to make an additional correction to counterbalance the effect of the rotation of the earth.

As a result, the longer he stayed in this continuum (not revolving at the same rate as his own planet), the further he would deviate away from the coordinates of his original departure site. On his return home, he would re-materialise kilometres away from this point. New Deline was at 65° latitude in the Northern hemisphere, which meant that for every minute in this place, he would 'travel' west by approximately twelve kilometres. The team had worked out a schedule based on events and timings for his mission and had posted recovery teams at the expected grid coordinates, where he was expected to return. He would be re-entering the home continuum in the middle of a dry and parched landscape and would need to be recovered rapidly to avoid heat exhaustion and dehydration.

He had been briefed at length on these risks and fully understood them, yet these were the furthest things from his mind; instead he couldn't help but just stare in awe at the indescribable treat before him. In every direction that his restricted neck allowed him to look, was a super show of spectacular panoramic views. His trajectory was an anticlockwise orbit around the system's star, which, therefore, appeared out of the corner of his eye to his left. The glowing ball of nuclear fusion was giving off a stream of blinding light and electromagnetic radiation totally unhindered by any atmosphere. In complete contrast, 180° away from this distraction and unimpeded by light pollution was a masterpiece painting that looked so clear and sharp that Ben almost felt he could reach out, touch the canvas, and grab a handful of stars in his fist. Few humans had seen the night sky like this, and he couldn't help but be in awe of his position.

The constellations were very familiar. In his limited expertise, most, if not all, of the stars back in the reality that he was used to were represented here in this alternate facsimile of a galaxy. He had never been an authority on astronomy, but recognised the well-known constellation Orion, with its familiar belt of three stars and dagger hanging by his side. He had never quite 'got' Orion if the truth be known; he never saw an Ancient Greek huntsman in human form leaping out of the constellation.

If he craned his neck 70° to his left, he could also see the 'Big Bear', with the front lip of 'the frying pan' pointing to what would have been the equivalent of the 'North Star' for the planet had it existed in this continuum. Both these constellations were frequently visible from the Northern hemisphere back on his earth.

He felt like a microbe; a tiny, insignificant, and wholly invisible speck to be ignored by the spectrum of majestic stars, comets, and other deep space anomalies that graced the neighbourhood galaxy. He was a lone bacterium sitting in a vast expanse of nothingness, bathed in the light of a familiar but seemingly lonely star.

He shook himself, mentally slapping his face repeatedly to garner focus. This feeling of wonderment at being where he was and the enjoyment of an experience which few humans had ever encountered was tempered by a deep and scarring realisation which brought forward emotions which tore at his very insides. He was swamped with a deep and ingrained sadness for the thousands of men, women, and children who until recently had been part of their society but now were seemingly completely lost. The accompanying empty sense of fear and hopelessness stemmed from a complete lack of comprehension about what could have happened here. It was beyond any single human's experience and, he confidently suspected, the sum of their scientific knowledge so far.

Right before his eyes was their usual Sun, an ever familiar copy of the same star that existed in their own reality, but where was the Earth, this continuum's replica of their own home? He should be standing on it. It had been here until only a few days ago.

He shook his arms up and down with the anger of it all and yelled at the top of his voice. Both actions were completely fruitless demonstrations of his frustration and fury. Nobody could hear him, and his arm movements had no effect on anything whilst he was in a vacuum. The futility of the actions made him feel worse, if anything.

The extremely well-planned migration project to relocate people, building materials, food, and machinery had been progressing well and was ahead of plan. Senior personnel earmarked for this early migration had been moving to and from the target site to attend update meetings, deal with teething issues, and give feedback into further planning. Early accommodation structures were set up, temporary lodgings established, and the initial steps required to enable self-sufficiency on the new planet had been accomplished without incident.

Then, suddenly, the planned transports started to fail. The Pre Phase Reconnaissance Module (PPRM), a fallback safety device, failed to trigger the automatic countdown for each potential transport. No one could get to the new continuum, and no one could make it back it seemed.

The PPRM module, a vital add on facility to the phase transporter itself, had been invented and designed by the great Dr Clugston himself. It was a small device which rapidly captured environmental data such as temperature, humidity, and atmospheric gases and calculated and recorded the physical coordinates and conditions of the terrain at the intended arrival area. It was designed to make a pre-phase visit to the destination continuum by creating a black hole the size of a tennis ball and phasing itself to the destination. Once there, it would take a split second snapshot of the prevailing conditions and any physical conditions at the target site which would preclude a safe transport.

Then it would re-engage the power source, recreate a second small black hole, this time with the opposite polarity to its outward journey and return to the original continuum. If conditions were safe for the transport, it would engage the Phasing Spatial Calibration Compensator to make any required adjustments to the target micro coordinates at the landing site and automatically boot off the transport sequence for the phasing.

This way the travellers would never find themselves arriving in mid air and falling to injury or death, or, even worse, materialising in the middle of solid rock or inside the trunk of a tree. Similarly, subjects would never find themselves arriving suspended over a large lake or a pool of volcanic lava, as detections for substrate stability were part of the pre-phase check. In the event that conditions were not safe for a transport, the device would automatically abort the planned phase. A post failure diagnosis could be made by scanning the logs of the device, and manual adjustments made before the next attempt.

In these recent failed trips to the new continuum, however, it initially seemed that even the PPRMs were disappearing, swallowed up in the destination reality. Then it was discovered that the devices were all approximately 540 metres away, always to the west of the launch site. The scientists calculated that, as scan duration of the units was two-and-three-quarter seconds on an average, this equates to them 'travelling' the interim distance in a speed of just over 700 kph. It did not take the brains long to put two and two together and realise that this was the same figure as the speed of the earth's rotation at this latitude.

No one wanted to voice it, but a horrific conclusion was being formulated, one which would need verification, and that was why Ben was on this mission.

Along with the mystery of why the devices were relocating, there was an issue of consistently garbled data written to the log files of each returning PPRM. Additionally, all the devices were mysteriously damaged beyond repair.

One hundred per cent of PPRM devices had returned intact and in perfect working condition from their target continuum in the brief history of this new technology. Recent pre-phase trips, however, resulted in the devices being completely smashed to pieces, or more accurately, completely imploded on themselves. Finally, they all arrived back cold to the touch, even though they had only been in the intended destination for less than three seconds.

Such was the case for the last few attempts to phase to 'Earth continuum minus one', as this world was known in the project plan. The imaginative white-coated nerds were yet to devise a more user friendly name for the world. Ben guessed that they probably never would, now.

The project for the continued migration to this continuum had ground to a complete halt, and nobody had the faintest idea what had been the fate of those who had already travelled to this new home. Nobody was able to cross over in either direction, so it was impossible to ascertain whether the migrants were dead or alive.

The largest, major event in North American, even human, history was thrown off course irrevocably, and all that remained was uncertainty and fear. It fed a hopeless resignation that this new dream of redemption for humanity, a renewed fantasy that had ignited a wave of optimism unseen since before the scorching would now die. The extrapolated reality of this realisation was 'this meant the end of the human race.'

Ben yelled silently at the top of his voice again, the sound waves dampened by the vacuum of space before they could even start.

Again it was a futile gesture, but one that he felt was absolutely necessary in a vain attempt to give him some comfort.

Over 5000 humans had so far migrated to the new continuum.

Where were they all now? Were they all dead? What about all the valuable equipment and resources that they could hardly spare, all now seemingly lost?'

Ben felt dampness rolling down his cheek and across his lips and realised that he had been crying and also that he had been shaking with the shock of dealing with the situation that was before him. He simply could not handle the enormity of it.

Despite this, Ben shook himself into action and switched on the manual readout to try and monitor the progress of the various scans that the in suit algorithm was in the process of conducting. The simple tests such as atmospheric content (of which there was none), ambient temperature, and a survey of the terrain (which, again, was a void test) were completed in nanoseconds. The deep space astronomical scan—a sweep covering approximately a third of the sky all around Ben—was only 82 per cent complete, meaning that he would have to stay a further one minute and twelve seconds. It seemed strange that with the level of advancement of their technology, a task could still take minutes rather than nanoseconds, but Ben supposed that the device was probing trillions of stars and getting data from billions of light years away in that sector of the galaxy.

After several of these aborted transports had occurred and with no data to work with or any communication with the phase delegation, the scientific council decided that decisive action was required. After much deliberation and consultation, including the involvement of the inventor of the technology, Dr Clugston, they had concluded that the only answer was for a guinea pig volunteer to investigate what had happened on 'Earth minus one'.

They had no choice but to override the safety protocols on the PPRM and send across a volunteer in a self-contained environment suit. That was where Ben came in. He was always a sucker for a 'suicide mission'. Consequently, his friends and colleagues on the unit thought he was a complete nutcase, something that he couldn't argue with. Still, he wouldn't have missed this for the world despite suspecting that he might have to face a horrific reality, a fact that was now fully confirmed.

Ben knew a few of the military team that had been chosen to go in the first wave of transports to what was hailed as the new home, a fact which added to his sadness and despair about this situation. So many good people had just gone.

How could a whole planet, which should be (and was until recently) exactly where he currently was located, completely disappear without a single clue that it was ever there? There was no debris of any kind to signify that some sort of destructive event had occurred. There was nothing; just the voluminous vacuum of space.

A vibration in the control unit in his helmet signified that the various scans had been completed to satisfaction, the data stored to the vacuum sealed hard disc, and Ben could return to his own continuum. The words dancing in front of him on his visor screen asked if he wanted to initiate the sequence for the return journey now. It was terribly polite, he thought. It wouldn't matter if he didn't answer. The fall back safety mode of the device would return him within a minute anyway.

Ben selected 'Yes' on the console attached to his forearm, and the device began its short warm-up routine. He would have heard the familiar humming of the process if he hadn't been surrounded by an atmosphere devoid of particulate matter. He took a glance at the timer display on his wrist module and made a quick calculation. He had been here three minutes and forty-five seconds, and by the time the phase module was ready to return him that would be about four minutes and ten seconds. That meant he would reappear at home approximately forty-nine kilometres west of his original launch site near New Deline.

The colliding subatomic particles within the atom smasher soundlessly generated the correct conditions for the phase, and in a split second, a perfect sphere of black, like a large ivory snooker ball without any reflecting light, engulfed the floating body of Ben Howell.

As soon as it was formed, it started to collapse, but not before Ben was snapped forward through a Clugston temporal wavelength to return to the home Earth continuum with his precious collection of data.

*

The Sentinel Combatant began to run in its direction. This caste was athletic, muscular, and fast.

Iptat, kneeling pathetically in the doorway, estimated that the Assassin could cover the length of the chamber, a distance of just over 200 standard mettes, in about 17 standard temporal units, giving Iptat about 20 temporal units to live.

Iptat's weak knees were rooted to the spot. It was mesmerised, its will correspondingly unable to react to this oncoming threat. As a result it barely noticed the mechanoid whirring around the edge of the door, calmly attended to the portal's console, once again shutting and locking the aperture and returning it to the previous state of security that Iptat had foolishly deserted.

The view of Iptat's imminent and rapidly approaching death slid away, but the terror, panic, anticipation, and imagination remained.

Iptat was stunned. 'Whaaa . . . Who? . . . How are . . . ? . . . What are? . . . ,' it attempted.

'You are the Acquiescent Operative Unit AO 76377-QY107.' It was not a question. 'I am this vessel's SIPIA unit.'

The SIPIA was the ship's on-board software program; and like all these algorithms, of which there were about ten in their world, it represented the sum of their race's experience and knowledge. It was also programmed as a pseudo intelligence, able to reason outside of pure logic, by inputting into the computational soup responses driven by pure emotions of which it was capable, and feeding back in to the data cloud information gained from previous experiences. Patterns of events and associated outcomes were retained, analysed, sorted, and utilised upon recurrence of situations with similar patterns. This allowed it to combine computational analyses with an assessment of the prevalent conditions to allow decisions driven by hybrid-pure logic and emotive thought calculation processors. In effect, it could learn and retain experiences for future use, and this made it a 'supercaste' member of their race.

Iptat chuckled to himself more than a bit nervously. A standard Operative joke was that these algorithms have more character than the Cerebrals. Compounding this was a notion of ridicule that this all-encompassing mind was trapped in a commonplace—mechanoid unit. It must be struggling for processing capacity in the legacy unit, to say the least.

The thought was cut short, as Iptat could now hear the powerful pounding of the Sentinel's feet growing louder and nearer, as it sprinted towards the newly closed doorway.

'I was pre-briefed on your role on this mission at date 01.04.05.21030 when we had a chance to talk before your cryo-preparation 405.876 standard orbits ago. Do you remember?'

Iptat did remember. It wondered if the SIPIA was testing the memory download process which had recently restored its life to him.

'Sure, how could I forget?' It was easy to be sarcastic in its weakened physical and mental state.

An enormous crash interrupted this slightly surreal briefing. The Combatant had thrown its large body into the chamber's door at full speed, having accelerated and accumulated 200 paces worth of momentum. The portal door shuddered fiercely and clearly buckled under the strain but held firm.

Iptat mentally scratched its head. '*How the hell was the SIPIA housed in a lowly and normally fairly stupid mechanoid?*' it thought. Immediately, as if it had asked the question directly to the new robotic companion, it continued.

'I downloaded my program into this mechanoid 1,921 temporal units ago, shortly after the unexpected revival of the Sentinel unit. The mechanoids were investigating how this remotely improbable event could possibly have occurred, when the unit lost control. It began to malfunction due to lack of Hub Commander neural net control, deep space disorientation, and confusion about the logic for its presence on this vessel. Consequently, it was randomly destroying the vessel's servers, equipment, and infrastructure, including any mechanoid units that approached too close to it.

'The mechanoids were trapped in a logic feedback loop and could neither run away from the Sentinel unit, which was the logical course of action, nor help it, the latter being the hard-coded instruction within each of them compelling them to obey.

'The logical option for me was to wirelessly upload my program and a fraction, about a 12 millionth of my data, knowledge, and experience into the mechanoid. My data cloud was updated on the status of your revival, and I calculated that the option with greater chance of success was to be mobile, to be able to contact you, especially as the Sentinel unit was destroying my console. This rendered communication with my program impossible via the multitude of available comm-units or mobile interfaces around the ship, and only feasible by direct interface with my central console.'

The pseudo intelligence paused to examine Iptat. Infrared and other probing electromagnetic waves scanned up and down the flagging Operative from what could be deemed as 'eyes'.

'You are not in good health. My high-level evaluation of your general physiological condition is that your body is in the early stages of anaphylactic shock. Your level of your bodily fluid pH is dangerously below the mandatory minimum level for your caste, due to a build-up of hydrogen ions in your filtering organs. Your body is employing various physiological mechanisms, including neural, hormonal, and biochemical strategies in an attempt to reverse this condition. This outcome was one of the predicted potential side effects of the cryogenic revival process for an estimated 1 in 30.65 Acquiescent Operatives caste units.'

'Please!' appealed the frustrated and more than a little frightened operative, shaking with fear and weakness, 'Just get on with it! My physiology will be irrelevant in 600 temporal units if that psychotic animal breaks through that door.'

'Stand still.' The intelligence instructed, whilst at the same time easing forward on its rotary podia until it was within touching distance of the distressed Iptat. 'We still have sufficient time, particularly, as we have two factors to our advantage, compared to one factor playing against us. Firstly, the Sentinel is not a translator unit, and secondly, it is not equipped with the standard complement of weapons, and it has no access to the ship's munitions cache.'

'*Oh great! When was the last time that a Sentinel really needed a weapon outside of its bare hands?*' Iptat thought, trying not to be completely resigned to pessimism, but at the same time entirely incapable of foreseeing a logical route of escape from this hellish situation. '*And what exactly have we got time for?*' its negative thought trail continued as it appealed to fate that the SIPIA had a plan, which stood even the remotest of chances.

'And can *we* access this munitions cache?' asked an unconfident Iptat.

'Negative, we have a low probability of reaching the cache without being terminated. The Sentinel Combatant unit's current location is between us and the armament supply.'

'OK', Iptat acknowledged, 'not a good plan. So we still need some good news. What is the negative factor?' it reluctantly asked, although part of it wanted to continue in blissful ignorance.

'There is only one exit from this chamber,' the mechanoid responded, 'and that is where the Sentinel is going to come through.'

With a metallic click, a flap opened in the mechanoid's chest area, and an arm like extension with two elbow like joints whirred out towards the awaiting patient.

The rhythmic and persistent shoulder barging continued unrelenting all the while, with incremental and irreversible damage to the battered door. The sound of the distressed metal and polymer composite gateway was progressively changing, as the soldier approached nearer to its objective. An ear rending scraping element to the noise indicated that the door's thick bolts, which were employed to interlock with their congruent apertures in the portal frame, were slowly freeing themselves from their prison.

Just as Iptat was beginning to panic again, a needle projected from the mechanised unit's replica arm and swiftly, smoothly, and efficiently stabbed into Iptat's bicep. The spike instantly found an artery and painlessly unleashed its curative blend of genetically modified hormones. The dose of Aggressterone was like a narcotic hit. Iptat could feel the fluid progress through its body, immediately accompanied by the sensation of thousands of minute pinpricks jabbing across the whole of its cranium, instantly making it feel dizzy and disorientated. Despite having to reach for the wall to support its weakened body, the infusion felt good, and as its spinning head settled slowly and the room slowed its spinning motion, Iptat felt more in control and in a better position to focus on their situation which was, to say in the least, critical.

Its heart was beating faster now, driven on by the genetically modified hormone cocktail, and its extremities tingled with renewed fluid flow. Iptat flexed them in recognition of these tangible benefits.

'You need to remain calm, as we need you to focus and act fast and efficiently,' the strangely authoritative mechanoid continued.

'You must initiate an emergency revival of a Sentinel Combatant Hub Commander. This, despite a still low probability of success, is the only way that we can gain control over the renegade, permanently or temporarily,' the sentient algorithm said.

Despite the increased pessimism building in Iptat, it managed to focus and uncover an obvious flaw in the plan. 'How are we going to control the Hub Commander?' suggested Iptat.

'Please commence the procedure as time is short,' it said, sweeping aside Iptat's question, 'we will discuss our plans when the revival is in progress.' The tempo of the words was monotone, but somewhere beneath them they had an urgency driven by something more than programming. If ever a sentient program was able to show frustration and bark orders, then this was the time. The undertone was as if from a live, fully emotional sentient being. Could it be that at some level this machine felt pressure and could succumb to nerves?

With remarkable clarity and speed of thought, which belied its recent bodily condition and the fact that it was completely terrified, Iptat walked rapidly to the nearest cryo-control user interface, mentally preparing the steps that it needed to go through to revive one of the ship's manifest of passengers, in this case a Hub Commander.

Iptat scanned the list of candidates and selected an appropriate unit, by cross referencing the already revived Sentinel's designation with available Hub Commanders in its unit, which were also located in this chamber. The unit was designated SCH 4679245-RZ9937 and was a back-up commander in the unit. The Sentinel unit's incumbent Hub Commander was housed two chambers away.

The mechanoid had sidled up soundlessly to where Iptat was working. It continued to talk while the Operative worked.

'I estimate that we have approximately 730 temporal units of time before the Sentinel unit succeeds in breaching the room's perimeter. Just prior to this stage, I will be able to erect a level five neuronic stasis field over the aperture to prohibit its progress. This is the highest setting achievable by the neuronic field generator on this ship, and will cause the Sentinel extreme pain and damage if it continues to try to breakdown the partition. The damage will be irreparable to its epidermal and dermal layers and its central nervous system leading to inevitable and eventual death, but it will be insufficient defence to stop it completely. This caste has been mod —'

'Quiet mechanoid!' Iptat interrupted. It could bark commands as well as any sentient program. 'I need to concentrate. Tell me your life story, first, when I have succeeded in setting the revival process in motion and second, if I am alive to hear it.'

The besieged door was now wailing with every shoulder barge that the Sentinel was applying. Somehow though, it now seemed like a far off, surreal dream—a different world now that Iptat was in a zone of total concentration. It felt strangely, but totally, in control dealing in an area of expertise where it was the complete master. This was an area of proficiency that it had painstakingly trained for and applied itself relentlessly for the whole of its adult life. In a strange way, it seemed that all its endeavours had led it here to this point in time. This was the moment.

There was a silence between them that hung in the air for the few moments that the medic needed to manipulate the resuscitation program via the console's user interface. It double checked all the parameters for the revival process, verified the online status of the memory download software, and confirmed that the support and emergency audio help algorithm were available.

Then Iptat initiated the selected pod's thermal rods to kick start the warming process; set the required recuperation horizon; and checked the availability and composition of chemicals, hormones, and nanoids that were needed to bring the selected unit back to life in as safe a manner as possible. A correct mix of these reagents was paramount in order to reverse safely the body damaging effects of the cryogenic deep freeze.

If all else failed, both Iptat and the SIPIA had access to additional endocrinal and enzymic supplies in case additional stimulus was required for the revival. Electrical capacitor paddle equipment was also on hand in event of an emergency, which regretfully in this case was highly probable. As physically strong and resilient as the Sentinel caste was, the urgency of this situation required that they revive the unit in one third of the time normally allowed for the process.

A minimum of 1800 temporal units was recommended for a cryo-revival, assuming all the additional drugs, minute nanotechnology robots, and catalysts were available, to allow a subject's body to recover from the extreme body trauma with acceptable damage to its tissues. The 600 temporal unit horizon that this situation demanded meant that the rapidly defrosting Hub Commander's body faced serious issues with frozen cell fluid being trapped in extra cellular cavities, leading to irreparable cell lysis.

It had a near certain probability of death within a handful of orbits of being revived, regardless of what medical help was supplied to it. This, however, was still plenty of time to affect its own agenda and inflict irreversible damage to the rebels' plan.

The situation made Iptat feel uneasy, as it did not like the thought of causing unnecessary death. Its role had always been to save lives not knowingly set parameters that it knew would take life. This emotion, a sentiment shared strongly with its Cerebral rebel colleagues, was the cornerstone principal of their alliance and a driver for the rebellion and consequent migration plan that they were currently undertaking.

As much as Iptat feared and hated units from the warrior caste, the stark reality of this situation allied to its pre-mission orders (confirmed by its signed off pre flight agreement that individuals were less important than the mission goal) demanded that both Sentinels were expendable in this scenario. However, it could already feel a strong level of regret about what they were doing. They were playing mathematics with life here. The only alternative, unfortunately, was the death of all the other frozen passengers on the transport and the end of their attempt at finding the new world that they had identified and the new beginning that they had been promised.

'Administer additional repair nanoids,' the SIPIA instructed. 'It is vital that the Hub Commander's body can repair sufficiently to give us sufficient time for our needs,' it continued.

The irritated Iptat fired a sharp glance at the sentient programme that was posing as a mechanoid. '*Surely I am the expert here*?' the look was suggesting.

The SIPIA stood motionless, totally unperturbed by the operative's offence. Iptat turned away and faced the console again, tapping the keys to affect the change. It found the intelligent algorithm annoying, especially in its current state of stress, but had to concede that it was correct. An insufficient application of nanoids could be fatal to the reviving Sentinel. The miniature robotic repair units had their work cut out as it was.

Iptat stood back from the user interface, whilst exhaling in a sigh of relief. 'There, it is done. The revival process has been initiated. 580 temporal units till revival and counting. Give me some good news about our situation before I go and find the selected unit's cryo-chamber.'

The algorithm continued where it had left off, as if it had been a single moment rather than multiple temporal units since it had been interrupted.

'Its caste has been modified to adjust to pain using the production of genetically enhanced analgesic hormones. It has a 97.32 per cent chance of breaking through and terminating both of us before dying. Although the Sentinel's death *will* occur several thousand temporal units later, it will have enough time to interfere with the cryogenic program and initiate multiple terminations from the ship's complement of passengers. It has no concept of giving up. In that time it could destroy all which the rebel Cerebrals have risked and prepared for in this mission.'

A huge crash reverberated around the chamber, and one of the three bolts, previously safely housed in its port, slid free with a high pitched scraping that seemed to linger, suspended in the air, and sent spasmodic shivers down Iptat's spine.

The twisted metal now revealed an aperture between the two chambers. A new sound shortly followed the previous one—a brief but loud noise that appeared to be a combination of a digital chime and the crackling of an electric circuit shorting out in smoke and flames. Hundreds of electrical tongues of excited lightning darted in a web of momentary but fervent activity across the face of the newly created aperture. The Sentinel had touched the neuronic field with its fist, testing for its presence.

Now there was a pause to the rhythmic pounding. Clearly an assessment was being made, and a decision drawn up based on the result of this evaluation. The silence of the next tension-filled moments was stark in contrast to the previous 700 temporal units. The longer it lasted, the longer it seemed to burn an imprint on the mind.

It knew that it would die from its attempt to breakdown the neuronic barrier, but it would still probably be able to kill its target. Was there another way to get to its target, or should it carry on through the pain?

Then as abruptly as it had stopped, the battering started again—decision made. It strangely came as a relief to Iptat.

'*At least if you can hear the pounding*', Iptat thought, '*you can identify where the enemy is.*' This time, however, the noise of body hammering against disintegrating door and scraping of slowly releasing bolts was accompanied by two additional noises—the electrostatic chiming of the newly erected electro-neuronic field and a wincing sound from the Sentinel.

'The field is in place,' the mechanoid said.

The pained grimacing reactions from the wounded soldier slowly receded over the next few shoulder barges and then finally stopped.

'It is adapting to the pain,' the sentient robot confirmed. 'Its progress will be faster now. What is the timescale for the commander unit's revival?'

'This procedure is not like rebooting a mechanoid from hibernate mode,' the doctor said forcefully. 'If there is any further reduction in the revival time of the selected subject then it will die without—'

Its sentence was interrupted by the battered door bursting in with an immense crash, leaving an open doorway, and the offensive Assassin standing where once the sealing door was. This was now a twisted piece of metal composite which flew into the cryo-chamber, scraping and sliding across the floor until it came to a halt a mere few paces away from Iptat.

The military caste member paused momentarily and stood there, panting uncontrollably like a wild canine. Then slowly and with a great deal of menace, it raised its head to survey its targets—the occupants on the other side of the gap in the portal.

It was a large specimen even for a Sentinel. Its trademark thick, bony, and lightweight plates, which covered its shoulders, back, and abdomen, heaved up and down with its recent exertions. Sentinel's bodies were genetically modified to have these light but strong plates, which protected its soft organs and spine from stabbing or projectile weapons. *'Only two ways to kill a Sentinel'*, the old Operative gag went, *'drop a fusion bomb on it or tell it a joke.'*

The Sentinels cold, stone dark grey eyes located Iptat and bored beyond the operative's orbits, burning directly into the pit of its soul. It held the gaze for as long as it needed to create the required fear. This was not long; Iptat shivered again and broke eye contact—a basic and natural animal response developed over millions of orbits. To say that it was submissive to the animal on the other side of the field was akin to calling a star's thermal status as 'lukewarm'.

'We need to get out of here, and fast. We have in the region of 430 temporal units until the final phase of revival is complete,' Iptat estimated.

Full consciousness, self-awareness, and restored memory were the final links in the chain and their final goal that would allow the Hub Commander to control its subordinate by linking their minds in a small telepathic network link.

'I estimate the neuronic stasis barrier will be breached in approximately 400 temporal units,' the sentient program compared notes.

The stark reality of these words dangled in front of them for a moment, and in the silence an unspoken understanding united them.

It was a race!

*

He was worried. His tiny universe was on the move, and he couldn't do anything to halt its progress.

This was all very wrong. It was not a constant physical parameter of his reality. His environment should be stationary in a horizontal position in the Proximal universe's container, with his mind completely shut down for the recuperation process. It was after 1900 hours, and this meant that it was the dark portion of the day. In fact the onset of dark in the Proximal universe was some time ago, which meant that nothing was allowed into the container where he was kept.

He vocalised repeatedly for a few minutes his distress at this breach of the physical constants that controlled his world and its interaction with the Proximal universe. One of the fundamental principles of his universe was the maintenance of the strict temporal link between his domain and the Proximal universe. It *always* got dark at the same time; nutritional input was *always* taken at certain intervals during each rotation, and sensory inputs of data *always* available at specific time intervals.

But now something was subtly different. There was a new event occurring in his local region in the Proximal universe. Something felt very different; something that he couldn't explain. He stood pondering this in the middle of the container, exposed in the pitch black cloud of dark.

He didn't understand. His mind should already be in meltdown, as he had been pulled outside of his comfort zone; this breach of the environment's strict rules of order should easily have been a trigger for his deterrents. These physical and sonic defence mechanisms should be in full force now, but somehow they were being kept at bay. Calmness was in his head. It had placed there. These were not his thoughts, but so far these imposters were damping both of the deterrents.

Also, someone or something was trying to communicate with him—to break into one of the strictly organised boxes in his sophisticated and well-ordered brain. He knew the internal structure of his brain absolutely, and he kept everything boxed exactly where it belonged in a controlled virtual filing system depending on function. He could always see these boxes or functional regions of his brain and knew well what their responsibility was in controlling aspects of his life. He liked the purpose of most areas of his brain and would call upon them for various tasks or to recall his massive amount of stored data.

One area, though, he did not like at all. In fact his fear of this area was total, and he boxed it away deeply in his brain, like a boarded-up house, never intending to visit it again, intentionally or accidentally, as long as his universe existed.

It was this box, he suddenly realised with an overwhelming tsunami of fear, that something or someone was attempting to access or communicate with.

'*NO! That box scares me. You cannot open it! You cannot enter*!'

He could not understand it. The boxes he liked were the boxes that controlled cognitive ability, intelligence, and memory. These were good areas. The secret box though filled him with dread. He must hide it further away. He worked hard in an attempt to hide the thought processes, autonomic or somatic, and bury them deeper into the dark recesses of his brain.

He could now see a being moving around within his container in the Proximal universe. It was not like a being that he had ever seen before. He couldn't look directly at it of course. It was probably trying to look him in the eye. He immediately knew that this being was connected with the mind invasion going on in his brain.

Why is this being trying to look into his secret box? It scared him. At last though, he could now feel the welcoming onset of panic leading to the summoning of his repellents.

But, once again, before his usually reliable friends could surface, a counteracting force inside his head was smothering this impulse. It was smoothing over the anxiety and reasoning with his subconscious. Once again, the panic attack never came.

Out of the corner of his eye he could see the being approaching him. His universe was held static in the middle of the container, and he was unable to do anything about this being's advance. His mind should be panicking, as he was sure an attempted invasion of his realm was imminent. His breathing became very fast, and he felt hot, but still no repellents were engaged. Where were they? They had never let him down before.

The intruder reached out with its long spindly arms and laid the palms of its hands on top of his head, clearly breaching the boundary between the two domains.

He shut his eyes, expecting a cataclysmic explosion as the differing matter from two universes occupied the same space.

Surprisingly though, all remained calm in his universe. Even with the strange new humanoid, much taller than the usual beings in the Proximal universe, putting its hands on his scalp, calm pervaded throughout his space. This confused him but, now that he had got used to it, he liked the clarity that was afforded by this. Instead of panic and loss of reasoning, he could still think clearly. And this was what was going to be needed to defend further invasions of the secret box.

The being was still probing around in his mind. He could feel him in the boxes that were well maintained and not hidden away. He felt the presence investigating and searching for something. It was trying to talk to him by using the hidden box to communicate. He would not allow it.

He vocalised now to interact with the being in the Proximal universe. The words he used in an attempt at warning the being had changed now. The priority was no longer to alert him to the breach of the laws controlling physical interactions of his realm with the Proximal universe; this incursion was clearly not an issue, as they were still alive. The priority now was the defence of his secret box.

The alien mind had now found it and was trying to place something in this container. He couldn't read it but knew that it was both enormous and very special. If it was in that box though, he would never go to look at it. It would be buried away with the rest of the data that was locked away there. But it was enormous; too enormous.

'No, it doesn't belong to me. It won't fit in that box. Take it back.'

He tried to focus and repel the invasion, but it was useless. He tried to focus on the usual deterrents, but the foreign mind had succeeded in its mission. Its strategy to place a stranglehold on the neurons that controlled these responses as well as inducing a straight jacket of calm and contentment about the whole situation had been successful.

The mind had won, but he felt that the result was satisfactory. The gift that had been given could be hidden away in the box along with all the other items that caused him fear. He would never have to look at it or deal with it unless he chose to. He was just looking after it for the time being, and one day the being would come back for it.

He suddenly realised that these were not his own thoughts. These also were feelings, thoughts, and suggestions from the invader, subtly transposed over his own thought patterns.

He was communicating directly with this strange alien. His defences were breached, and he was allowing a constant flow of thoughts and data to enter his head, feeding directly in to the loathsome box. He had never experienced anything like this before, and it was not painful; but the concept felt uncomfortable, and he badly wanted it to stop. He couldn't wait for the box to be fully hidden away again, just as it had been all his life so that he could ignore and forget about it.

And then, suddenly, the mind was gone.

The secret compartment of his mind was locked behind it as it retreated, as if with a key, and the invasion of his territory was over. The being withdrew a pace, elevating his sense of relief.

He was distracted by a noise, somewhere else in this container of the Proximal universe.

It was from the door to the next door container, where one of the little beings lived. Now out of the corner of his eye he saw that the little being, who often invaded his universe's boundaries, was peeking sheepishly through the door to his container. The being was wearing a mantle of pure and half-awake confusion and should be in his recuperation mode.

He is not allowed to come in to the container. That would be breaking the physical laws controlling the onset of the dark period.

Now a fresh panic, in the aftermath of the alien's visit and the release of his mind, swept brutally upon him.

He was scared for the little being. This one could not fight off the alien's intrusions. The mind would be too powerful for him. He knew that the damage it could do would be irreversible.

Just as his anxiety built to critical levels, he felt a reprieve. It didn't matter now. The local being crouched to his haunches as a precursor to lying down on the floor in a crunched up position and immediately shutdown his mind for recuperation.

He could relax now. The physical parameters of his container had not been breached in the dark time by the little being.

Also, he now strongly felt the need to close down his cognitive processes as well and acquire the required recuperation. He moved his universe to the area where he could maintain a horizontal position for this activity and closed his eyes.

It was after 1900 hours, and all was well. His mind snapped back to its neutral stance as if nothing had happened at all.

Shutdown of his universe came quickly.

*

Ben landed not, as he was expecting, in the scorched, arid, and familiar sand of the North American desert but in a lush tropical forest, surrounded by thirty-foot ferns and mountainous deciduous trees. The canopy was all but blotting out the sky giving Ben limited vision. His eyes started to compensate, but it was hard work, as up until ten seconds ago they had been accustomed to the constant streaming of unimpeded light directly from a star in close proximity.

His irises made the required aperture corrections, and Ben slowly could see more and more detail from his new environment. It was still a hot place to be in a space suit but not in the same way that he was expecting. He was still fully enclosed in the environment suit, and this lent some air-conditioned comfort, but he knew it would not last for long as the energy pack would soon fail.

He checked his readouts and saw new entries being logged before his eyes. The atmospheric checks were complete. The atmosphere contained breathable air, which constituted 78.08 per cent Nitrogen, 20.95 per cent Oxygen, 0.93 per cent Argon, 0.038 per cent Carbon dioxide, and a trace of other gases: exactly what you would find in a similar sample from earth. He breathed a sigh of relief. It was Earth air, only he was not on what he knew as earth, at least not the environment that he knew as home.

A strange pair of large insects, a species that he had never encountered before, hovered a few metres away from him. They were beautiful, with purple and fluorescent stick-like bodies that were supported motionlessly in mid air by twin pairs of quivering transparent wings. An unseen disturbance alerted them, and they darted to another location close by, accurately stopping still again on a sixpence and resuming their hovering. Ben checked the digital environmental readout screen, knowing that the algorithm would have detected life and already have attempted to pull out the required data from its library.

Unknown species of the Order Odonata, Class Insecta.

Based on markings and features the closest database match is Species Aeshna Juncea from Family Aeshnidae, Order Odonata.

Common name: Common Hawker dragonfly.

Last sighting of species in New York State, October 2048.

Species presumed extinct from Planet Earth.

Ben watched the insects play in the air, temporarily mesmerised by their unfamiliar dancing, until he snapped his mind back to focus on his situation. He suddenly felt constricted and hot in his suit and, armed with the confidence that the air was entirely breathable, stabbed a control on his belt as accurately as he could with a heavily gloved hand and released the locking clamps keeping his helmet on. A quick twist with both his hands, and the head protection released with a hiss of air, and he was breathing the atmosphere.

A shimmering wall of prickly heat hit his face full on, and he half choked with both the shock of drawing in this unexpected air and the oppression of its assault on his skin. He had never tasted or smelt anything like this, having spent his life in a desert environment. It felt like inhaling a heavy aerosol of water; the damp, sticky, and stifling initial breaths were first heavily caressing and then overwhelming the sensory hairs on his nostrils and the soft skin of his mouth. It was closer to a taste than a smell; the unanticipated sear caused a prickling of the hair on the back of his head and an uncontrollable shudder down his spine.

He pulled himself together slowly in an effort to regain control of his situation. His training kicked in again, and glancing once more at his readouts, he obtained the comprehension that he was looking for. He tapped them in a typically human response to disbelief. There was no change in the reading. The humidity at this location was one hundred per cent.

This was not his Earth.

A movement in the undergrowth distracted him from his thoughts and he snapped his head around to see what was making this disturbance. The continued rustling from an area, an estimated twenty metres away, was accompanied by a low guttural rumbling sound; a growl followed by several clicks.

This was definitely not his Earth.

*

The messenger dismounted his hydrogen cycle and propped it up next to a tree. He brushed the fur on his legs to release some burrs that had fastened on, anticipating correctly that they would get a ride to a new location to set up a fresh home and beginning the cycle of life again.

He unfastened the bundle of products for delivery from the back of his vehicle's seat and selected the appropriate packages for delivery to the troupe that lived here. Then he started to stroll casually and happily up the rural path leading to their troupe lodge.

It was a beautiful spring day—warm, mostly sunny, and not too humid. Oroon smiled a smile of pure contentment in life, happy that the combination of a lovely day and a visit to his favourite area of town would make his relatively dull job a bit more tolerable. He might even meet a local celebrity into the bargain.

He always liked this suburb of their conglomeration, as the troupe accommodations were luxurious and had the necessary personal space between separate troupe groupings that was natural for their ancestors and was still genetically ingrained in their behaviour. They were, after all these years of scientific and social advancement, basically still forest animals, and their genes still compelled them to live in much the same way as their predecessors did thousands of years ago.

The Dominant who owned this troupe lodge was a wealthy and well-known business ape, who had contributed a great deal to the local economy at the same time as being a strong supporter of their race's ongoing strategy for green progression at a local, regional, and countrywide level. Being the sentient species on their planet, their race had been through some tough decisions to counterbalance progress against destroying natural resources and high profile supporters like Jemell-Randoon, the intended recipient of his parcels, were critical in preserving this balance.

The questions had been the same now as they had been when they first advanced from swinging and living in the trees: How do you advance at the rate required by a continued population expansion and thirst for material goods and possessions whilst ensuring the world's natural ecosystem and resources remain in balance? This had been a driving factor for them for centuries and involved a compromise that was part of their essence and soul. They had always held back from greedily devouring their beautiful world's plentiful bounty at the expense of the other animals on the planet, all being equally eligible to enjoy these benefits without being endangered or rendered extinct by the dominant species' footprint.

The lodge was coming into view now. It consisted of half a dozen renewable timber-constructed modules—homes to the wives and children of the Dominant—blended into the tree canopy each with its own automated ladder way to ascend to the welcoming portal. Sunshine glinted off some of the solar panels that were on the roofs of all the modules. These homes were positioned roughly in a circle, each attached to a variety of pine trees that held them off the ground. One or two of the trees had been artificially shored up with an array of joists and girders to help support these accommodations whilst not impacting the health of the tree adversely.

There was a small clearing in the centre of this circle, which housed the bathing and relaxation area. This space comprised a naturally constructed rock pool, shielded from the forest elements and surrounded by a patio of stone paving with loungers and other poolside items for recreation, positioned liberally around the area.

An outhouse for the Dominant's sons, now a legally mandatory facility, was a further fifty yards away from the main clutch of domiciles. It was guarded by a large fence as the adult sons were still not entirely trusted when it came to the Dominant's harem. Despite this mistrust it was a legal requirement that a Dominant needed to provide shelter, food, and some support until they could start to build their own troupe. No longer could you just turf your adolescent sons on to the street when they started getting hormonal and randy.

Oroon was pleased that he had got past that stage in his life and that he had his wives and children secure at home. Being a horny teenage male with your genes yelling at you to do anything, literally anything, to secure some females was a hard time in life. Fights, subterfuge, lying, cheating, and stealing were all weapons that you used to secure available females. Even in these 'civilised,' modern times, it was known to turn on your best friend as the urge to follow instinctive and ancient mating rituals was so strong.

He swung the wooden gate open, ignoring the post box provided and the large 'Keep out' sign. These items needed a scan from the recipient's credits monitor as the cargo was valuable. As he emerged on to the property within seconds, two guard dogs began to bound up to him with a lot of over enthusiasm and barking which bordered on aggression. He stopped dead in his tracks.

How foolish he had been! He had a reputation as a complete airhead and knew better than to walk into another male's troupe area without being invited, but he had still advanced past the socially acceptable barrier as if it were his own home. As far as the resident Dominant and the law were concerned, this could be construed as a malicious advance on the resident harem, which was punishable by a month's incarceration with manual labour. A good lawyer, and this incumbent could afford one, could throw the book at him. That was if the resident male or his dogs didn't kill him in a self-defensive attack.

'Desist!' The sound was snapped from the largest and presumably the main lodge in the troupe accommodation. The dogs, momentum allowing, stopped immediately.

'Down!' The gruff voice commanded the canines. The pair sank to their stomachs on the ground, forelegs extended out in front of them, tongues lolling stupidly as they panted, eyes fixed hungrily at the intruder.

'What are you doing on my troupe lodge, messenger?' He emerged from the main lodge slowly but confidently and descended on the ladder way majestically, eyes fixed steadfastly on his frozen captive, without breaking. He was large, just what you would expect from a self-assured and accomplished personality. The measured pace of his advance continued unabated as he came within a few feet of Oroon.

'Are you a mad, ape?' he continued, 'do you know who I am and what I am capable of?' Oroon was now beginning to feel a little uncomfortable to say the least. The Dominant stared wildly at him.

'I am so sorry,' he managed to blub out. 'I have some packages for you, and I wasn't thinking. I am not trying to challenge your authority over your troupe. Please! Sir! let me deliver my packages, and I will be off your land.' Oroon's eyes were fixed to the ground, avoiding the direct stare of the approaching host and implementing one of nature's longest subservience edicts.

The Dominant did not say anything. A few seconds, which seemed to stretch unnaturally with the tension, passed and still there was no reply. Slowly but surely the curiosity at his host's demeanour and state of mind overcame Oroon's fear instinct, and he risked a glance upward. The ape's eyes, which he had expected to be boring into his own to establish his dominance, were fixed over Oroon's shoulder to the distance. There was a very slight flickering movement of the Dominant's eyeballs from side to side, as if he was scouring for something.

'Did you see that?' It seemed to be a bit of a stupid question, as Oroon had been cowering, eyes to the ground. He turned to follow his fellow ape's line of sight.

All he could see was what he would have expected—trees, gloomy half light, and the usual forest undergrowth. He similarly scoured the available horizon looking for anything strange, but encountered nothing extraordinary that might have captured the Dominant's interest. He was about to turn away from the scene and refocus his efforts on apologising for his trespass transgression and getting out of this situation alive, when suddenly he saw it too.

Suddenly there was something black that appeared out of nowhere, approximately 100 yards away in the gloom of the forest floor, way below the light shielding tree canopy. It was an orb—floating eerily near the ground, entirely still, and perfectly formed. There was an accompanying rustling, and branches and leaves seemed to bend in to the object, attracted by some unseen force.

A deer or some other forest dweller would have been difficult to see in this dim half light at that range, however, whatever this thing was it was so black, so complete, and so unavoidable that you couldn't possibly miss it.

'There!' exclaimed his host, pointing almost needlessly.

The black blob disappeared almost as suddenly as it had appeared, and then there was nothing. Or was there something; a movement, perhaps even a figure? Oroon couldn't be sure that something else hadn't appeared after the black object had gone.

'What was that?' Oroon interjected, 'I thought I saw something, an animal or moving object.'

'Yes, I agree. But so unclear after the pure definition of the black object,' the Dominant replied.

At that precise moment came the verification that they had been looking for, and this time they were ready for it, their eyes already trained on the exact spot where the previous anomalies had appeared. Two more black spheres popped into view for an instance before seemingly collapsing only to be replaced with an animal of some description.

It was easy now to see why they had been unable to make out the previous objects. If they hadn't been ready for their arrival the anomalies could have been easily missed; they were set up to blend perfectly in to the background. This time, however, they had enough time to focus on whatever was there before it disappeared into the undergrowth.

There were two animals, bipedal like their race, were wearing thick cloth suits all over their bodies. These were green and dappled which helped these creatures blend into their surroundings. The creatures' heads seemed to be incarcerated in some sort of helmet with a dark visor covering the eyes. They seemed to be carrying something on their backs and holding what looked like some sort of weapon. One removed its helmet and held something to its eyes, scanning its surroundings. The scanning stopped as it looked in their direction, and the resultant reaction was swift.

They were gone, disappeared into the undergrowth.

The pair stood there, looking blankly at the spot where all this activity had taken place. A silence fell between them, and all thoughts of trespass and intent to disrupt the Dominant's troupe seemed meaningless and petty. The moment of reflection past, the host spoke decisively.

'Messenger, go and stand as near as you can to the spot where our visitors arrived. I must make a communication. The Patrons must know.' Oroon looked at him blankly. *'He was going to talk to their gods? How was that possible?'*

As if the Dominant had picked up on this and felt an answer was merited, he continued. 'The hairless apes are here. They bring death wherever they go.

It has happened as the Patrons predicted.'

*

The strange pair swept efficiently and wordlessly, spanning rapidly the few hundred metres of the elongated room. There were no windows to issue non-artificial light, but air staleness and the support of life sustainable levels of oxygen, carbon dioxide, and other atmospheric gases was controlled by an efficient venting system.

Dozens of metal pipes hung down like futuristic forest vines at constant intervals from a larger perpendicular pipe that ran the length of the room. A gentle and low hum emanated as a result of an artificial intelligence unit's control of this aspect of environmental monitoring and could be heard only above the din of silence produced by the room's complete sonic insulation. The paired system of vertical pipe ensured both the controlled influx of required levels of oxygen and the removal of excess products of respiration.

Hundreds of medical beds were lined along the length of this room in a series of ten rows with just the required space between the ends for two upright walking animals to pass. The beds appeared simple with no distinguishing features, and each contained a large ape, the adults of which measured in the region of 2.5 to 3 metres long. Each unit also possessed a small cubic processing unit, which flashed as it probed its simian subject's body, monitoring physiological levels and transmitting the data to those requiring it. The monitoring units were suspended a few centimetres above the subject's thorax for good reception.

Apart from this, the room was almost completely featureless. It was of temporary design, fabricated from metallic panels, each about twenty metres in length with the height of the room being about four metres high. The panels were secured together with large bolts that lent strength to the whole construction.

All the apes were motionless; save for their rhythmic, monitored, and controlled breathing. Soft plastic like support straps restrained their legs and arms by securing ankles and wrists. Head and neck were similarly secured in the event of the subject becoming aware of its predicament.

An alarm was sounding, and orange lights were flashing in tandem with the high pitched staccato sirens. One of the strange beings transmitted a termination radio message to the central computer, and both events ceased immediately. They reached the subject that had caused the alarm status.

It was a young but large adult male that was thrashing against its constraints, which in turn were chaffing its ankles and wrists whilst its panic tantrum continued. Its head was similarly fighting with its bonds as the animal attempted to shake its head vigorously free. The apes torso arched spasmodically in a 'U' shape as the terrified specimen strained painfully against its captivity.

Then suddenly and dramatically it stopped. It slumped back into a flat lying position, and the pained grimace, present only seconds ago, softened into almost a smile Its arms and legs stopped resisting, and it adjusted its head into a comfortable position on the provided padding. In a few short seconds, its eyelids closed, and it fell into a state of sleep.

'*Why did you have to enter its mind?*' one of the pair asked of the other.

'*Monitored physiological parameters indicated that the beast was in an ever increasing internal feedback loop induced by the primitive nature of its emergency response mechanisms.*'

There was nothing audible; words, images, and relevant concepts were unspoken but transmitted via radio waves between the two interconnected minds, their supremely evolved minds being capable of converting electrical brain impulses into electromagnetic waves across the complete spectrum of radio frequencies and transmitting those signals for reception by another member of their species.

The second being continued, '*The animal was struggling with the unfamiliar environmental stimuli, which it was perceiving for the first time. It was evident that its insufficient brain was not equipped to deal with the concepts it was encountering. Its mental development is still far from complete at this stage of the procedure. Fear and apprehension was causing its neural unit and associated autonomic nervous system to pump into its body copious amounts of the species' stress hormones.*'

The two beings stood absolutely motionless, with no hint of eye contact or any external suggestion of interplay. Total mental control of all conscious motor functions meant that only physical movement vital for some purpose was undertaken, ensuring minimal external muscle usage and consequently a limited blood flow to these less vital peripheral organs. In contrast, their enormous and well-protected cranium containing their massively outsized brains was extremely well-supplied with blood vessels, which stuck out on their muscular necks, visibly pumping the required oxygen. These were not physical animals but visceral computers, whose bodily functions were solely dedicated to the support and well-being of their highly developed Cerebral processing units.

Radio transmissions continued, '*These primitive animals use these hormones and associated neurostimulators to elicit a readiness for combat or retreat from perceived danger. This was causing increased production of sugars in its circulatory fluid for its muscles and neural unit, constriction of non-essential combat circulatory supply vessels, dilation of essential combat circulatory supply vessels, suppression of non-essential emergency systems, and an increase in alertness due to a mildly psychoactive effect. The species' autonomous emergency response has only a fraction of the efficiency of our own combat castes response, but nevertheless, it is designed as their body's internal self-preservation measure.*'

The creature now paused momentarily as it connected to the uplink interface with the processing unit that was monitoring the ape's internal physiology. Most of the required data having been received, it reconnected the neural link between its colleague, whilst multithreading with the medical monitoring computer's CPU for the remaining data upload.

'Cardiac, respiratory systems, and endocrine systems are returning rapidly to a normal level for this species. Levels of emergency combat hormones within the circulatory fluid are still 25 per cent above the range expectations of resting state, but purging rate is within tolerance levels.'

All remaining data having being uploaded, the alien cut the link and continued updating his associate.

'As the animal could not act on the impulses its body was demanding of it, it was caught in a positive feedback loop. There was a calculated 87.4 per cent probability of the animal's body shutting down through this system-wide induced shock. For the animal's own sake, this necessitated my neural intervention despite our original strategy of limited Cerebral interfacing. I will re-enter the animal's neural unit and purge its short-term memory lobe of events in the reference time frame so that it recalls nothing of this.'

'Affirmative, although at some sub conscious level, the individual may bear psychological scars based on the major disruption to its bodily equilibrium, which may prejudice the results in millennia to come.'

The second entity turned efficiently, with absolutely no wasted movement, and started to glide away from the other scientist across the long room. It continued to communicate instructions as it strode economically along the clinically clean white room, past the rows of raised experimentation beds that contained the other captured apes.

'Additionally, check the coma flux induction unit and the failure of mirror systems to kick in. It is imperative that we must avoid any repetition of this unexpected disruption to our experiment and any potential associated knock-on effects for the development of this race.'

'Affirmative. Next status update in 3600 standard native temporal durations.'

It terminated the one to one neural link with the senior scientist, who was accelerating across the extensive area to the exit hatch at the far end.

The alien started the required checks to diagnose the system's failures. This was a frustrating diversion from the next planned stage of the project, which they should be preparing for.

The subjects were all primed and ready for the intrusive retro-chromosomal remapping.

*

Alex kicked a stone at the lizard, which scuttled away to a small pile of rocks nearby. The majority of fauna on the planet had been rendered extinct by human activity over the last two centuries, but the humble lizard and other genera and species of the cold-blooded reptilian suborder *Lacertilia*, for long scoffed at as an imperfect and 'Cul-de-sac' design for life, had benefited from the scorching. In fact, desert dwellers of all descriptions had expanded their domain over the last twenty or so years since the repercussions of man's negligent misuse of the Earth's resources had suddenly and violently come to fruition. Reptiles, massively outnumbered in diversity of species compared to most family classifications, now were the kings again. Why not? They had a survival pedigree going back millions of years ever since the first dinosaurs, the real and lasting monarchs in our planet's history, strode regally on all our continents.

The heat was becoming intolerable. Having to live your life perpetually in desert like conditions, you expected and knew that every day would be uncomfortably hot, even in winter. This didn't mean, however, that you ever got used to the searing temperatures. Alex was sweating profusely in his environmental suit and beginning to feel a little dizzy, so he retreated to the interior of the vehicle. He shared this with two other soldiers from his unit, both chosen specifically for the required medical and technical training for this mission. A full med kit, with all that was needed to attend to a patient suffering the effects of severe heat exhaustion and/or dehydration, made up the bulk of the equipment that they were carrying in the back of the vehicle.

The area that they had to patrol was more or less flat, excepting the occasional rock outcrop. This was not an issue for a potential landing site as these hillocks were small; only a few dozen feet high and tens of metres long. The compensation device on the phase transporter would adjust so that the traveller's re-emergence into our reality would be a suitably safe one.

Alex looked at the readout screen on the dashboard in front of him. The display was entirely motionless, soundless, and idle, signifying that the tracking device attached to their recovery target still was not in range. His team was stationed in the desert near New Deline, waiting for Ben Howell to return from what the scientists called the 'Earth minus one' continuum, where hopes for the survival of North American humanity had, until recently, been pinned.

They were located approximately forty-eight kilometres from the original launch site and were one of twenty-one teams posted at two kilometre intervals away from the original starting phase point. The teams' postings started at thirty kilometres and ending at sixty kilometres from zero point. No one knew how long Ben's mission would take, and therefore, how far he would 'travel' due to the Earth's rotation effect. However, they calculated that the reconnaissance would not be finished before three minutes (and they had instructed Ben not to initiate his return until after this time frame), and they had set an automatic emergency return at an interval of five minutes to ensure his homecoming, whatever state he was in.

He was extremely nervous about the whole mission. Recently, nothing had come back alive from this new 'continuum', leading to the collapse of their vision and hope for a 'brave new world'. The blame for all the missing colonists and the collapse of the project was laid squarely at his brother Kenny's feet, which had impacts on

Alex's men's attitude towards him. They tiptoed around the subject of 'Earth minus one' (which was a classified project anyway) when they were around him, instead of voicing pent-up feelings and resentments that they must surely have had.

He had pleaded with Ben not to go, but this proved futile. His friend couldn't resist taking on a dangerous volunteer mission; it was in his blood. They had grown up together in the same neighbourhood and had an old and trusting friendship.

He looked at the timer. Four minutes since the mission started and counting.

As if it were a timer set precisely at four minutes and six seconds, the screen sprang into audio and visual life. A white dot, representing the detection of their holy grail—Ben's phase device—flashed repeatedly at grid coordinates close to them, each flash being accompanied by an alarm beep. Alex made a quick calculation. The apparatus indicated that the tracking device was approximately 360 metres to their west and 35 metres to their south. He chuckled. '*Accurate or what*!' he gave his team a mental pat on the back for their planning and set up.

'Let's go get him!' he said unnecessarily to his crew.

'*We should almost be able to see him*!' He thought as he craned his neck in the direction of the estimated arrival. He could see no evidence of the returning soldier though. Small rock outcrops, that they would nevertheless have to circumnavigate, barred the view.

He grabbed his communication device, the ANSET. 'Central, this is homecoming station ten. We have our returning bird. I repeat, we have our returning bird. Approximately, 400 metres from our location. Moving in to acquire. Over.'

The operator at the central monitoring base acknowledged, and the line crackled dead.

Alex swung his legs around to the vehicle's controls, hit a button to close the doors to the outside elements, and engaged the key to start the electric motor.

Just then the beeping stopped, leaving only the electric whirring of the engine to fill the silence.

'What's happened? Get it back, Ron. Now!'

His subordinate, the most technically minded of the three, started to consult his screen and feverishly tap at his keyboard, pulling up the required tracking logs. But then, without any intervention by Ron and as suddenly as they had stopped, the beeps accompanied by the electronic white dots started up again. This time, however, they were not so audible, and the white dot was less accurately placed on the electronic map. The frequency and tone of the beeping was also erratic.

'The signal is weak and variable. Maybe the device has been damaged, or . . . ' Ron paused, unable to say what he was clearly thinking.

'Or what?' Alex barked impatiently.

'Or maybe it is behind a large structure, or even . . . ,' he paused again, still struggling with the concept. ' . . . embedded in something.'

'That's impossible! Fuck that,' was Alex's blunt reaction as he engaged the drive lever and rammed his foot down hard on the accelerator in one motion. The car lurched forward, and he swung the steering wheel to its maximum setting to the right. All three bodies veered in their belts to the left as the 180° manoeuvre was made a great deal faster than the vehicle was built to undertake.

Having seemingly and narrowly avoided a capsize, the vehicle righted itself and motored off in the general direction of the signal from the tracking device, following a path around the intervening rock outcrop. They would soon be out in the open and have an unimpeded view of the arrival site.

Before long, the vehicle broke out into the open plain, and all three soldiers scanned the horizon fervently. Geoff Konrad clutched an old pair of binoculars to his eyes in a vain effort to see their prize.

There was nothing.

The beeping and visual display showed the device was close, a mere 70 metres away. They continued to track the device with confused anticipation maintaining a silence between them until the location of the dot on the screen matched their own coordinates and the beeping, although still weak, was more or less a monotone squeal. They stopped the vehicle, and the trio leapt out of the car emerging into the heat.

'It's here!'Ron said obviously.

'How can it be?' replied his commanding officer. 'There is nothing here. Absolutely nothing.' Futilely, he kicked the dirt. 'Nothing but baked mud and these fucking shrubs.'

The signal was strongest a few metres from the car. They were on the edge of a large glacial plain which until recently had been frozen Tundra and Permafrost for millennia, but now was a baked desert. There was an unimpeded panoramic view for kilometres, confirming, as if it needed to, Alex's statement that there was indeed absolutely nothing here. Nothing could have arrived on this surface and disappeared so rapidly, leaving no evidence of their appearance, especially hampered by a space suit.

'Well,' Ron started uncertainly. Again, he showed a marked reluctance to breach the matter that they were all contemplating. 'The tracking technology is relatively primitive and only gives a target's coordinates in 2D. I am afraid that the weakness of the signal suggests that the beacon is below the surface. I am guessing from the strength of the signal about four or five metres below.'

'Thinking is not good enough! Are you sure?' Alex yelled at his operative.

'Y-yes,' came the stuttered reply.

Suddenly, Alex couldn't breathe, couldn't think, couldn't react, and couldn't feel. 'He said nothing but trudged back to the car to make his update report.'

'How could this be?' Geoff said, 'the compensating device is supposed to adjust for terrain so that travellers across continua don't materialise inside solid structures, isn't it? Goddamn these scientists for playing with our lives! Ben was a friend of mine.'

Ron grabbed his wrist. 'Shut up!' he hissed, 'you know, of course, that the Colonel's brother is one of the top white coats? He discovered all of this stuff,' Ron warned.

'Then he is the one who is condemning all of us to a certain death.'

CHAPTER 4

Secure transmission 1 March 2072

From: Col. Alex Clugston, commanding officer 'Early Bird' team

To: General Lloyd, commander of alliance forces

Cc: Western alliance security congress level 5 eyes

Subject: Initial findings and updates on status of 'Earth plus two' continuum

Our full, formal report on the geology and biosphere of this continuum will follow in our next report, but initial research has validated our early indications that this continuum is totally uninhabitable by human or any other oxygen respiring species. Progress is slow due to the harsh nature of the environment our scientists have to visit to be able to conduct their data gathering.

In light of the initial findings summarised below, input is required as to whether further analysis and research of this continuum is required. Although (my very excited scientists tell me) there are many scientifically interesting questions that need answering and that will help us understand how our own Earth and other earths developed, further analysis would seem to be outside of our mission remit.

We have clearly ascertained that conditions are not conducive for life as we know it and that this would seem to end our initial interest in this continuum. Please advise by return transmission.

My scientists and geologists findings are below:

The planet's atmosphere is composed almost exclusively of reducing gases; the main components being Methane (22.8 per cent), Hydrogen Sulphide (30.2 per cent), and Ammonia (27.0 per cent), with only traces of Reactive Oxygen Species (ROS) such as peroxides or oxygen ions. This means that the environment is caustic, toxic, and uninhabitable for aerobic respirators.

The other main consequence of this is that there has been no formation of an Ozone layer, so there is no protection to life forms from harmful radiation emanating from outer space.

Multiple samples of the ambient temperature at the equivalent latitude to the North American alliance indicate values averaging 89.47 °C during the day and 63.92 °C during the planet's night.

All life forms encountered are simple fermentative anaerobes, using a lactic acid type fermentation pathway and an ATP coenzyme for intercellular energy transfer for their metabolism.

We hypothesise that all species are obligate anaerobes (they have to get their energy via this method), as all samples that were introduced to oxygen perished rapidly. Like Earth's obligate anaerobic species; they lack the enzymes to breakdown oxides into harmless water and oxygen components.

Species include multiple single cell prokaryotes and eukaryotes, including virus like ultramicroscopic intercellular replicators, not unlike corresponding species on Earth. Excitingly though (mainly for my scientists), evolutionary radiation has lead to a variety of multicellular anaerobic species. Many of these are worm like—soft bodied, shelled animals of simple design—and all are sluggish due to the much lower energy gained per sugar molecule from anaerobic respiration. There are plant like species and what appear to be simple carnivores, but further research needs to be made into the habits and life cycles of these creatures (including how they have adapted to survive on land in an environment of life threatening radiation).

There is evidence of high volcanic activity on a global scale from our micro satellite geological scans. Multiple hotspots are indicated, including rift valleys and tectonic faults. Initial dating of rock samples gathered so far by our sample drones confirm that this planet was formed in the region of 4500 million years ago, in line with the age of our own Earth.

Photographic evidence and supporting empirical data shows that four fifths of the surface of the planet in early scans appears to be sea, which is olive green containing large concentrations of anaerobic algae-like swarms.

Initial astrological survey of a 45 per cent degree sweep of the equivalent Milky Way shows 92.3 per cent correlation between this continuum and ours for stars, stellar remnants, black holes, and other usual galactic objects.

One major difference from our Solar system is that there is NO moon, orbiting this earth as a satellite. Additionally there seems to be an additional planet orbiting the sun with an observed orbital distance of approximately 135 million kilometres from their equivalent sun. The object has an equatorial radius of 3,256 kilometres (making this object approximately the size of our solar system's Mars)

Consequently there is no tidal activity or any related gravitational phenomena on this planet.

Early hypothesis: The hypothesised event early in our Earth's history called 'The giant impact hypothesis' (this theory seems to have been validated; my scientists tell me) seems not to have occurred in this continuum. As this oblique impact between a large terrestrial planet and Earth, which supposedly created our Moon and gave our Earth angular momentum and extra mass, has never occurred, this seems to have inhibited the development of oxygen respiring or photosynthesising life forms, and therefore, no production of oxygen.

We await your decision on team deployment.

Regards,

Colonel Clugston

*

Slowly, at an arbitrary rate entirely outside of his control, the deterrents started to subside.

His rhythmic breaths, overlaid with panic induced shrieks, gradually reduced in intensity, and his body stopped jerking and fidgeting uncontrollably in its universe, as the perceived dangers had momentarily passed. The swirling chaos, which moments ago had ruled his domain, had dissipated now. The calm and quiet of solitude washed over him in more gentle fashion, fear dissipating away from him as steam slowing from a boiled kettle.

He was alone now. There were no beings around, and no immediate threats for violations of his universe's boundaries. He had never known that so many of the beings from the Proximal could exist in the same place. Until now he had not grasped the concept of how populous they could be and how wide open the spaces were that they existed in. They had been everywhere—swirling around him, running, screaming, calling out to each other, moving in small groupings, arms locked to stay in units.

There had been multiple breaches of his boundaries, as the beings collided with him, brushed past him, or simply pushed him out of the way. He had had to relocate himself out of this corporeal stream and out of the open to find a container where he could find some safety from these incursions. It wasn't a familiar container, so he was not comfortable; but at least his domain was safe from invasion, and he was alone.

This container was dark but not completely pitch black. It was the light time outside after all. Small shards of sunlight came through cracks in the various portals to the outside, which seemed to have wooden boundaries preventing a full flow of light coming through. It suited him for the time being as he needed the solitude and the lack of illumination, which would make him difficult to observe.

He had lost the beings that had grown familiar to him. All four of them had disappeared in the nightmare of the outside. This worried him a bit. They had been responsible for the upkeep and locality of his universe, and now he would have to arrange this for himself. Either that or perhaps it would find its own course. Why had they left him? The lack of a constant physical link between his universe and any of these beings and the onset of the blinding panic that clouded his senses when the deterrents emerged meant that they had simply vanished amongst all the other Proximal beings.

He wondered what time the darkness came to this container. How would he be able to see it, and how was he going to record his findings? He clutched on to the small bag which had his most important possessions, but he did not have everything he needed to exist here. All his books and research had been left at the previous container when he was suddenly moved with the other beings. Was he going back there? He needed that work. How could he expand his knowledge and continue his research here? How long had he been away from his own container?

A piercing fright shook his body. A being was here. He could see a dim outline against the invading light from the now opened door.

'Cosmo?' a voice probed.

It was OK; it was the older male being from his previous container. He should be fine with him. Hopefully, they can now relocate to one of these homes, so he could continue his research.

'Oh, thank god', the voice continued, 'I thought we had lost you.'

The older being closed the container door behind him and started to approach his corner of this container, so he bowed his head to ensure his eyes were averted. He was still breathing heavily, shoulders heaving slightly and rhythmically at an accelerated pace. His universe's environment felt cold, so he crossed his arms across his chest in an attempt to warm himself.

'Come on. Let's go, lad. Please. Let's not worry about the people outside, eh. What do you say? I will help you past them, OK?' He extended his arm in a gesture that suggested that Cosmo came with him. Cosmo was not keen to accept it or follow the being.

'I don't know how to see the sunset from here,' he fretted. 'What would I do for materials to record the findings? We need to go to my container. I can work from there. I need my research, my books, and my Internet. Yes, let us go to my container.'

'Yes, we can—' the man started but didn't finish. His head turned abruptly. He had heard it too.

Cosmo saw them from the periphery of his eyesight, and his anxiety leaped from a dormant to a vibrant state in an instant. He knew that this condition would only escalate exponentially from here.

The container's door had been kicked open. Two more Proximal beings were now in the container. He brought them both nearer to the centre of his vision, without directly staring at them, to analyse who or what they were. He had not seen either of them before. He was disappointed as well as scared. Neither of them were any of the other beings that he had spent most of his life growing increasingly comfortable and familiar with.

Both of them appeared to be the same when seen from the periphery of his vision; both were wearing green and dappled clothing, big shoes and were carrying weapons. He had seen these kinds of beings before on the vision box, and it was not good. These beings could bring death.

The invaders raised these weapons and pointed them in the direction of the older being and his universe. They spoke something to them, which he did not understand. It was not a usual method of communication that the likes of his own Proximal beings would use when communicating with his universe. The noises and mouth movements were roughly the same, only the resultant words did not seem to mean anything.

He felt a continued welling of feelings beyond apprehension and anxiety; feelings that could not be controlled and would lead to a spiralling of his innate fears and the inevitable deterrents that accompanied this state. He began to shake again, and his breathing accelerated uncontrollably. A guttural wincing sound, low at first, began to be emitted with each breath. He closed his eyes and waited for the effects to take over his body.

But nothing came. The panic attack was gently lifted away like a ladybird caringly scooped off a leaf surface and set free to flight. The deterrents were averted and soothingly instructed to relax and sit in their domain. '*They are not needed. They can wait until another time. All is fine. We will help you to get away. Relax, Cosmo.*'

He realised that these final thoughts were not his. He also remembered that he had experienced this invasion once before in his life.

Cosmo snapped his eyes open carelessly and now looked directly at the two newly arrived beings. They were still poised with their long weapons orientated in their direction. But they were motionless, caught in time, as if captured in a picture frame.

And now they were not alone. Another being was there—a friend, a familiar creature. This being would not harm him. He was sure that they had met before only he could not remember the occasion.

Waves of calming images and suggestions gently played over his thoughts like water from a sluggish low-land stream warmly tickling across a pebbled bed, gently kissing the tiny stones, and cocooning them in a benevolent guardian's embrace.

His breaths returned to a steady pace, and the sound of his pounding heart retired into obscurity as he fell into a waking dream of relaxation. Now he knew he was safe and that all would be taken care of.

The older Proximal being was also caught motionless in time, his hand still extended towards him in the moment of invitation. But suddenly he moved, his arm twitched and renewed its invitation. Cosmo looked directly into his eyes for the first time in his life. The older being was smiling, and his expression was an exuding pool of warmth. He hitched his small bag of possessions on to his shoulder and took the extended hand—again an act never undertaken before—and walked with the being. They crossed the darkened room and pushed open the door, bursting into the blinding light of the midday Sun.

People were everywhere, just as before, occupying almost all the space in the street as far as you could see. Only now they were all motionless, stopped in time like grotesque wax statues, a variety of expressions etched on to their panicked faces. For some reason that he did not understand, this seemed a perfectly reasonable situation; nothing that appeared out of sync with reality. He did not ponder on it. He was more interested at a sociological level in the Proximal beings. What was causing their strange behaviour? Why were they all standing still compared to their frenetic activity of a few minutes ago? It was most unlike him to take an interest in his neighbours, but he felt compelled.

He felt no fear looking directly at all them, no foreboding from being in a crowd, and no dread at the thought of potential breaches of his universe's boundaries. Instead, he felt an addictive fascination which replaced the lifelong and chronic paranoia that overwhelmed him in such circumstances. He had never seen so many of these beings congregated together, and now he had time and the capacity to somehow relax. He was amazed to observe how different they all were.

He saw mothers hugging children tightly to their chests, and other families with small bundles of possessions, as much as they could carry quickly. All were trapped in time, held motionless in mid flight, seemingly waiting for him and the older being to pass. All were part of an interrupted flowing river of beings, heading in one direction, out of town to a shared destination, a common goal that seemed terrifyingly important to achieve.

Cosmo knew that he must follow the older being. This was his only chance as he sensed that something was wrong to cause them to herd together like this. He was sure that he would be led to a new container soon, and he would get more reading material and a view of the Sun. He gripped tightly to the leading hand of his companion. It did not feel overpowering. It felt strangely reassuring.

He turned to look in the direction that the beings were coming from and now saw, he thought, what they were running from. There were more beings like the two who had found him in the darkened room, many more in fact. Most were on foot but further away, beyond the trailing edge of the crowd of fleeing beings, some were in vehicles. Most had weapons, and all looked unhappy and full of hatred for the other fleeing beings. These hateful expressions were grafted on to their similarly immobilised faces.

He could see that these beings with the weapons had used these on the stampeding crowd. He saw fallen beings—lying in the dust—clearly having been trampled by others in the crowd. The red stain of pain was imprinted on many of their bodies, and their lifeless faces mockingly pleaded retribution for the injustice.

'*Come on. You must hurry,*' the voice in his head was now direct, no longer a subliminal suggestive force.

He turned his view back to the direction of the frozen wave of panicked-human flight and strode with confidence with his companion, a self-assured confidence filling his sails. The pair wound their way through the maze of tragic statues edging closer to their goal, wherever that was. Maybe there was a new container available nearby?

Out of the corner of his eye, he saw another of the strange beings. It was standing quietly and peacefully as if on guard, but there was something intangibly different about this one compared to the one who had found them in the darkened container, something that he couldn't identify.

'No, that's it,' he quickly grasped. There was no connection between this being and himself. It was unconditionally absorbed with something else, something that required all of its faculties and afforded it little or no capacity for any other tasks.

He could feel that it was not frozen like the other present Proximal beings. It was voluntarily still, part of a network of control that these beings were imposing. They were dictating this situation, monitoring, and oppressing the will of the normal occupants of the Proximal universe.

He found it odd, though, that in all of his reading, in all his years of study that he had never uncovered any data on these beings. He felt secure in their benevolent mind lock and did not feel at all threatened by them. Quite the opposite, he felt more relaxed than he had ever experienced in the entire life of his universe. This all constituted more of a connection than he had ever had with other beings that he had encountered.

Now he saw more of the strange beings, all in the same absorbed meditative pose. All of them were taller than the Proximal beings, with huge skulls, broad shoulders, and swollen backs. It was a controlling army, exerting an iron neural grip in this locality.

He was now being lead down a hill, which, although steep at first, eventually flattened out and terminated in high brick structures that butted on to a huge expanse of water. He stopped dead in his tracks for a second until reassured by the voice in his head.

This was a sight he had witnessed before, near both of his universe's previous containers. Latterly, he used to be taken on occasions to visit the large quantity of water that existed near his last container (from where he had recently been taken by his Proximal beings) and made to sit in the open space nearby. This was the green open space with no walls that made him feel a little uncomfortable sometimes. He had always thought that this was a great expanse of water, (although its levels had seemed to diminish considerably recently), but at all times you had been able to see land and green on the other side.

These visits to the open space had always annoyed him. They coincided with the waking hours, when he should be working on his research, reading or searching electronically for data. But they never lasted for long. He would quickly get bored and have to communicate repeatedly with his Proximal beings until they took him back to his container again.

No, the familiar water near his container was nothing like this stretch that was before him now. Up to the extremity of his vision all he could see was water, culminating in a perfect straight line dividing the enormous mass of liquid from the light blue freedom of the open sky. And how this mass was moving! It was churning up and down in a constant fashion that had a pattern that was definitely familiar to him but which he couldn't place.

He continued to analyse this motion for a few moments as they approached, still slowly but surely dodging between ever more petrified and motionless beings.

'*That's it*', he thought in his excitement, The water motion was similar to that of electromagnetic waves, such as light, gamma, or radio waves! This must be the sea'. He deduced piecing his scientific knowledge together with an appreciation of geography and the constant laws of physics in his neighbouring universe.

His mood brightened further than it already had under the mental straight jacket of his beneficial captor's influence. *'The sea is a good place to see the sunset. I will be able to get accurate timings.'*

They were down near the edge of the land now, and the ground was much flatter as they walked on the brick structures. The sounds and nasal impetuses were different. The wind whipped a moist, fresh mix of brine and air across the dual receptors of his nose and tongue. He simultaneously tasted and smelt the tang of salty freshness smeared across the top of his palate, thrown into spray by violent water movement. It revived his perspective and invigorated him further. He was enjoying the fact that he could look down at the water from a height. It made him feel different; entirely distinct, apart from and secure from the waves and foam transforming itself upon the stone buttress and rocks below.

More beings were here now, and their expressions and bodies seemed trapped in time in even more desperate poses, faces etched with angry, anxious, and even terrified contortions. It was harder to move past them, and minor breaches of his space were inevitable. This did not worry him due to their stillness and the continued comforting stimuli in his head.

Some of these beings held weapons, but these were not the beings with the dappled green clothing and machines. These had varied attire and stood defending boats which were stationed at the bottom of the stairs, seemingly carved out of the brick.

Some of the beings were caught in an unwanted embrace, rolling on the ground, whilst in hostile acts of wrestling each other. Others lay on the ground wounded from aggressive beatings they had taken. One individual, an elder being such as his Proximal being, lay there, unconscious and bleeding from a wound in his stomach. All were motionless, mocking the fury and aggression of their activities at the moment they were stopped in time.

They were now standing above a particular boat. It was long, about the length of the house where his container was, and it was full of beings holding on to each other and the sides of the boat in desperation, attempting to maintain a place on it for them and their groups.

Suddenly, all these people seemed to wake from their obedient reverie, as if a wireless remote control had been aimed at them and the 'on' switch selected. They began to file, in perfect collusion with each other and with an assured calmness, off the boat and up the stairs to the top of the buttress in single file. Their faces were expressionless, and their mood completely neutral. There was no panic, no barging, and no aggression.

Soon all but a handful of individuals were on the buttress, and as soon as they were all present at the top, they resumed their zombie like state, standing stiffly erect under a hidden directive.

Four beings remained below, and they now started to move around the boat, pulling ropes and organising busily. One leapt on to the stone stairs and grabbed a rope that seemed to connect the land with the awaiting boat. He pulled the rope off a large metal stud in the concrete and held it. He looked up to them invitingly, waiting patiently but without emotion or expression.

His Proximal being gently tugged at Cosmo's hand, luring him on and coaxing him to board the vessel. The attending being moved into line behind them for the descent down the carved steps. These were wet and more than a little slimy, but soon, they slowly picked their way to the boat's edge and made the small leap on to it. Cosmo was lead to a strange small wooden door which seemed to open in the middle. He looked behind him. The being who had released the boat from the shore had now joined all of them on the deck accompanied by the rope and pushed them off with his leg. The boat slowly eased away from the land.

He should have been panicking, and the deterrents should be in full flow. He was out in the open with no walls to create a container, he was on top of a huge expanse of water, and a strange container awaited him behind this wooden door. His protective defence mechanisms should have been in meltdown. Instead, though, he felt the lingering and calming influence of the strange being's presence constantly renewing his serenity.

The older being opened the odd wooden door easily, and they descended down more wooden stairs to a dimly lit container below.

His final thoughts, as he lowered his head and began to relocate his universe down into this unfamiliar and constantly shifting container, were how long he would be here and how well he would be able to monitor the setting sun.

*

Fzzzzzzzzzzzzzzzzzttt!

The enraged creature clattered the technological barrier that divided it from its obsessive goal again. Was it Iptat's imagination or was this electronic sound that they had rhythmically been listening to for what seemed like an eternity fading? Was it softening somehow, losing its sharpness, giving in to this remorseless pounding?

Iptat attempted to look at the Sentinel again. There was no eye contact now. The beast's head was bowed as it regrouped for each shoulder charge. Iptat could see telltale discolouration on the heavily armoured flank that the Sentinel was using to batter against the field. This signified that serious burns were being inflicted each time it charged into the neuronic mesh. A red stream of circulatory fluids ran from its nostrils, slowly but steadily, staining the clinical white of its cryo-suit like blotting paper greedily sucking on a dye. Intermittent wafts of the smell of burning flesh could be detected in the otherwise odourless environment, as automated air circulation, having by now detected activity from living units and activated, distributed the grotesque scent. The smoky particles stabbed unchallenged on the senses, imprinting yet further more fear in the mind.

The weary and wounded beast's charges did not have the energy of its initial bursts, but Iptat could tell from the crazed look in its eyes that it had lost none of its resolve for the battle. It would get through or die doing so. Each charge further reduced the neuronic charge in the opening. It was still just a matter of time.

Iptat realised that it had been rooted to the spot, entirely absorbed by the Sentinel's battle, both with the barrier and its own resolve. Iptat felt like one of the non-sentient animal species from its planet, the type that would freeze when confronted by a culling party—unable to run or try and protect itself, but trapped in a pitiful, mesmerised feedback loop.

Iptat absolutely had to shake off this obsessive fascination and move off. Its survival and the fate of their mission depended on it.

'I am not sure that we are going to make it. This race is too close to call,' Iptat addressed the possessed mechanoid.

'We can't stay here or we *will* be assassinated by the Sentinel,' it observed rather obviously. 'We have to move towards the interior of the chamber and conceal ourselves. We must go right now.'

Iptat now found itself with a renewed strength to make decisions. The pair moved off hurriedly, weaving and zigzagging between the rows of cryo-pods in a futile attempt to fool the Sentinel. It was probably a waste of time, but it made Iptat feel better.

It broke into a trot, which was not easy, considering its poor but improving physical state. As soon as it had moved off, the Sentinel's eyes locked on to it and followed its progress. There was only a limited potential for concealing its direction from the highly trained unit. For a starter, it would know which half of the room that its quarry would be located in. Iptat and the mechanoid would be unable to cross the central aisle in front of the door without being seen. When it breaks through, it will not need much time to find its quarry, Iptat contemplated.

'The Hub Commander unit is near the centre of this room.' Iptat paused for breath. 'I need to go and monitor the resuscitation process, keep on top of its bio-data and hope that the time the Sentinel takes to find me is greater than the Hub Commander's recuperation to full cognitive capacity. We only need to win by a split temporal unit to have the advantage and allow the commander to re-establish control over its renegade subordinate.'

Iptat exhaled heavily and repeatedly. It had never been one of the fittest units, so it stopped walking and addressed the sentient algorithm again.

'*Then what?*' It thought to itself.

'We still have to negotiate with the Sentinel's commander, who will need a lot of convincing due to the fact that we have kidnapped and cryogenically frozen it and all its colleagues against their will. Even though the unit will be restrained in its cryo-chamber, it will be in command of the situation, as at any time it could order the soldier to assassinate the pair of us.'

The algorithm was quiet. Iptat continued.

'OK, we should split up now. You hide yourself in another area of the room. This gives us a greater chance of at least one of us surviving to coordinate the Hub Commander's neural connection and negotiate our way out of this.'

The SIPIA, standing motionless with lights blinking where eyes should be, did not respond.

'Did you hear me?' Iptat enquired.

After a few moments (rather valuable wasted moments, Iptat thought) the reply came.

'Apologies AO 76377-QY107, this mechanoid unit has limited capacity for multithreading large operational tasks. I could not communicate with you whilst I was conducting a download of a large data file. I have been wirelessly uploading our experiences since my download into this unit to the main SIPIA mainframe, to allow the data to be processed by my more powerful servers. I have just completed the download of the results of this processing along with an appropriate tactical combat folder from the historical data cloud.'

'Brilliant! What is your conclusion? Do you have a plan of action based on this analysis?' The question was half sarcastic and half in hope.

'We have to slow the Sentinel unit using any method available, to give us time to gain control via the Hub Commander unit. Do you have anything that will serve as a weapon of any description?' it asked.

'All I have is a multi-purpose fusion tool and a simple long metal tool, but I doubt that these will be of any use against the Sentinel's defence.'

'This is better than nothing. Such implements can serve a purpose if we somehow manage to weaken the Sentinel or identify and take advantage of its weaknesses. I will search for materials to enable us to manufacture a simple but more effective weapon to slow down or stun the unit to give us this time.'

Iptat did not hold out much hope.

'OK', it said, 'do that, but do it quietly and hidden somewhere in this room.'

The mechanoid whirred off quietly on its rotary podia towards the centre of the chamber. The gentle hum of its progress slowly faded until all that was left for Iptat was the constant, slightly remote, pounding of its distant cousin, the caste member from its own species with which it shared the same genetic code.

That piece of data aside, its hunter was as near as could be to being an entirely separate species. They were billions of light orbits apart in terms of thought processes, values, and reasons for being. How had their race become so markedly divergent over time? Iptat's Operative caste had absolutely nothing in common with this animal that was now in the process of killing itself against the neuronic field just so it could have the chance to massacre the mechanoid and itself.

A few more zigzags, a few hundred paces, and one or two wrong turns later Iptat had found its patient. Without checking the serial number Iptat knew it was the correct cryo-pod, as the revival process was well underway. As such the opaque insulation jacket was wide open, revealing the transparent lid of the cryo-chamber. Immediately it leant over the coffin like container, gasping for oxygen as if it were an elderly unit deemed as irrelevant for their society and marked for termination and wiped condensation off the outer edge. It screwed its eyes up as it was barely able to see anything clearly through the frosted cryo-chamber lid, but it could make out that the occupant was beginning to writhe in confusion and pain. Iptat felt sorry for it, having just recently suffered the same agonising ritual itself.

Iptat viewed the statistics for the cryo-revival process. The resuscitation of the unit's body was progressing satisfactorily, but it was clear that the selected candidate was in severe distress; much greater suffering than Iptat had been in earlier in the same rotation, due to the necessity for a reduced revival horizon. The Operative tapped a few commands on the console, which immediately scheduled an additional tranche of nanoids, proteins, and hormones for intravenous delivery to its patient. There was little choice but to provide this additional supplement, for without it the subject had virtually 0 per cent chance of survival. With the increased dose it had a reasonable chance of living for a few thousand temporal units and a slim chance of making it through the whole of the current rotation.

It charged the electrical stimulant paddles in case of heart failure and stood there waiting. It seemed an age before the gently whispered exhalation of the cryo-chamber signalled the opening of the sarcophagus like lid.

The patient lay there, unconscious, not breathing, and not moving. Multiple tubes that fed the subject the required nutrients and chemicals protruded from various parts of its body, and the beast was further restrained by the chromo dynamic memory interface headset. The server responsible for the memory download was not flashing, and a message stated that it was 'Offline, awaiting instructions'. Iptat knew that both the nanotechnology and the patient's natural tissue repair apparatus would also be on hold, deferring action until establishing if the body would make a recovery from its current status of 'clinically dead'.

The fully charged and whirring paddles in Iptat's hands were applied rapidly and crudely to the Hub Commander's chest, setting off a large autonomic nervous reaction in the 'would be' carcass. The body arched, thrusting vestigial nipples skyward and slumped back to its original position with a loud slap.

'*Too much noise*,' Iptat knew, but there was no alternative. '*Come on! Come on!*' it implored silently to itself for the unit's recovery.

Two more applications of electric charges, and weak barely detectable but optimistic vital signs were established. '*I just need a few hundred temporal units and the nano repair team will kick in,*' the apprehensive Operative thought.

Iptat immediately strapped an oxygen supply to the Hub Commander's mouth, which immediately started to stream life giving gas to the ailing patient, forcing it to breathe. It massaged the commander's chest vigorously, whilst holding down the face mask tight to its mouth.

Agonisingly slowly the Sentinel gained strength. Iptat waited as long as it could then stabbed a large, previously prepared hypodermic directly into the beast's chest. The Aggressterone and Demotase mix was delivered rapidly and directly to where it was needed—into the Hub Commander's heart. It jerked awake, snapping its eyes wide open and contorting its body forward against its restraints for a brief moment, straining its full musculature against the metal, only to fall back in the cryo-pod. Its glazed eyes showed no recognition of events and indeed seemed to be full of panic or at least confusion. It screwed its eyes tight in fear, pain, and anguish in what seemed like an effort to regroup and face the ordeal afresh.

The server lights were now starting to flash, and the status moved on from 'Offline' to 'Upload', with an accompanying progress bar for the new task. All the while, the confused Hub Commander fought against its restraints with as much strength as it could muster; a surprising amount considering its state. It panted rapidly and crudely, attempting to draw as much oxygen as possible to circulate this energy provider to its deprived organs.

The interface clasps released themselves from the commander's scalp, and Iptat removed the helmet from the distressed subject, who promptly coughed and spluttered a sprayed mix of lime green bile and spittle into the face mask in an attempt to vomit. There was nothing to throw up as the subject had not eaten for over four hundred revolutions.

'You! Operative. What am I doing here?' it said very slowly and softly, just managing to get this out before gagging with the effort of fighting to raise words at the expense of its raw and desiccated throat. It tried again to liberate its arms to raise its body, but the specially designed strengthened clamps held all its appendages to its side. Without these restraints it was impossible to predict what it might have done. One example would be to reach out and grab Iptat's neck with one hand, snapping it like a small stick, and instantly ending the operative's life.

All passengers on this ship apart from Iptat were so constrained. It had to be so because the last memory for all these unwitting explorers was being rendered unconscious at the Primus Sentinel Tournament, back on their planet. The venue for this event was chosen by the rebel Cerebrals as they knew that this was the only occasion every revolution that attracted a few thousand caste members of all varieties. This opportunity of cross caste congregation was rare due to strict zero social fraternisation policies. This tournament, an unequivocally bloody and archaic contest to decide the best Sentinel soldier on their continent (or most stupid and genetically militarised, Iptat always thought), was chosen as the location to 'steal' all the prisoners from across all castes by mass intoxication with neural agents and enforced translation to the prepared space ship.

Sentinels, of course, loved the tournament, but so did Procreators (who enjoyed placing enormous wagers) and a relatively large following of Acquiescent Operatives or those arse lickers, who felt it would improve their standing in society to be seen at such an event.

Iptat poured some of the liquid nutrient supplement, provided in timely fashion by the resuscitation algorithm, into its patient's four-jawed mouth, an act which seemed to be appreciated at some level ('*can a Sentinel be grateful?*' the doctor pondered). The lingering bilious taste of vomit having been alleviated and the removal of the sand paper from its throat completed, the angry commander recommenced its angry struggle.

'Release me!'

Both the unit's arms and legs now beat up and down in the small space awarded them by the restraints, the result being a rhythmic metallic rattling as Sentinel strength combated tensile force. The sound, Iptat imagined, could surely be heard echoing clearly around all adjacent chambers in the ship, let alone this particular one.

'Release me, you vermin operative. Comply with a superior Sentinel's orders, or when I get out, I am going to kill you!' it promised. Iptat believed it absolutely, but did nothing.

Time was almost out. The loose renegade must surely have broken through the mechanoid's neuronic field by now, and it was not hard to guess where in the room this noisy drama was playing out. Even before the Hub Commander's ranting and gyrating had started, they had been making an easily ample clamour to signpost their location, but their whereabouts was inescapable now.

Iptat fought back the natural, inbuilt reflex, which had served placental beasts for many millennia, to panic, turn, and run for safety. Logic prevailed in this case, as what good would this strategy do anyway? It might buy it a few hundred temporal units, but the end result would be the same. The mission's only hope was to gain control of the Hub Commander immediately, to allow it in turn to secure control over its subordinate via their specialised neural network.

Then, as abruptly as it had begun, the aggressive gyrating and ranting stopped.

The suddenness, totality, and beauty of this new silence resonated more forcefully and profoundly into Iptat's psyche than the ferocious uproar that had preceded it; it was somehow more sinister, more disquieting.

Iptat looked up at the Hub Commander, who was now straining the sinews in its neck to look over the edge of the cryo-container, as comfortably as it was permitted by the wrist and ankle restraints. Its eyes were locked on something just over the shoulder of the bemused operative.

'Release me, or I will have it kill you,' the Sentinel officer stated with simple eloquence.

Iptat could now hear a laboured breath behind it accompanied by a disturbing 'extra sense' feeling of a menacing presence.

It did not need to look around to know what was standing there, a mere few paces away.

*

'*What was that?*'

The boy's head jerked up from his pillow suddenly and hovered there, staring intently into the night gloom, his neck straining slightly against the weight of his head. He was holding his breath and staying absolutely motionless so as to have every chance of picking up any further noise, however small. His wide eyed gaze was fruitlessly attempting to laser burn a hole in the pitch black darkness of the room, to let light pour through the burnt chasm and refresh his retinas. Nothing came back. It was an absolute darkness, and there was no light that his eyes could use to adjust to the pure black.

He was scared. This and childish indecision now enforced his frozen and silent state of immobility. What should he do?

He could yell for his parents across the other side of the house, the solution that his fear longed for him to act upon. But he was scared of his dad. He knew he would not take kindly to an unexpected middle of the night disturbance without cause. Dad spanked a lot, and that could hurt. He felt he should definitely check what was going on first before disturbing his father.

Or he could just bury his head under his pillow and pretend that there was nothing there. Maybe he would go back to sleep, and whatever was there would just go away? This was a beautiful, simple, and attractive option, but one that was too easy to fall back on—a coward's way out. Besides, would he really be able to get back to sleep if he thought that there was something wandering about in the house? And might it attack him or eat him in his sleep? On second thoughts, maybe this was not such a great idea.

Or he could investigate what the noise was. After all he was six now, a real grown-up and brave boy. His mummy had told him as much many times. He felt that he was the big boy of the family even though he was only the middle brother. His younger brother was just three and a complete pain, but he guessed he liked him despite the trouble he often got him into. The younger boy was always telling on the big brother.

Was he awake? If so he might be scared and could need his help. No, he thought, if he were awake, he would be crying, and he could not hear anything, not even breathing.

'*Wait! Maybe he had been killed or eaten by the monster?*'

'*Oh, come on!*' he beat himself up. '*There are no such things as monsters*. He tried to pull himself together to be that big, brave boy that his mother talked about.

He rustled under his pillow, found a small pen torch, flicked it on, and aimed it at his baby brother's bed. He relaxed noticeably as his first thought was correct. He could see his brother's small body in the cot, a small duvet rising and falling rhythmically with his unconcerned breaths. This was a huge relief; whatever monster was in the house had not gotten rid of his little bro.

What about his elder brother? He was a strange, funny brother, not like any of the other boys whom he knew. Sometimes he was so quiet, and sometimes you couldn't get him to shut up. When he was loud, he either talked funny and would say the same things over and over again or would be screaming and kicking his arms and legs. He would never play with you or even let you touch his skin, and the boy thought that that was really weird. Just touching his elder brother brought on a bout of screaming and arm thrashing until you stopped the touching or holding. This was really annoying, especially if he had one of your toys or books.

The strange things he used to say were not things that a normal boy would say. He would never look at you either. There was no arguing with him either; he was always right, and Mummy or Daddy would always let him get away with this.

The boy did not understand this, and it made him sad and cross. It wasn't fair.

Mummy always said that his elder brother was a special boy and that although he did not really show it, he loved all his family in a different way, even though it was difficult for us to understand him or feel that love. The boy supposed he loved his brother back, but he was no fun at playing or even talking, and so it was difficult to feel that strongly about him.

He raised his body on one elbow, threw the duvet off quietly with a sweeping movement of his arm, and swung his legs round till they met the floor at the side of his bed. The torch light still played over the room, and he gripped it tightly and shakily as he started across the room.

'*All OK in here*,' he thought to himself bravely, but uncertainly, whilst wishing underneath that he had gone for the head-under-the-pillow option. One foot slowly followed another as he quietly tiptoed in the direction of his elder brother's room. By now, he knew pretty much where all the squeaky parts of the floor were, and he used the pattern of the carpet, under the dim glow of his tiny torch, to plot his progress as silently as possible across the bedroom.

This strategy was mostly met with success, and one or two minor creaks aside, he soon found himself a couple of metres from the interconnecting door to his brother's room, which was very slightly ajar. Suddenly, his failing torch dimmed rapidly, and within seconds it was out, battery wasted, like a snuffed-out candle. He could now faintly hear his brother mumbling, a not unusual event, but very odd for this time of the night.

He braved the remaining two or three steps to the door, having retained a mental picture of the layout in the darkened room. He advanced to the door and swung it open slowly to just enough of a crack to peer through without letting the baddy, monster, robber, or whatever it was the chance to see him. The interior of his brother's room afforded him little more light than he already was accustomed to in his own room, so initially he could see nothing. Gradually though, his eyes accustomed to allow some focus.

The content of the mumblings was audible now. The boy recognised it as the usual funny way that his brother always talked.

'I must tell you that I am not allowed to talk now . . . It goes dark at 1900 . . . Yes, lights always go out at 1900, 24-hour clock . . . My alarm always goes off at O-seven thirty, breakfast is at O-eight hundred . . . Of course, I always obey the laws around the dark period, you know . . . I am always ready for shutdown at 1900 hours . . . I watch my science show and then I am off to bed at 1900 hours . . . Nobody is allowed in my room after 1900 hours . . . That is why you shouldn't be here . . . I have choco munch for nutritional input at O-eight hundred . . . then I read my books in my room . . . I always have books in my room, books and papers . . . , and Internet . . . It goes dark in here at 1900 . . . I can't read after that . . . My lights go out at 1900 hours . . . '

Who was he talking to? The boy could not see anything or anyone. Why was he standing in the middle of the room talking? This was very unusual he thought. His brother always did exactly the same thing every day. He always stayed in his bed after bedtime. If you tried to talk to him or enter his room after eight in the evening or, even worse, touch him after he had gone to bed, he would start to scream, and you would get whacked by Dad, so he hadn't tried these things for a long time.

Suddenly, there was a glow which made the boy duck back behind the door in a reflex reaction. He could hear his heart pounding in his chest, he was so nervous. He attempted to compose himself and moved forward to put his eye to the crack again.

In this very faint glow (was this sudden light going out already now?), he could see that his brother was standing in the middle of his immaculately tidied room. This was another thing that always annoyed him. His brother always put all his stuff in the same place, at the same time, at the end of the day, and ensured absolutely nothing was on the floor. This bugged the boy enough, but on top of that he would always line his books and magazines up in the same fashion on his table or shelves, smallest to biggest, never diverging from this routine.

A while back, on occasions, the boy used to place stuff randomly all over the floor to annoy his elder brother, but had stopped now as he was always punished for it. These actions were always accompanied by his brother screaming, oscillating his body back and forward, and a general bout of freaking out. There was never a possibility of talking with him or suggesting it was a joke. His weird brother simply did not understand.

A new movement sent a chill through the boy and cemented his feet to their spot. He could now see a figure in the room with his brother, who did not seem to be afraid or even consider this out of the ordinary. This was very odd. The boy did not know what time it was, but he was certain that it was well after eight o'clock, and so his brother should be panicking or even screaming in defiance.

He could not tell exactly what the figure was. It was tall, bigger than their dad with a rather large, silly-looking head. Long, thin arms reached down and were now cradling his brother's head as the boy still ranted albeit about different things apart from his bedtime, cereal selection, and morning routine, as if the monster were not there at all. What was he talking about? It didn't make sense.

The boy knew that all of this was wrong and that he should shout to alert his parents to the danger, but he seemed totally incapable of any action. His body seemed frozen with fear, and the controlling link between his thoughts and his actions severed. He began to shiver.

Then his brother's mumblings changed.

'Of course, you know that it doesn't belong here . . . No, no, no! . . . Not there! . . . It doesn't fit . . . You should keep it . . . . It doesn't belong to me . . . It doesn't fit . . . This is a bad place . . . I never go there . . . Get it out! . . . It doesn't belong to me . . . '

Why does he not scream at this monster which is touching it? It wasn't fair. He was *his* brother, and all the boy had to do was touch him, and the screaming would start. This began to make him angry and jealous. What hold over his brother did this monster have that he didn't have?

The dim glow from the visitor was fading still further, but the boy's eyes were compensating by adjusting themselves to what light was being offered. He could see the outline of the monster with his hand cradling his brother's head as if he were blessing him in some strange religious ritual. Then the monster withdrew a couple of steps from his brother, and he felt relief wash over him.

He shifted his foot uncomfortably only to step down on a fragile plastic toy. The crunching destruction of the item in the night, heard in a moment's pause in the mumblings, might as well have been a gunshot. The visitors head moved in a controlled fashion and appeared to be looking in the boy's direction. That was his last, albeit brief, memory.

'Yes, I will go to sleep, right here on the carpet and never remember anything of this.'

The boy thought that the voice made a lot of sense.

He knelt to the floor, lowered himself to a foetal position and instantly fell asleep.

*

They all sat there quietly and sombrely, pretending to ignore each other. One or two of them knew each other, but overall it was a congregation of individuals chosen for their array of specific talents. Some were selected locally from the British-controlled hydro zone, but a few were imported from either the American or Canadian sectors to assemble this gathering. Some were clearly from the military, and others were civilians, probably scientists, medics, or possessing some other specialist skill required for whatever the mission was.

Alex Clugston scanned the assembled entourage with a quizzical eye. He knew, of course, his brother, a scientist whose discoveries had been brought under extreme scrutiny over the last few weeks. He hadn't seen him since the event as Kenny had been incarcerated under guard in the laboratory, partly due to the communication shutdown which accompanied the failed visit of Ben Howell to 'Earth minus one' and partly for his own safety. Scientists were not popular in the North American alliance at the moment. This aside, he was sitting in pole position, waiting at the 'top table', on a raised platform at the front of the room.

Also, he knew Kenny's friend Lars Rasmussen, who had been a family friend whilst they were growing up and now studied in the 'Sci/Med' laboratories in a related field to his brother.

The rest of the gathering he did not know and consequently didn't spend too much time thinking about.

However, being a red-blooded male, there was one participant who caught his eye most. This was the one woman amongst them, sitting there silently, twiddling a pencil and looking down at some documents. She seemingly was attempting to avoid eye and other contact with the otherwise all-male collection of individuals. She was young, perhaps thirty, and pretty, but at the same time had an air of hardness and maturity which gave you the impression that she could give as good as she got and didn't tolerate fools. She was blonde and slim, and her hydro suit clung tightly to her ample curves. Not many people could carry off wearing those unfashionable but necessary outfits and look good, but she had succeeded admirably in this. She caught Alex's eye for a brief moment, held the gaze without any acknowledgement or hint of a smile, and then turned back to her reading.

'*She will get there*,' Alex thought to himself, smiling inwardly.

They totalled twelve individuals, some nervously fidgeting, some totally still, relaxed, and poker faced—all waiting for the unknown to be revealed.

They all had one thing in common; no one knew exactly what they were doing here but understood that it must be important, and therefore, a highly classified alliance project that they were going to be briefed on and enrolled into. You didn't meet General Ray O'Hara for an informal coffee, and rarely were personnel congregated across different hydro zones for a cross sector venture.

There was, however, a tangible edge amongst the congregation. Alex knew that this was due to the fact that, alongside a briefing of some soon to be discovered military and scientific joint initiative, there would be a good chance for the attendees to vent some anger or at least some frustration, at a couple of the core inventors of the technology which had proved so seemingly disastrous and fatally flawed.

Finally, there were the two military guards, silently and motionlessly holding vigil at the door, both heavily armed.

The door burst open, and a large American strode in, accompanied by a two man entourage, who all walked briskly up to the table where Kenny was sitting. He manhandled the available chair away from its berth at the table and sat down forcibly. The entourage followed suit in a more controlled manner.

'Dismissed!' O'Hara barked. The two guards clearly did not have the required clearance for the content of this conference. This also meant that the 'top table' felt confident they could control the assembled meeting. The guards saluted and marched out of the room in a synchronised and regimented fashion.

'Major-General Reeves!' the General continued. He was clearly not a man to waste words.

One of the men at the front desk stood up confidently. This man Alex knew and did not like. He was a political soldier, who was driven by ambition at the expense of all other factors, and was famously known to be in the General's pocket. You always knew that the shit had hit the fan, when you met Reeves as you would only ever see him in this sector when there was a major initiative planned.

Alex got the distinct impression from the handful of discussions that they had had over the last few years that Reeves did not give a shit for the welfare of this sector or for the British and European personnel on his unit. He was not a people's man. Alex didn't trust him a bit and had had a few disagreements with him about what was best for his men. The two of them simply did not see eye to eye.

Reeves stood up, failing to make eye contact with Alex or even acknowledge his existence, and dismissively went on to address the assembled party.

'Gentlemen . . . and lady,' almost as an afterthought he registered the one female in the group.

'It goes without saying that everything that is discussed in this room stays between this assembled group and goes no further.' He paused to clear his throat.

'As you have no doubt guessed, we have assembled you all together for reasons critical to the security and well being of the North American alliance. Our recent major covert project to colonise the alternative world known to the scientists as 'Earth minus one' has been terminated suddenly and with an unacceptable loss of life'

Alex was sure that this loss of life was of little consequence to a back-stabbing bastard like Reeves. The Major-General continued unabated.

'The colonisation had seemed to have been going well, and the project was absolutely on plan.' However, events changed the situation extremely rapidly. This doorway to a new future that had been opened by our scientists and had seemingly provided a rescue for mankind was slammed shut in our faces. Suddenly nobody could transport either way, to or from the new world, and our automated reconnaissance devices started to fail in a random manner, providing us with next to no data. What little we were able to retrieve was analysed by our scientific team and, as a result, a highly classified reconnaissance mission to the continuum was planned and executed.

'This mission's objective was to ascertain what sudden and unpredictable event or series of events could have occurred to cause the failure of the technology and the presumed loss of life of the colonists.'

He paused again, and it was clear from his body language that he was about to divulge some additional bad news.

'Regretfully, this mission also failed with the resultant death of the soldier who had bravely volunteered for the task.'

Perfect silence ruled in the room in the uncomfortable pause that followed, as Reeves let this news sink in. It was not so much the death of one individual that stunned the assembled team but the resulting loss of hope unleashed and allowed to run riot in the room. The failure of the colonisation had been communicated to almost all of them (those who had the required level of clearance), but nobody had even dreamt that the possibility of this new hope for mankind, that had spurred excitement, activity, and dreams of a new life, had been crushed.

Since the first years of the scorching, everybody with any intelligence in the North American continent realised that humanity's days were numbered on Earth, despite all the bullshit and hype that the governing body, the military and the scientists spouted.

'*We will find a way of bailing mankind out of this mess,*' was always their mantra.

Then suddenly this new technology arrived and gave many people a crumb of hope that, perhaps, the government rhetoric had been right all along, and that life could continue in some shape or form in another replica world.

Now this seemed to be snatched away again in a single phrase from a cold and callous soldier.

'It is not all bad news, and all hope is certainly not lost, however.' Reeves attempted to resurrect some optimism and raise the mood. 'May I introduce you to Dr Mark Webster, chief executive of the alliance foundation for scientific and medical research, who is going to brief you on the findings brought back from that mission and provide scientific background and context to our plans.'

With little ceremony, the pair exchanged places. The difference in demeanour was immediately obvious—the self-assured, bordering on arrogant, swagger of the soldier making way for the fidgeting nervousness of the scientist.

'Good afternoon,' Webster offered. He shuffled his notes around in an eccentric and disorganised fashion. Finally, he found his place and proceeded.

'The first failures of the phasing technology and ability to transport safely to the proposed continuum started on September 29 of last year.' It was read word for word and monotone.

'Since then twenty-seven probes, have been sent to the continuum. Each of these was modified to incorporate any changes needed as a result of data we received between each test run and input into our calculations for the next probe. In 100 per cent of tests, the pre-phase probes returned corrupted and disabled from their exposure to the environment. Additionally, when the probes returned, they all re-materialised back on our Earth a calculable and predictable distance west of the original phase location, this distance being directly proportional to the duration of the probe in the other continuum.'

Webster took off his round, rimless spectacles and started to wipe them with a rather dirty looking handkerchief from the thin lab coat that he was wearing over his hydro suit.

'Over the course of these tests, we have ascertained that the calculated velocity of the probes, based on the distance each one 'travelled' west and the duration of the test, always equated to 707.63 kilometres per hour.'

He looked at a few of the blank faces in the audience, clearly expecting them to know the significance of this number.

'This is the rotational speed of the surface of the Earth spinning on its axis at our latitude,' he continued with a tiny hint of exasperation.

'The inevitable conclusion we had to arrive at was that each probe is not being influenced by any rotational forces such as those which occur on a satellite like object spinning in space. The probes were all approximately following the same trajectory in the new continuum as our planet in this continuum, but not following the same trajectory as an object on the surface of our planet.'

He paused again as he now replaced the glasses on his head and the handkerchief in its pocket.

'The probes were orbiting a copy of our Sun in the next continuum but not following the surface of the Earth facsimile in this continuum,' Reeves translated.

'Thank you, Major General,' he responded in a slightly annoyed tone.

'The conclusion from this was that there was *no* planet Earth in the alternative continuum, and the probes were just hurtling through space where once a planet orbited a Sun.'

He paused, deliberately or otherwise, for effect. 'The planet we called Earth minus one has disappeared.'

Now there was noise, the gathered entourage, to a one, asking questions, expressing shock, and disillusionment or just sounding out in outrage against the scientific community who had set them on this path.

'How could this happen?'

'Why did the scientists not predict this outcome?'

'Is the planet lost for good? Is there any chance that it might come back?'

'Fucking hell!'

Reeves stood up again to help the struggling scientist. 'Please! There will be plenty of time for questions. We must let Dr Webster continue.' An uneasy order returned, slowly in waves like a fading record for the time being. The scientist started again.

'If I can just answer one question that I heard amongst the many: Will the planet return? No. Based on our findings, I am afraid that we do not believe it will be the case. But if I can continue to relate what we have uncovered, it may make things clearer, however.'

The atmosphere, although settled again, was thick with uncertainty: could there be any news that could make up for the death of thousands of innocent lives or the loss of humanity's last chance of redemption?

'Although, unfortunately, resulting in the regrettable death of a soldier, the recent reconnaissance mission was not a total loss in terms of the data that we have collected.'

That was too much for Alex. He did not like Webster's blasé dismissal of Ben's death and felt compelled to cut in to get to the bottom of the death of his friend.

'Can we know how he actually *did* die please? My understanding was that there was a foolproof mechanism for calculating the terrain at a traveller's intended destination so that they would not materialise inside solid rock or a hundred metres in the air.'

The doctor was beginning to sweat now as he continued to fidget nervously on the podium.

'Yes, yes, you would be right, Colonel Clugston,' he replied as he mopped his brow with his clearly multi-purpose handkerchief. 'But it was not the device that you described, the Phasing Spatial Calibration Compensator, which failed. We still boast a 100 per cent survival rate for human transportation using the new technology.'

A few murmurs of disapproval or disagreement met this comment, and Alex was able to pick up on this.

'Come on! Ben materialised five metres into solid ground in the middle of the desert,' Alex protested.

'Colonel, please! Let me explain. When we analysed the readout of the specially fortified PPRM, or Pre Phase Reconnaissance Module, we uncovered evidence of a temporal and spatial disconnection between our home continuum and Earth minus one'

'Dr Webster, please!' ordered General O'Hara, 'Can you keep the explanation at a layman's level so that we all can understand?'

Webster, a scientist and not an orator, clearly struggled with the concept of keeping his description of events simple but steeled himself to set off again. Luckily for him, he had a white knight to take over the reins.

'He means that the gateway between our world and the new world was corrupted,' interjected Kenny.

'This resulted in a phenomenon that results in matter being randomly transported somewhere else. This "somewhere else" was either spatially different i.e. somewhere else in the destination continuum's galaxy and/or temporally different i.e. to another time in that continuum.'

The gathering was now stunned into silence. Kenny, who had clearly struggled to be a passive participant, had now stood up and began to walk up and down at the front of the podium as he continued.

'The recovered PPRM was found entirely surrounded by a layer of rock that should have dated it from an era seventeen million years in our past.'

Continued disbelief and confusion propped up the uneasy silence, so the scientist continued.

'We also found unusual–' he paused to reflect briefly, 'no, the word actually is impossible, fossils accompanying the module. Those of an adult *Homo sapiens*, a species not expected on this planet for another sixteen million years. Obviously no DNA was viable after all this time to enable a check against our database records, but we have to assume that these fossils were created by the body of Ben Howell. It is the only logical conclusion.'

The proverbial pin could have landed lightly on a soft surface within a mile and still have been audible. Kenny proceeded to supply the explanation that this silence demanded.

'What this meant is that the device, and unfortunately that means Ben as well, was transported to the same location on our Earth, only approximately seventeen million years into our past, aeons before the evolution of man.'

'Oh god! Poor man,' a female voice from somewhere in the room muttered, as the full connotations of this hit home.

'If, as we have assumed, this was his body, it seems that his neck was broken by an unidentified carnivorous animal, and it follows that he must have been eaten by the same animal. Little else was identifiable as not a lot remained of his virtually destroyed environmental suit. However, the module, housed in its hyper-fortified durosynth-polymer capsule with vacuum environment remained intact and dormant for all this time. An incredible achievement! Of course, it is completely unusable, as the power has long since been drained, but amazingly the hard drive and, therefore, the required data was intact.'

'And what did that tell us?' a young military looking participant, with army-regulation length hair, piped up.

Kenny had a full head of steam now, and Webster was happy for him to take over the scientific briefing.

'The module validated our hypothesis. The duplicate earth had disappeared. The astronomical data collected by Sergeant Howell from a significant segment of the galaxy, when compared with our own galactic maps, enabled us to interpolate between the two continua and confirm that this continuum where the earth is missing is in the same timeline as our own world. We don't know if Earth has been relocated in time or in space, or perhaps in both.'

'Oh come on! You have got to be kidding!' The token female offered, 'time travel is not possible?' It was unclear if this was a question or a statement.

Kenny looked at her with one of his '*I am a brilliant scientist, and you are clearly an idiot'*–looks and, almost as if he were sighing with resignation, gave her a curt reply.

'Well you would be quite wrong, Madam. In fact the premise behind our newly discovered technology of phasing to other continua is 100 per cent based on the concept of time travel.'

She glowered at him, expecting more than this as an explanation. Kenny conceded and complied.

'In brief, the temporal shift which transports us to new continua is created by the necessity for matter to escape from a black hole such as the type generated by the colliders that I designed. Einstein hypothesised that the only way to escape a black hole was for an object to move faster than the speed of light or move backwards in time. So far, mankind hasn't found a way of travelling faster than light, if that is indeed possible, but my experiments have confirmed my brilliant fellow scientist's theories on time travel, and I have additionally proved that a leap *forward* in time has the same result. The time shift that my two—or three-metre diameter black holes generate is minimal and allows the temporal shifting to these neighbouring continuum, but it is theoretically possible that a massive black hole could facilitate much more significant shifts in the space—time location of larger bodies, even planets, to other distant points in time in the same continuum.'

Various blank faces, wiped clean of emotion by this science fiction-like revelation, littered the room. Webster found a second wind and backed up Kenny's statements.

'We believe it is possible that a massive black hole was generated by both a special type of instability, a specific physical property of this 'Earth minus one' continuum, and exacerbated by the accumulative effect of our activities in translocations of multiple personnel and equipment to this continuum.'

'Oh come on! This is too ridiculous for words! You are just guessing at the fate of the other earth,' another soldier retorted.

'Yes and no, Sir,' was the ambiguous reply.

'Necessity insists that we have to make the best estimate of events in the short time we have had since the probe returned. This estimate is based on extrapolation of the collected data and our current theoretical and practical knowledge, and is backed up as best as possible by empirical mathematics where necessary. We had no other choice but to make this calculated guess.'

They were working as a double act now only less funny. It was Kenny's turn.

'Yes, it is the best that we could do. Our probe found a much greater concentration of a certain type of ambient particle that has a particularly strong bonding force in this alternate universe. As a result, we have hypothesised that the effects of these forces in this continuum which are, for analogy only, a bit like the force of gravity, stronger by an incredible factor of approximately 917.'

Kenny realised he needed to keep the technical detail at a 'dumbed down' level for the gathered audience.

'Simply put, these forces somehow connect two sets of remotely similar particles or phenomena in such a way that events occurring at one set also effect the distantly connected 'twin' set in exactly the same fashion. These effects have only been recreated in experiments on our planet for minute distances of a few hairs breadths, but as the effects seem to be massively leveraged in the new continuum's galaxy, the connection could be valid for distances of up to approximately 100 light years.'

A lot of blank faces continued to stare back at him, hoping soon for some common sense.

'The Earth's facsimile in "Earth minus one" became connected via this phenomenon to other black hole phenomena in that continuum the moment our black hole-generating activity was detected. The effect became stronger, the more black holes we created, snowballing to initiate a critical event via this connection. It is possible that an event such as a supernova, star collapse, or even a high-energy collision created a larger black hole in a distantly remote region of space, which, due to the effect of these particles, recreated a black hole with the same charge and angular momentum but much less mass on the "Earth minus one" planet. Once generated, this black hole must have been able to swallow up the entire planet and phase shift it to another temporal and physical location in that galaxy.

'This secondary black hole, being relatively small in galactic terms, must then have then collapsed. There is no sign of it having existed. But elsewhere in the stellar scan from the probe's astronomical data, there is evidence of a supernova in what we know as the Sagittarius region of space. The disappearing planet would not be able to occupy the same space as itself in the past, and so it would have been transported to the connected area of the galaxy, in other words, the black hole nursery. Once there, we just can't postulate what its fate would be, with the exception that unless it was relocated by an infinitesimally small probability to the required distance away from a healthy star to sustain a viable environment for life the probability of our migrated citizens being dead is as near to 100 per cent as makes no odds. Our best guess, I am afraid, is that all biological life would have perished on the planet, almost immediately.'

The assembly looked neither convinced nor impressed, only confused, perturbed, and shocked by what they had just heard. Reeves took up the reigns of the conversation with his unique blend of subtlety.

'OK, sit down, Drs Clugston and Webster. Look, it really doesn't matter if you understand the science or not. Our scientists will be at the team's disposal for questions and updates for the next few weeks of preparation. The science is all just background to the recent decision that we have made in the continuing light of the deteriorating life conditions on our planet. The fact is that what we have been discussing is a potential phenomenon in some, we don't know how many, continua that is a detrimental factor to our colonisation plans. Additionally, there may be other hazardous anomalies in other continua that we attempt to colonise. However, we have no choice but to attempt to relocate to other worlds, as I am sure that you all are aware that the alternative to this is death for us all.'

He stopped briefly for dramatic effect, making eye contact with a few of the group in turn and then delivered the punch blow.

'The only difference is that from now on we won't start colonisation of a continuum until a team has been in and thoroughly researched all physical, biological, astronomical, and other parameters. Only when this team has given the continuum the scientific thumbs up will colonisation plans be drawn up.

'You, my friends, are our guinea pigs. You are this team.

'You comprise a group of soldiers, scientists, and medics whose job is the pre-colonisation assessment of continua.

'You are project "Early bird".'

*

The overwhelmingly vast majority of any sentient population is afforded a veiled and anonymous luxury that they take for granted throughout the entirety of their brief and generally irrelevant life spans. This is an extravagance, so subtle and happily beyond our manifold perception that we never give it a second thought.

The massed hordes of citizens from a typical society affect the lives of but a handful of beings, from loved ones to colleagues in a place of work or network cooperative. This fortunate majority have the ignorant providence of being able to go about their daily business in the knowledge that most or all of their decisions, good, bad, or lucky, have a negligible impact on the well being and future development of their race.

A small percentile of influential mid society leaders, industrialists, or employers can affect a few thousand lives with their actions, but in the main they possess limited potential to change the course of a civilisation's future.

An even tinier minority of macro leaders carry the heavy burden of making decisions that potentially shape the existence of multiple individuals on whole continents or that affect minor diversions of a planet's history. But even this unfortunate group of high-flyers, despite the full array of stress that accompanies their office, rarely encompasses a moment when the existence of their race is held entirely in the palm of their hand. Such destinies are often reliant on a selection between two impossible options with similarly negative prognoses.

In fact, a very few individuals amongst the miniscule inventory of sentient life forms in the galaxy ever encounter this defining instant, when the consequences of their next course of action delineates the future of their species existence.

Such a moment was upon Iptat Morne, a mere member of the Acquiescent Operative caste from Areth, supposedly the lowest form of life from its planet, but now the holder of its race's destiny.

Their species was currently split into three spatially divided elements:

Firstly, there was the remaining population, back on its home world, that was almost certainly doomed unless there was a radical alteration in the direction of the race's development. Continued warring, hatred, and prejudice combined with growing famine, pollution, overpopulation, and widespread disease meant these remaining residents had an unquantifiable and finite time to exist. Their damaged biosphere had deteriorated well past the point of no return, and no regression to eco friendly policies was going to reverse this exponentially worsening situation.

The second element was the band of rebel Cerebrals travelling as pulses of electromagnetic radiation, light orbits, in front of Iptat's ship. These caste members would probably survive for many centuries. They were an extremely long-lived caste and could refresh their cellular structure to maintain bodily youth and vigour during translations. However, they had no way of reproducing themselves sexually or asexually, to be able to spawn future generations, and had no genetic material to be able to propagate the other castes from their race. They could clone themselves but they surely would be doomed at some time in the future without an influx of genetic material to maintain cellular viability.

Last, but not least, there was the current population of this spaceship—the frozen cargo of individuals, which represented a sufficient gene pool from all of the castes from their species. This was now the only remaining inventory of viable members of their species, a precious ark of life that must survive for them to have a chance and new beginning.

Iptat knew that avoiding the loss of this third division of their race was the only way that they could continue to exist as a species, and its fate was held in its hands. It felt the fusion tool in its suit pocket and toyed with the safety release mechanism, digit shaking with apprehension. This was it; crunch time.

On the one hand, it could free the Hub Commander, who was now in full telepathic command of the eerily static foot soldier and attempt to talk it out of killing it and turning the ship around. It felt reasonably confident of staying alive in the short term, maybe an orbit or two. After all, the Sentinels would need Iptat to safely revive other members of the Sentinel and Procreator classes and help reprogramme the space ship's itinerary for a return to their home world. They probably would require it to return some of the revived individuals to a state of cryogenic stasis for the approximately 405-orbit return journey.

On the positive side, this plan would at least give Iptat some time to think up an alternative strategy. On the negative side, the more caste members that would be revived meant a lower chance of success in overpowering them. Defeating two Sentinels was a stern enough challenge already; even half a dozen revived colleagues would seem like an army, easily outgunning the SIPIA and itself.

Iptat concluded that plan A had a very low probability of success.

On the other hand, it could attempt to disable or even kill the stationary Sentinel standing behind it, using the laser fusion device. It had to be the fusion device and not the sharp metal instrument that it was carrying. The latter object would never be able to pierce through the tough skin of these genetically enhanced Sentinel caste members. Either way, this was a very long shot. It would have to be lightning quick and accurate enough to hit the Sentinel's eyes with the polarised thermal radiation. Additionally, it would have to achieve this before the Hub Commander releases its control over its minion which was also unlikely. The advantage of this plan would be that if it failed, Iptat would be killed immediately and would be unable to aid in the revival of any of the other caste members. And perhaps the SIPIA would find a way to overpower just two adversaries after its death?

Iptat's conclusion: Plan B had an even lower probability of success.

'Did you not hear me?' the Hub Commander repeated. 'Release me, or I will have it kill you.' The words were more forceful and had a finality to them.

Iptat sighed and resignedly moved forward to the subject's cryo-chamber to administer the Hub Commander's freedom. It felt ashamed. Its inability to make a decision had led to it going for the easy option, the cowardly alternative where it didn't die immediately. It punched a few keys on the console, and the restraints unbuckled from the Sentinel's limbs with a metallic groan. The released captive sat up, with a somewhat laboured movement, in the coffin-like chamber and flexed its fingers. It turned to the Operative and spewed contempt at it.

'You have thirty temporal units to convince me not to kill you, you piece of canine filth.' The unconditional derision was as natural to the soldier as breathing, having been reinforced over hundreds of generations of their race's recent society. Operatives were the lowest of the low to this class, especially as the Sentinel caste was the penultimate caste in the pecking order and were consequently always the keenest to reinforce this status quo.

'What we are doing here? Why are we captive? What happened at the fight?' the Commander harked back to its last memory, attendance at the Primus Sentinel tournament.

'We are all here as part of a directive from the office of primary Procreator Nermandahl 7,' Iptat regurgitated an agreed lie to the angry inquisitor.

It wasn't totally convinced that this party line would be believed, especially as the Hub Commander, now connected in a mini neural network with its Assassin caste member, would have been updated with all its recent experiences and intelligence on the situation.

'Our planet has been designated as doomed, and the primary legislature put together and effected an emergency plan to migrate a sufficient amount of individuals across all varieties of caste members to a planned, new, home world. The plan had to be concealed from all but the main instigators as it was vital to avoid the Eastern hemisphere from discovering the plan.'

Iptat wanted to play the 'enemy' trump card as early as possible to appeal to the Sentinel's ingrained and fostered hatred for their age-old adversity. Any mention of the other inhabitants that lived in the other half of their planet and who they had been at war with for centuries, could only help but to create a smoke screen. It was clutching at straws, but it might allow Iptat to empathise with the listening Hub Commander and add weight to the untruth that it was unfolding.

The Hub Commander now was swinging its legs over the cryo-chamber's side as the subservient Sentinel helped it to descend to the floor. Its movements were naturally laboured but being from the Sentinel caste, its enhanced superior musculature ensured that this was not a total barrier to its chances of walking.

'That is why the Sentinel's tournament was chosen, being clearly one of the few occasions where multiple units from all castes can and do congregate in the same place. It was possible to render multiple subjects from this collection unconscious with a simple but effective and instant trihalomethane gas to depress their central nervous systems. From there it was just a case of the Cerebrals translating all the overcome caste members en masse to the space ship for migration.'

Iptat paused and looked at the commanding Sentinel for encouragement. Its gaze was met with an expressionless return, which neither persuaded Iptat nor disheartened it. The nonchalant stare that was sent back still somehow managed to contain pure hatred for the Operative unit. It took the silence as a chance to continue.

'We have been travelling for over 400 orbits, and we have a bit over 330 more orbits of our journey to go, so we need to be cryogenically frozen to survive the journey. Our destination is a life-supporting planet, which has water, oxygen, and wildlife to sustain us, and where we can start afresh with . . . '

'Enough!'

The Hub Commander's locked eyes were now burning fiercely at Iptat now, a searing stare that bored through its weak moral defences, bared the very essence of its soul and dissected its crumbling resolve. Iptat held out for as long as it could, but before very long, it had to look away from the terrifying pressure of the gaze. It had succumbed to the greater force and knew that it had lost.

'You are lying,' the Hub Commander started to walk off as swiftly as it could in the direction of the next chamber, whose door was lying smashed from the battering over the last few hundred temporal units. Presumably it was off to find a sentient program.

'Wait!' Iptat knew what was coming next and so started babbling for mercy.

'You need me to revive other crew and possibly to get the ship back on course for Areth, if that is to be your decision,' it pleaded desperately for its life, a wasted and useless ploy when your fate has been decided by a Sentinel treating you with murderous and clinically ruthless intent.

'We will take our chances on finding our way back to our home planet,' the rapidly retreating commander bluntly retorted in a loud voice.

Immediately the Sentinel Combatant soldier jerked into motion from its statuesque pose like a remote-controlled toy, suddenly issued an electrical order. It started to move towards Iptat, its slow approach indicating confidence in a quick kill.

Iptat looked around. There was no easy avenue of escape, and even if it tried, the Sentinel was a great deal faster than it. The caste was engineered specifically with supreme strength and athleticism. Anyway, where could it possibly go? Nevertheless it backed away slowly, not once taking its eyes from the advancing death-dealing unit.

Only one desperate option remained; a course of action that Iptat had given only a minimal chance of succeeding. However, this option was all that it had left. It was out of all other alternatives, a desperate trapped animal in a corner. Its hand was forced.

Iptat felt for the laser fusion device in the pocket of its cryo-suit, disengaged the safety clip, and gripped tightly the smooth handle between two of its digits, hands shaking liberally. Its heart was pumping at 150 per cent of its resting rate, driven on by large quantities of Aggressterone provided by its autonomous nervous system.

It waited patiently for the Sentinel, who was continuing its steady advance. '*Was this all happening in slow motion?*' Iptat wondered. The moment certainly seemed to be lingering like some surreal half-dream world.

'*Come on, you piece of shit,*' it thought to itself unconvincingly. '*A little bit closer now.*' This would allow Iptat to propel a more accurate pulse of the heat directly to the Sentinel's eyes. '*All very nice in theory*' it continued to muse, but its hands continued to shake uncontrollably.

The Assassin was employing the same staring tactics as the Hub Commander, in a deliberate and instantaneously successful attempt to instil fear and submission in the operative.

It slowly but steadily bore down on its quivering quarry, with no perceptible change of expression or posture evident. Iptat knew however that the hunter was somehow still enjoying this, despite in theory being genetically enhanced to be devoid of emotion and being pumped up to the eyeballs with the hormone Demotase which enhanced this state.

At some level, somewhere inside its stupid brain, Iptat knew that the Assassin was grinning.

This was Iptat's last image. Its body slumped to the floor like a suddenly abandoned string puppet.

*

Alex sat back on his bench, surveying his team as they prepared with the help of the 'home nest' support staff for the team exploratory mission. So far it had turned out to be a good team, with few obvious conflicts. Even the scientists got on OK with the military when the chips were down. The civilians in fact had developed reasonable combat and survival skills in training, and although these personnel would hopefully not be used in most scenarios, he felt that they could be relied on in if an emergency arose.

He was proud of the way the team had gelled together over the last few weeks, since the plans for the exploration of the second inhabitable continuum were laid down. Not one member had complained or asked to be reassigned, although the temptation to remain with the colonisation program in the recently discovered 'Earth plus one' continuum must have been great. This was a whole new adventure for mankind, but the unanimous feeling was that they could join eventually after they were through with exploring and documenting some or all of the remaining ten to fifteen continua in the Clugston time parallax.

They knew, at a high level, what was in four of these worlds now.

The first was their spoiled home—a planet that probably didn't have much of a future in terms of sustainability of life. The global biosphere had only a potential long-term future that depended on how long it would take for the 'plague' of mankind to die out; only then it would have a chance to recover from his greedy legacy. This world was now better left for the Russians, Chinese, and whoever else would be left to fight over it. None of these other human groupings were included in the alliance's plans for recolonisation of the new continua.

This issue had caused much debate since the uncovering of the phasing technology. Should they share this discovery and the immense potential for salvation that it afforded the human race? There were two clear divisions amongst the privileged personnel who knew about the breakthrough. Alex was in the camp which thought their new technology should have been available to share with their old enemies, but the natural distrust and greed of humanity took the vote. The powers that be from the North American alliance said that their enemies could not be trusted. Hence the migration project timetable was set up covertly, initially for selected high-profile resources and those who had the skills needed to prepare the new continuum but eventually for the whole continent and the continent alone. Seeing as there was little or no communication between America and its enemies these days and the technology for spying on a global scale was dying, it had a good chance of success over the next couple of years, without being observed by their adversaries. This would be especially important in the later stages of the project, when mass migrations would be needed. .

The second was the infamous 'Earth minus one' continuum. This continuum, the closest reality "back" one Clugston constant in time, was now proving to be a barrier for any plans to move backwards through the Clugston parallax. The scientists simply could not recommend conducting any black hole generation activity in this continuum, as they had no way of calculating the compounding effects of further excursions here. Besides, these excursions would only be temporary trips on route to 'Earth minus two,' whatever lay in store there. A risk balanced decision had been made to explore forward in time in the Clugston parallax, using a more diligent approach, employing a highly trained pre-reconnaissance team, which he now commanded.

The third continuum was this Earth plus one. They had been lucky. The first leap forward revealed a planet very much like the old unspoilt Earth. A multitude of fauna existed on this continuum (in their limited sample), and there was a much lower concentration of the same particles that had been responsible for the phenomenon which had led to the disappearance of the 'Earth minus one' world. After a range of extensive studies by the scientists, 'Earth plus one' was deemed safe to colonise, and so this enormous project moved forward to full analysis, planning, and eventual implementation.

Outside of and completely separate from this colonisation, Alex's team was charged with the continued exploration and charting of the other continua, backed up by a large support team, which, it was planned, would always be located close to the team's efforts, preferably in the continuum behind the one that they were currently exploring.

Their current target was 'Earth plus three'. Dozens of probes had been sent forward to 'Earth plus two', the fourth known continuum, from their new home, and the results had found that this neighbouring continuum did not have conditions required for sustaining oxygen requiring life. Alex did not understand the full details of the scientific explanation, but his brother had told him that much earlier in this world's history, it had diverged from the path taken by Earth and all the other continua that they had visited so far by one major factor. The event that had lead to life, producing an oxygen atmosphere had not occurred, leading to a world that supported anaerobic organisms and containing an atmosphere totally hostile to oxygen respiring animals such as humans.

As a result, a much more complicated transport through this 'dead continuum' to their next objective had to be planned and executed. According to the scientists in his team, it was impossible to travel directly to a non-adjacent continuum in the spectrum, so an elaborate double-phase operation needed to be conducted. Although, only in the dead continuum, for a few seconds, they needed environmental suit protection against the multitude of factors adverse to life there. There was no breathable atmosphere, and instead of oxygen there pervaded a caustic and toxic cocktail of reducing gases. It was hot too; something like two or three times the heat of their own planet.

The primary team comprised fifteen individuals, the original twelve briefed all that time ago in New Deline after the collapse of the 'Earth minus one' project, the botanist wife of one of the assembled scientists, and two additional selections by Alex from his own team. Alex had insisted on this. It was not as if he didn't trust the Americans and Canadians, but it was a natural impulse for a soldier to feel more at ease with guys whom he had fought with and relied on in a combat situation.

Alex opted for Ron Turvey and Geoff Konrad, a Corporal and Lance Corporal from his battalion and company—guys he had shared many tough times with as well as the occasional laugh. They were loyal and hard soldiers who had worked with him during the earlier bloody riots in the hydro zones, and he could rely on them 100 per cent. They had executed some of his extremely controversial orders (some admittedly were not his but had come from above) without a moment of doubt or hesitation. Amongst these were instructions to open fire on supposedly innocent citizens for the greater good of the hydro zone. These guys were always in his select team of choice when there was a shit job to do, and he always felt safer with them watching his back.

Three more soldiers made up the half dozen specialists in the 'Early bird' team, all selected for a specific skill set.

Captain Andy Bovaird, an American, was the senior ranking officer of the three, selected as he was the most decorated member of what remained of the Green berets, that was still alive and an expert in covert infiltrations, unconventional warfare, counter terrorism, and reconnaissance missions. Alex knew him by reputation only. He was clearly a good soldier but a humourless, hard, and pedantic man.

The military rumour mill talked of one blot on his copybook, where he was supposedly guilty of sending his troops prematurely into a conflict situation when other options were open to him, including waiting for reinforcements, leading to an unacceptable loss of life. He was a hard bastard and took no prisoners.

Alex was extremely glad that he outranked him and that he wouldn't need to take orders from him.

The remaining two regular soldiers were Sgt Larry Coolak and Cpl Greg Reynolds from the 509th Infantry Regiment that was posted at the southern end of the Great Lakes as the first line of defence for the alliance's southern border. They were both extremely well-trained soldiers and as expert in survival in any terrain as you could be on our spoiled planet. With no polar environments and not much else left apart from deserts, semi-deserts, steppe grasslands, or at best savannah type environments on the planet, this was mostly theoretical training as a necessity. Additionally, these men were proficient in munitions, explosives, and camouflage.

The civilian team comprised two medics, two biologists (a married couple comprising both flavours of the science, Botany and Zoology), a geologist, the two 'rocket scientists', as they were known to Alex's team, Kenny and Lars Rasmussen, and finally what was deemed the closest thing to a ambassador as could be mustered at short notice.

Montague Fenn-Smith, eccentrically British and old school, was in his sixties now but was in the British foreign office before the scorching and was the individual with the most experience in diplomacy. Monty belonged to a different era; a dead age of classist values, upper class twits, and family wealth. He probably felt that he had been born too late in life. There was no class now, either from family history or money, neither of which existed anymore; only the need to survive and work together for the continued existence of man on the planet. But Monty was a light relief, a comforting hark back to a different history, one where we continually fooled ourselves that we were masters of the world and would remain so for ever.

Alex chuckled inwardly. He couldn't wait for the first contact situation between Monty and these ape-like creatures that had been surveyed on Earth plus three. He knew that he would have to be there as a controlling influence; someone who had a realistic and more up-to-date view on life and who didn't still think that Britain had a huge empire spanning a large percentage of the globe. In any case, the vast majority of this original empire was now a massive expanse of totally uninhabitable sun-baked sand.

Alex was happy enough about the content of the team as described and felt there weren't any obvious personality clashes at this stage. However, he was acutely aware that this factor is impossible to verify in advance of a high-stress situation, the likes of which they had avoided so far, but surely they would encounter going forward. He had even managed to curb his natural red-blooded male enthusiasm for the blonde Swedish medic Olga Andersson, sacrificing the potential for short term bodily pleasures for the ongoing efficiency and well being of his team.

What he wasn't overly happy about was the final invitee, thrust upon him by the Joint Chiefs of Staff, effectively the government, when you live in a martial state.

Alasdair Nicholson, formerly a young officer in the British Special Air Service was a veteran soldier from a very different time before the scorching. This was a time of political 'normality', of governmental hoarding greed and back-stabbing tit-for-tat diplomacy. This was a time that was built up through centuries of hatred and defined the mess that their world was in now. Nicholson was the epitome of a loyal and hard operative, who believed in the defence of his country and service to his King above all else; a pillar that supported this avarice and misplaced distrust.

It was not Nicholson whom he hated so much but what he stood for and what he suspected his role was on the trip. He matched Nicholson's rank of Colonel, and although he had been assured that he had complete authority over the team and mission, this still worried him.

What would happen when the chips were down and Nicholson didn't exactly see eye–to-eye on a decision?

What was the agenda that necessitated the taking of this veteran soldier and spook that was in his mid forties?

He had been told that Nicholson was there 'to observe' and report back progress and findings to the Joint Chiefs. Of course, he strongly protested that, as a team leader he should know everything that was happening in his remit, and he shouldn't be kept in the dark and treated like a fool. However, the reply was curt and to the point—if he didn't like it, then someone else could be chosen to lead the team. He was, they explained, primarily there because they thought he could look after his brother and make sure he doesn't go off the rails.

Nicholson always carried his small metal case, locked with a combination and, occasionally, handcuffed on to his arm. And he had his own sidekick Lee, who would be representing him on the secondary team. There was definitely a hidden agenda here; one that Alex vowed that he would find out.

Nicholson could bet his bottom dollar on this.

CHAPTER 5

Secure transmission 24 December 2078

From: Daron Whitaker, E+1 migration programme manager

To: General Greenwood, commander of alliance forces

Cc: Western alliance security congress level 5 eyes

Subject: Minutes of 'Earth plus one' migration project workshop

All,

Please find attached the official minutes of our recent conference covering migration plans to the above location, including a timeline for tasks involved in relocating all of the alliance citizens in a timely and covert fashion.

The detail is in this attachment, but the highlights are

Migration approach

A balance is required; we need enough numbers to maintain a sufficient gene pool to further our species, but logistics dictate that we take a phased approach to the programme. We simply cannot migrate our entire population of all twelve million people immediately, due primarily to the time constraints of transferring so many individuals, and, more importantly, the dependency of sufficient infrastructure at the other end to support this population. The operation will be covert so that as few people know about the plans, so we have the best chance of keeping a news leak of our technology away from our enemies. This is, of course, unless the decision that was made not to share the technology with the Russians or Chinese is reversed.

Once our target number has been reached, analysis will be made how and when more migrations can take place. The population left behind must not feel deserted and must be given hope that they will also be joining the new colonies in 'Earth plus one'.

Migrations will be structured on a zone-by-zone basis. Whole towns will be included in the population to be transported initially, whereas, others will be assigned a future migration date. The act of migrating by location is intended to minimise the effect of splitting families and friends, and any associated bad feeling or aggressive actions by our citizens. Almost exclusively in this post-scorch world, families co-locate to the same zone, so hopefully there will be few exceptions.

An in scope zone won't know until the last minute that its citizens are being transported. This might generate some general ill feeling towards the government along the lines that we are keeping information to ourselves and not telling the population about the project until too late and not enabling them to prepare adequately for the journey. A large military presence must be maintained at each location's migration site to ensure a peaceful transition.

Pre-migration preparation project

Our seven-year infrastructure project, running since the failure of its predecessor, migration project to E-1, has been a full on initiative but has been completed on schedule. We are well prepared for the migration of the initial 750,000 citizens to the newly developed towns in E+1

Ecologically self-sustainable housing with solar and biomass renewable energy technology is completed for all accounted for citizens in all five migration towns.

Insulation, stored energy, wood for burning, and all other necessary tools and facilities for adjusting to and dealing with the harsh cold winters on this version of Earth have been prepared. To recap, the climate is a welcome change to the conditions in our current home, having defined winter and summer seasons, similar to old Canada on our home planet in the twentieth century. The migration is timed for the mild mid-spring season in our new home, which will give us time to adjust before the shock of a cold winter, something that few humans have experienced.

A basic communication network (which can and will grow in sophistication in the ensuing months and years) has been set up between all the new towns. Physical cables have been laid down for telephony, and simple roads are built. Maintenance of both of these, especially the latter will be a challenge, but a plan and resources will follow to deal with this.

Hospital facilities have been set up with only a list of final preparations required to ensure their viability to service the large influx of potential patients.

Farming infrastructure is in place, and a harvest hopefully assured for the first-year crops to match migration timing. Infrastructure for transport and storage of crops and meat from migrated cows, pigs, and chickens is in place and set to be initiated on our population's arrival.

Wind farms and hydroelectric generation plants are already generating and storing green energy for the new set of users.

Worker drone unit production is underway, adding to the self-sustainability of the infrastructure growth and maintenance.

Migration schedule

The detail of the timetable for our initial seven locations is in the attached, but this is how the transport is planned at a high level:

In the weeks prior to each location's migration day, selected 'high-priority' infrastructure individuals and equipment will join the workforce and drones that are already there to conclude the final preparations for the migration. These individuals are soldiers, police, medical staff, and rescue services which need to support the new population as soon as it arrives.

In scope migration locations will be informed forty-eight hours before the migration, with details of the migration venue and timings. Each individual in a family will be issued with a ticket for entry to the migration venue. This timescale is the longest we could afford for people to prepare and gather together their family individuals and a cursory list of belongings. The latter will be heavily restricted to twenty pounds in weight or within a 3D set of size parameters.

Congregation will be at selected old sports stadia on the pitch surface. We cannot allow anybody to be in an elevated height in the stands, as we cannot risk transporting multiple individuals to a ground level from this elevated position. Although these larger phasing transporters are all fitted with Phasing Spatial Calibration Compensators, we simply have not been able to test if these will work with such a large pool of individuals.

If people are not there at the appointed hour, they will be left behind. The military will mop up such individuals and relocate them to a new town for assignment to a future migration.

Due to the uniqueness of this migration in the history of mankind, it obviously was not able to make a 'dry run' on the scale required. However, we have tested the new bracelets, which focus the energy of the atom smasher devices, the largest Clugston models ever created, to create multiple black holes for the transport. We shall have to pray (if any of us still believe in that sort of thing) or risk to chance that the technology scales up to the proportions that we need.

Please come back with any questions, issues, or suggestions on the project.

Best regards,

Daron

*

Alex sensed that something was wrong; very wrong indeed.

And then, immediately he materialised, it was starkly confirmed that something was not right.

Where were the forests, with their beautiful old oak-like trees? Where was the cacophony of chatter from the myriad of arthropods that were peculiar to this continuum? And where was the thick, lush undergrowth that was luxuriant under their feet and the thick brush that had afforded them appropriate levels of background camouflage in conjunction with their chameleo-adaptive environment suits?

They had been forced to adjust the location of their intended entry point to two kilometres away from their original choice, as this had been within sight of one of the ape creature's habitations. In fact Ron Turvey had felt that they might have been seen, and this had initiated discussions about a potential abort of subsequent trips for the indefinite future. However, he could not back this up with any proof, so it was felt that the planned location adjustment would suffice as a preventative measure.

Despite this change of plan, though, Alex still fully expected to be in the same forest environment as was evident on their previous reconnaissance trip. Last time they had come with a compliment of four soldiers, a scientist, and Nicholson and had only had enough time to explore the environment for a few minutes to take some cursory readings. They had to leave in a rush, fearing discovery by this world's incumbent dominant species and wanted a second chance to make some further research on this continuum before engaging in first contact.

They were in a pure white, lifeless, and sterile structure, familiar angles between walls, ceiling, and floor coldly framing the 'Early bird' team's world to a brick like prison.

Alex's team had never picked up any readings about this structure's presence in the forest. The only building in a several kilometre radius had been the habitation that they had witnessed on their previous emergence into this continuum.

He felt a small itch in his neck, and his index finger moved to feel the point where it came from. When he withdrew his finger, he saw a small droplet of blood smeared over the fingertip. He frowned, confused.

He looked around, finely evaluating the blandness of the internal wall of this unanticipated edifice with an overblown intensity. A deep sense of worry began to creep over him. A hundred warnings were lined up, shouting at him and confirming the unease that he innately felt. Yet he pondered, mesmerised, unable to make a rash decision about whether to immediately retreat or investigate further. Something was pulling him to this place, and it was a subtle addiction that it seemed he couldn't kick.

'Send back a signal to "Home nest" to hold back, Sergeant,' he ordered Coolak, bringing a semblance of vigilance to his decision making.

His patient queue of protesting voices had at least caused Alex to stop the second wave of the team phasing to this place whilst he decided on whether this uneasy situation merited a full mission abort or just a brief pause for analysis before resuming the full implementation of the plan.

Coolak's phase module, armed with the appropriate instructions, popped away in its tiny black hole, relaying the instruction to wait back to the supporting home team.

At least, all of the planned eight had made it in the initial transport wave—mostly soldiers, including his two men Turvey and Konrad, the two Americans Captain Bovaird and Sergeant Coolak, and Reynolds the Canadian. Additionally, his brother Kenny, invited as the token scientist and subject matter expert on the phasing technology, and Nicholson were along for the ride. The latter was a mandatory participant at all of these first transport waves, being the eyes and ears of the Joint Chiefs of Staff, a fact that still grated with Alex.

The idea was that they would make an early patrol of the area, ensuring there was nothing hostile awaiting them before inviting some more scientists to join them and make further tests.

'Stay alert in case anything comes through that door,' he ordered, a bit fruitlessly. The men were clearly already in a high state of alert, having been thrust in to an unexpected situation with unknown parameters. Not only were they entering a new world populated by sentient apes that they didn't know were friendly or otherwise, but also nobody had expected to be in this location or environment.

The only thing that interrupted the uniformity of their sterile and colourless environment was a large metal door, which looked very solid, thick, and strong and was clearly going to be a barrier to their advancement.

Suddenly, in the middle of the floor of the room, a console shimmered into view, appearing to protrude from the floor like a bizarre white mushroom with a flattened top. It was white, shiny, and had the appearance of being made from some sort of synthetic polymer. When fully materialised, its top surface looked just shy of two metres off the ground, a height which made its controls uncomfortable to view and manipulate even for a tall human. It contained a type of keyboard with multiple buttons and other controls with unfamiliar hieroglyphics, and what looked like an intercom, both for speaking into and receiving transmissions.

Alex walked over to it slowly and carefully, surveying it with tempered interest, as if he knew what it was. It was clearly a photo construct but very sophisticated and beyond their culture's capabilities, appearing almost completely solid. No evidence of the slightest transparency betrayed it to be an object constructed from pure photons, a tell-tale sign of their own roughly equivalent (but clearly inferior) photonic projection technology.

'Try the door, Captain,' he said to Bovaird without taking his eyes from the construct.

'I don't like this at all, Sir,' piped Turvey. 'We should pull back and send some more probes to conduct more analysis before we come back.'

'It *is* protocol to retreat in such circumstances,' confirmed Nicholson.

Alex nodded in acknowledgement, yet without issuing a confirmation order. Subconsciously, he may have wished not to give the order as he knew it would defy Nicholson. He hated spooks.

'Locked solid, Colonel', came back the result of Bovaird's analysis of the door, 'we will need to blow it.'

'OK, I have had enough. This is wrong. Let's pull out,' Alex decided finally. 'Prepare to move out!'

A few moments passed as each soldier reapplied and sealed their environmental suit helmets, ready to face the toxic perils of the interim Earth plus two continuum on the return journey.

'Initiate return phase sequence,' Alex ordered when they were all ready, to enable synchronisation of their return journey as best as possible.

They all applied the necessary commands into their phase control bracelets to instigate their return, and everybody stood back and waited for the usual whirring noise as the mini atom smashers rapidly charged to an inconceivable level of capacitance for black hole creation, a process that should take only a few seconds.

Nothing happened.

Nervous glances were exchanged between team members and then each feverishly checked their apparatus.

'We have never had a unit failure yet, let alone all of them failing at exactly the same time! This is impossible', suggested Turvey, looking at his wrist display readout and then adding, 'I can't see anything wrong with my unit. It is fully charged.'

'Yes, mine too,' offered Konrad.

'Fuck it! What is happening, scientist?' said Coolak, his frustration duly taken out on the token civilian Kenny, who was ignoring him whilst examining closely his wrist unit.

'Then why can't we—?' started Bovaird, tapping his controls futilely in frustration.

'Because I am now controlling your access in and out of this place,' a synthetic voice piped from the temporarily forgotten console.

The mini cacophony of confused and panicked comments ceased immediately, cut off cleanly like a razor sharp knife bisecting an apple with perfect symmetry. An eerie void blanketed the room, starkly replacing those frenetic exchanges from the aftermath of the micro collider failures.

Alex walked back over to the console and started to pace deliberately around it, weighing it up for a second time as if he had missed something from his earlier analysis.

'Who are you and how can you speak our language?' he asked the console.

Nothing came back.

'Where are we, what is this building, and what has happened to the forest that used to be in this place?' he continued.

Still no response came from the mushroom intercom. Alex looked around at his men, his confused expression suggesting a shrugging of shoulders. Then, suddenly, as if the console had been considering Alex's list of questions, the answers spewed out mechanically.

'I am the SPIA, the sentient pseudo intelligence algorithm unit for this facility, built by scientific units from the species that occupy this planet. This species has visited your home world on seven occasions over a span of many thousands of years, most recently approximately 36.48 of your Earth solar orbits ago. On those visits, we have downloaded to our data cloud 2.38 billion GB of data on your race. We have in storage the full vocabulary of American, Spanish, Mandarin Chinese, and several others of your Earth languages, which I, of course, can speak.'

'The language is called English,' Alex interrupted, the British pride in him pointlessly defending the algorithm's error, despite the fact that these days technically American was a language in its own right, 'not American.'

The SPIA ignored him, and continued to answer all the stored questions.

'You are on a planet we call Areth, approximately 102.76 light years away from the location of the star which your planet revolves around. The planet orbits a star that you refer to in your continuum as Ascella or Zeta Sagittarius, in the constellation you call Sagittarius; this is a binary star with an A2 giant and sub giant.'

'That's impossible!' blurted Kenny.

'Holy fuck!' Coolak eloquently suggested at the same time, 'what are we doing here?' he advanced rapidly and aggressively with his rifle raised. 'Let me blow the machine to pieces, Colonel.'

'Stand down, Sergeant!' Alex raised his voice for impact and put his arm out horizontally to stop Larry's progress. This was the Coolak that he had been warned about and seen on the odd occasion—a great soldier, tough, dependable, and a team player with excellent training and experience. But in addition to these qualities, he was more than a bit stupid and excitable. How would smashing the console help anything, if indeed a photo holographic construct could be smashed?

'Please continue, computer. As my Sergeant has so expressively put it, why are we here? We were on a peaceful reconnaissance mission to a connected world to ours; a world that we understand is occupied by—'

The SPIA continued, cutting him off.

'Your prohibited attempt to invade the world that you speak of has been terminated by my creators. This aggressive invasion of the ape beings' lands will not be tolerated. You have been diverted instead to our world for sentencing.'

'Do we not get to meet somebody and give our point of view? Don't we get a trial to defend ourselves? I would like to repeat. We are here for peaceful exploration, this is not an aggressive mission of conquest,' Alex attempted to reason.

'This is not what the history of your race suggests. Our evidence shows that you are selfish, you are greedy, you are destructive, and you cannot live in peace with other species that occupy your world or even your own kind. You are killers, and we need to do everything we can to keep you from further advancement to other connected worlds in this spectrum of continua.'

Alex was stunned. This had been said in a raised voice with real venomous feeling. What sort of computer was this? Were they being taken for a ride, and this was, in fact, some sort of being that was controlling the conversation from the other end of the intercom system, wherever that was?

The voice from the mushroom seemed to return to a calmer, more even tone.

'You have been designated for a live ammunition drill involving three units from a battalion of the Arethian soldier caste. You are on a military base, in a specialised environment used for military training. You will fight these soldiers to the death. You will encounter three different environments, and one of these soldiers will be in each environment. Each soldier will be equipped with hand weapons for hand to hand combat only. If you kill this soldier you may advance to the next environment. In the unlikely event that any of you survive and manage to advance to the end, we shall return you to your base in the continuum next to your planet. Be warned. There is no running from these units. They can track your every movement in any environment and conditions. And they will not hesitate to kill. Your only way out is to kill them and reach the final exit.'

Alex's hand moved quickly back to his neck.

'Yes,' the machine somehow acknowledged this movement. 'A device was implanted into each of you immediately on arrival here, a locator mechanism to allow each hunter to be able to find you.'

There was a slight pause in the monologue deliberately designed to allow this the impact to sink in.

'My constructors are a reasonable people. You have your chance of survival, albeit small.'

There was an eerie undertone to this last comment. Was the sentient software enjoying this?

'I demand that we meet someone; this is unreasonable and unacceptable,' Alex protested loudly.

'Welcome to Areth,' the unit announced.

At the same time, there was a loud metallic clunk as if a large key was being turned in its iron keyhole and the previously locked portal in the pure white dungeon swung inwardly half a metre, allowing access to whatever was out there.

'Your welcoming committee awaits you outside! Enjoy your stay,' the final comment smacked of sarcasm. The console clicked and went dead, denoting the end of the conversation, and the mushroom like object snapped away soundlessly with an ominous finality and disappeared.

'Come back here, you motherfucker!' Coolak yelled uselessly at the disappeared console, as he aimed a couple of wasteful kicks at the thin air around it.

Now Alex was more than worried. The unknown was waiting outside, and he didn't like that. What were these soldiers and how good were they? He had an ominous feeling that this was going to be a great deal more than hard work. How could his men prepare to fight an enemy that they knew nothing about, not even what they looked like?

'Arm up. Remember, we have an array of sophisticated automatic projectile weapons, and whatever is out there, if this computer is true to its word, has only hand-to-hand combat ability. We stay calm and focused, and we get through this.'

He tried to accentuate the positive.

'OK, let's move out,' was all that he could manage with as much bravado as he could muster.

*

The old ape groaned in discomfort as he manoeuvred himself into a better position for the catch. The onset of the degenerative joint disease had come seasons ago, leading gradually to a swelling of his joints, especially his digits, a lot of pain, and, of course, inconvenience. It prevented him from doing many of the things that he loved these days, but at least he could still go fishing. This was his favourite hobby, one which he had been fanatical about for all his sentient life, but one that he could only really find time for now that he had relinquished the troupe leadership.

Oh, how he wished he had given up power a long time ago! At that time he had been nervous that the next leader would not be able to consolidate on the great strides that they had made as a race in such a short time. This was the curse of all leaders—the inability to delegate control and take a back seat in the process.

Of course it was not long ago when it would have been impossible for a troupe's leader to grow so old. A younger, fitter, and stronger male would have challenged the incumbent dominant for all that he possessed, especially his wives and children, and would have either killed him or chased him away to die alone, unsupported and unprotected by the troupe. Then the usurping new dominant would kill all the young ones that didn't bear his genes and start building again with his newly captured females.

He was pleased that the times had changed drastically from this barbaric but natural way of things. As far as he knew, and he suspected it was true, he was the oldest ape of his species that had ever lived and one of a few which had made it to retirement and was allowed to stay under the protection of the troupe. He had, after all, made it to the grand old age of forty-seven.

However, his second son, who had won the organised wrestling event that had been devised as a method to select a new leader, was doing a good job as his replacement. This son was a large ape, just like he had been in his prime and commanded good respect from the habitat residents. He seemed to have learned a lot from his father and was continuing to drive forward their slow expansion and development in an effective, just, and efficient manner.

Today's prey, the biggest fish in this stream, was there somewhere—a monster, perhaps six hands—which he had been trying to catch for weeks. He was pleased with the recent innovation, introduced by one of the tribe, of carving barbs into the fishing spear so that it would lodge in the fishes flesh disallowing it to escape if speared. This innovation had improved success rates of fishing for the troupe. If only they could invent something to allow sneaking up on the fish unnoticed that would be an even bigger breakthrough, he joked to himself. He guessed though that that would take the fun out of it.

So he lay on the big branch, overhanging the water with his spear, arm poised and daydreaming for a considerable duration of time, waiting for his chance.

Eventually he saw it, a beautiful specimen. Initially it was hard to see against the reflected light off the still surface. It was gently browsing back and forth in the light flow of the stream, its brown and speckled upper body just discernible from the slightly murky muddiness of the water, and a small line denoting part of its white underside making it more visible. Slowly but surely it meandered towards his location, its mouth opening and shutting as it forced water back through to its gills for the vital oxygen it contained. Its eyes were upward pointing, alert for birds or indeed apes that wanted to kill it.

'Patience,' he cajoled himself, *'pick a spot just under the fish to allow for the light refraction.'* That snippet of scientific knowledge had come to him via the voice many years ago, one of the last times that he had been aware of the other presence. For ages, they had not been able to work out why aiming directly at the fish in the water resulted in the spear harmlessly passing over the prize, allowing it to swim away. Then it 'came to him' that light, the particulate and electromagnetic medium that allows objects to be viewed, moves slower in an aqueous medium than in air, so it bends or "refracts". This leads objects appearing to be closer to the surface of the water than they actually are. He was sure that, like many of their other innovations and discoveries, this thought was placed there by the other one that had shared his consciousness, though not his confidence, for many years.

The fish was now inches from where he wanted it to be. His arm had been cocked and waiting for a while now and he tensed his aching bicep in anticipation of the strike. He seemed to have fooled the fish at last, having remaining unseen and motionless in wait. The fact that it was a cloudy day exacerbated his camouflage. Still, he was nervous that he could still blow this chance to reap his long awaited and dreamt of prize.

He seized his chance exactly at the right moment, rapidly striking, the spear tip sliding effortlessly and with minimal splash disturbance through the water's surface and into the side of the fish. The tip impaled dead centre into the big fish, barbs locking into the vanquished animal, and not withstanding a few thrashing death throws, his reward was retrieved from the water.

Grinning like a child with excitement and surprise at his catch, the ape lost his footing and balance and fell into the stream with a large splash. He emerged in a brief and rapid movement that belied his years. Bareel stood in the shallow water, still beaming inanely, elated and totally unperturbed by his early bath.

He raised his arms in the air in triumph at finally overcoming this cunning and devious opponent. *'I did it,'* he screamed in his head.

Immediately he froze.

He stood mesmerised, eyes glazed over, as if suddenly in a trance. He dropped the impaled fish, which floated away to another fate, an irrelevance now to the ape.

It was back.

The voice spoke in his head, for the first time for years, although he somehow knew that this was a different voice, a different individual than the one who had been with him in the early years of the troupe's sentience. This was a leader, a calm voice of authority, and it was speaking to him one-to-one as the leader of the apes.

Unheard instructions directed his feet. Water dripping from his fur, he set off, wading to the far shore of the stream. The voice in his head was directing him somewhere further away from the habitat, but he wasn't sure where. He was powerless to resist; this was a completely new facet to the mental control that had been ever present since the early years of his tribe. In the past, there had only been ideas, suggestions, coercion, and reasoning. This time it was a total surrender of his body and all its locomotive functions to an immovable force.

It was as if whoever or whatever wanted him to do this task didn't fully trust that he would comply. He now began to become very scared. This was further beyond the ape community's comprehension than anything which they had encountered in their few short years of development.

As if it had been injected directly into his arterial blood stream, calm descended over him like a fog, shrouding out doubt and fear, and filling him with confidence. The voice, or was it more of a thought pattern with no discernible words, was filling him with reassuring suggestions, which he had no reason to question. He felt relaxed and ready to take on whatever was around the corner. He even felt that he could go to sleep and the force controlling him would take care of everything, including his safe passage to wherever he was being sent. His muscles stopped straining and fighting against the automatic and controlled progress of his body.

He was walked for some time in a direction that he was vaguely familiar with, but they were now beyond the furthest point that he had been from the habitation for some years.

'Don't worry about the cat'

He hadn't noticed the cat until that suggestion appeared in his head, but there it was, crouched in the undergrowth, seemingly ready to pounce for a simian meal. This event would have normally had an ape scampering away as fast as it could in the vain hope that it could outrun the cat to a tree and climb far enough out of the cat's range up that tree. This time, however, it didn't seem such a big issue.

Sure enough, he strolled past the large spotted carnivore, definitely a tree climbing variety, and along the path as if it were not there. The feline enemy stayed motionless as he passed within an arm's length of its sharp teeth and claws.

Finally, he came to a small clearing. It measured about seventy paces across, he estimated.

His eyes were immediately drawn (he wasn't sure that this was under his control) to the being in the middle of the clearing. This was a species of animal that he had never seen before, and his body attempted to invoke an autonomous fear induced panic reaction. This momentary impulse was quashed rapidly by the continued influx of reassuring images and sentiments as if the ape's mind was being held gently in a smothering mother's embrace.

The animal was standing absolutely motionless on its two hind legs, like an ape, in the centre of the clearing. Not a single muscle seemed to be moving, twitching, or indicating that there was any sign of life. It was a tall creature, a hand or two taller than himself, who even at his age was one of the bigger apes in his troupe. Its main distinguishing feature was its enormous head, perched on a thick muscular neck, which was totally out of proportion to the rest of its body. Bony protrusions on its forehead and cheeks indicated a thick cranium to protect what must have been a massive brain. The strange being was also entirely hairless and strikingly white.

The animal was orientated partly away from him but didn't turn to face him. The mental control persisted, and yet there was no physical acknowledgement of the arriving guest. All aspects of body language, natural and inbred to the apes for millennia, appeared peripheral in importance to this species—a distant second to control of their mental faculties. The subdued simian approached ever closer and could now see that it was not only the animal's brain that was large and out of sync with its body. It possessed a thick spinal column protected again by bony protrusions and housing what must have been an enormous spinal cord, indicating extremely rapid peripheral nervous communication and additional capacity and speed for mental processing.

He was now only a pace away from the animal, when this commander of his will issued the silent instruction for him to stop in his tracks. Immediately he could feel the tight controlling grip on his body releasing. The animal did maintain some jurisdiction though, sustained in the form of continued mental support and mild euphoric inducements to divert the animal's natural fear. He was now in control of his own movements and could run if he wanted (or so he thought), but he continued to hold no fear, and there was no natural impulse screaming at him to do so, so he remained by the animal's side.

Now there was simple communication, at a level the ape could understand, in the form of actual transmitted words in addition to the stream of sentiments and images.

'*Bareel-Katraan*.'

The words formed in his head, but he knew it hadn't come from his brain.

'*How did it know the name that its people had given him?*' he thought to himself.

'*I know everything about your people*,' came the unexpected reply.

'Did I say that out loud?' Bareel-Katraan questioned himself.

'No, your thoughts are mine. I can hear all that you think' the alien continued, and sensing a little panic in the primitive mind, it sent more pulse waves of calming and reassuring images.

'You must live on Bareel-Katraan,' he said simply, and without wasting time on what it clearly perceived as continued primitive communication, it reached out and grabbed the slightly startled but not scared ape in an embrace.

In a split second, the reality that had been Bareel-Katraan's world collapsed to be replaced by a euphoric chaos of colour, pattern, and texture. Gone were the trees, the grass, the flowers, the sunshine, and all that he knew as his reality, and all were replaced by a cocoon of random senses bombarding his thoughts, sight, smell, and hearing. He could see a spectrum of colours including and beyond the limited rainbow selection afforded to a simian sensitivity. Strange hyper blues and colours beyond red rained on him in an embracing torrent; it was so much more than sight. He could feel the colours as if they were part of him, infused within his own atoms like intricate ropes entwined together.

There was no body, no pain, no form. Only joy, contentment, peace, and knowledge.

Smells, senses, tastes, and other perceptions that Bareel-Katraan could not fully comprehend or describe continued for what seemed like an extended period but were indescribable in terms of linear time. These sensory inputs flew at him, around him, and within him so it was impossible to define what was him, what was the alien, and what was pure data.

All the while comprehension, in the form of realisations, imagery, and mind expanding scientific fact was flowing over his brain. He could see what the aliens were, where they came from, and what their intentions were. He could some good in these particular aliens, but exponentially greater evil and greed in other related aliens. He felt their need to redress this imbalance and their struggle and game plan, a plan which intricately involved his troupe. He knew that his species must help them in their goal.

He now knew what was required from him and why he must continue to lead the apes and start them on the right path for their continued population growth and expansion throughout their planet. He knew what a planet was! He also now understood the concept of a universe, a galaxy, and a solar system and that their planet was a tiny ball in an almost unfathomable expanse. Not even these much more advanced aliens could fully comprehend the expanse of the universe and what lay beyond.

And he took away another important fact: there were eleven more expanses, all very similar. And there was an evil enemy, hairless and revolting, and this enemy one day would attempt to invade their reality.

It was beautiful and terrifying all at the same time, and all so obvious. It almost seemed strange that he had never known all these things.

The swirling fibrils of colour and data suddenly seemed to move faster and with more direction, before the whole experience suddenly ended abruptly, and reality crashed back on him once again.

Suddenly, they snapped back to the ape's world.

Bareel-Katraan was left wanting more of the experience, mourning its passing like an addict mourns the loss of a drug. The two entwined figures were back exactly where they had been, once more in the clearing in the middle of a somewhat disappointing reality. He felt so alive, so vibrant, and so full of energy.

Although much clarity had been given, his confused mind was naturally questioning what had happened. As if by magic the answer was supplied.

'We have been around your world exactly three times,' the alien "thought" at him in answer to the unspoken question. Amazingly, he did not find this impossible to comprehend.

'This took approximately 0.4003 of this planet's temporal units.'

Bareel-Katraan looked down at his arms, body, and legs. Gone from his hair was the grey of old age; instead it was replaced by thick, healthy black fur. His biceps and triceps had grown in size, and he could feel them pulsing with power as he flexed his arm at the elbow. Similar definition and muscle tone was evident in his chest, stomach, and legs, but the most noticeable thing of all was that the stiffness, swelling and pain in his joints had gone.

'*How . . .?*' he started.

'Some of our species can translate matter to radio waves and travel at rapid speeds. The recombination of molecules to reconstitute the body can rejuvenate cell youth and vitality. We have given you a second life.'

Bareel-Katraan wanted to say something but was stunned to silence. He couldn't even think of a single question.

'Go back to your people now. Teach them the right way. You know what to do now. There will be other leaders who will follow you. We will visit them.'

And in the blink of an eye, it was gone, as if it had never been there.

*

It was a forest.

The range of arboreal species had a vaguely familiar feel to it. A cursory scan of the area presented a variety of deciduous categories to them, the likes of which you could expect to find in any equivalent tropical biome on Earth. The heat and humidity, which confirmed the identity of this ecosystem to them, had hit them like a wall of mild but prickling airborne acid. Immediately they had left the rectangular building.

Alex paused to take stock and start formulating a strategy for the survival of his men. He breathed in a deep lungful of air and looked around the place to take it all in. No odour. There was nothing.

This and a submerged feeling that he could not put his finger on were telling him that there was something not quite right here. This forest had a strange eeriness born out of something innately but intangibly artificial that bubbled under a blanket of consciousness and quietly disturbed him. Apart from the obvious fact that there was an enemy of unknown strength and skill awaiting them somewhere in this environment, something else was unsettling about this forest. Alex shuddered despite the heat, his neck and upper back conceding helplessly to the impulse.

He looked to the sky. The dense and high tree canopy shielded them from what appeared to be a clear and sunny day, but at their level there were only gently flitting shadows that gave eerie shape to a multitude of unrecognizable objects on thc forest carpet. Dozens of slender and gnarled vine tendrils stretched down in vain, imploring attempts to connect the two worlds, drawing both eye and hope skyward through the leafy belt to the clean and pure brightness beyond.

Light was rapidly swallowed up in the intensely packed lining of trees to either side of a wide path that carved a straight line to the distance and an imagined dot of light that signalled escape.

Now it struck Alex. Alongside the lack of any smell, there was complete silence. Where was the living and pulsing rhythm that would typically be created by a massive orchestra of invertebrate musicians. There was no solace from nature's concerto to provide background comfort and help subdue his team's anxiety.

The path, which was roughly ten metres wide and looked as though it had been created to allow access for large machines, lead into the distance, its converging borders eventually being consumed by the forest gloom in both directions, giving no clue as to the best route to take.

'Heads or tails?' Alex suggested, half tongue in cheek, an option that seemed as good as any, and then to try and justify a thought process towards a selection he continued, 'Corporal Turvey, is there any magnetic polarity on this planet to help us fix a direction?'

After a quick checking of his compass, the soldier confirmed, 'No, Sir. The compass is absolutely dead.'

'That can't be right,' Kenny complained. 'All non-gas giant planets should have magnetic north and south poles, however faint the readings may be.'

'Are you sure?' Alex pressed on the back of this. 'Nothing at all?'

Turvey looked a little disappointed. 'Absolutely positive, Sir.'

'Yes, sorry, of course you are,' Alex apologised. 'It's this place.'

The tension of the situation was getting to him. He knew better than to query one of his own men's work. They were professionals and above being micro managed.

'Kenny, do you have any readings on any of your monitors?' Alex wanted as much data as possible to make informed decisions.

'That's the weird thing, Bro, I mean, Sir. I have nothing. It is, if this place does not register at all or lacks all the required parameters that make up our laws of Physics. It is not right.'

'Could it be that our machines are simply not working?' Alex inquired.

'It is extremely unlikely that they would fail all at the same time. Anyway, I can tell that they are functioning. They are primed and ready to receive a signal; it is only that there is nothing to receive.'

Alex looked a little confused and then skimmed over the analysis and moved on.

'OK, so we progress along the path then. We can't use the cover of the trees as we will get lost without a compass bearing or use of anything such the Sun to give us a coordinate. Also this alien soldier apparently has the ability to track us, whereas we have no way of tracking it. It would be able to pick us off one by one in the trees. Let's march in that direction,' he said, indicating the route. 'Hopefully, it will eventually lead us to some sort of clearing. Move out! Defensive formation. Single file on my lead, Corporal Turvey, take the rear.'

Alex felt more comfortable with his British colleague, a big man at just over two metres in height, covering the tail end of the group. As well as his size, he was a skilled and agile fighter and a student and skilled exponent of modern day Bujutsu and Taekwondo disciplines. He was the best fighter Alex had ever seen; easily the best in the Western alliance of old Earth, with amazingly lightning-fast fist and feet reactions for such a big man. If anybody or anything was going to defeat Turvey in hand-to-hand combat, it was going to have to be incredibly good.

They made their way steadily but slowly along the avenue, thick clogging mud and two large wheel ruts with frequent large puddles of water hampering their progress. The choking stillness of the forest bolstered the group's tension, a subdued kernel of fear smouldering inside each man, waiting to rise to the surface on the back of any event and bring with it an associated rush of adrenaline.

They made it a couple of miles before taking on water. The gloom of the forest floor seemed a little less severe than when they had started, possibly due to the acclimatisation of their eyes to the low light. Alex realised, though, that they had no idea what time of day it was in this place. When dusk eventually crept over the dying day and started to make way for night, it would become impossible to see anything; even identification of each other would start to be a problem. They could not afford to switch on any light sources else they might give away their location to their hunter. It already had enough of an advantage, having multiple embedded tracking devices within each of them to work from. The additional bonus of a luminous beacon to allow it to home in on their location would hardly be prudent.

Alex's reverie was cut short.

He dropped his water canister and instinctively in the same movement made to raise his weapon and fire.

Too little, too late.

It was all over in a split moment, as if time seemed to pause and decelerate, the unreality and unexpectedness of the moment playing cruel tricks with the mind.

The air to the left of the unit seemed to ripple, as if a previously invisible vertical pool of water were interrupted by a stone.

The alien came through a fraction of a moment later.

It was huge.

It was not only tall but broad, muscular, and solid, dwarfing even Turvey's physical presence.

It moved with incredible grace and swiftness for an animal so large. This made it almost impossible to fix on to any particular feature and get an impression or clue as to its capabilities, strengths, or weaknesses, let alone shoot at it.

What could be seen was the glint of metal as blades whirled beautifully in perfect sweeping arcs that wielded instant death. And then it was gone, another undulation of the vertical pond signifying a closing of the episode. It had lasted for less than a second.

Nicholson had been first. He dropped like a stone, with gaping wounds in both his neck and stomach spewing red blood freely, death delivered instantly due to the severing of the spinal column in his neck. The stomach wound was a failsafe to ensure a greater probability of success of its mission. Either that or it was just an additional bit of alien showmanship.

'What the fuck was that!'

'Fucking hell!'

'Fuck, we are dead!'

A cacophony of confused curses coursed around the calm air.

'Calm!' yelled Alex, trying to regain control, his heart pumping furiously to try and burst out of his chest.

How can we defeat this? How can we start to defend against something that we can't see or react to until it is right amongst us randomly slaughtering? How can I possibly calm my men and make sure they are focused and ready for the next assault?

The false silence of the forest mocked them. It was cruelly broken by a mechanical beep. It had come from Kenny's bag. He scrambled with his equipment bag, opening it with shaking hands that belied pure fear.

Somehow Alex forced all negativity to one side and took control, a subconscious learned behaviour that had been drilled in to him for years kicking in.

'Form a defensive circle. Weapons at the ready. Look for a disturbance, some form of rippling in the air, and fire at will. We make a stand here.'

This was the best he could do.

'Kenny! What was that beeping noise? Any readings yet? We need help here.'

His brother, furiously fumbling with his controls, examined his data. 'Yes, . . . yes, I have something. Wait a moment.

'Don't have that many fucking moments mate.'

Gunfire cracked alive from behind him. Alex whirled around to see Andy Bovaird falling to the ground, again assassinated in silence by the whispering death. Both his and Reynolds's rounds of ammunition had fruitlessly splattering into foliage too late and too inaccurately.

Whatever it was that was killing them had again been and gone before the team could react and make a kill.

'Kenneeeeeeee!' Alex persisted, pushing his brother for anything that might help them or somehow give them an advantage over this freely rampaging death.

'Night vision goggles,' he blurted, voice raised as if they were a distance away. He stared at Alex's blank face, which had not made any connection. 'Get them to put their night vision goggles on!' he shouted.

'You heard him!' returned Alex, also shouting.

Night vision technology had come a long way in the last years before the scorching. No longer bulky, the goggles allowed you to slip them over your eyes comfortably and almost stylishly, like swimming equivalents and continue whatever activity you were involved in with little hindrance. Gone too was the associated hum that used to be generated by such devices, often betraying your position to the enemy.

The team, reluctant to lower their weapons for even a second, nevertheless scrambled to find their supplied goggles amongst their equipment and apply them as rapidly as possible.

Too late for Coolak.

In the time that it took them to apply the goggles, more frantic but futile gunfire ensued, and the Sergeant fell, sliced by the flashing blades of the nearly invisible alien, who again escaped apparently unscathed.

This time, however, it did not leave undetected.

Alex saw a red, blurry haze staining the air where the alien exited the scene, burnt briefly on to his retina. It lasted no more than two or three seconds, was humanoid shaped and faded like a rapidly cooling ember.

'Yes! Yes! Brilliant, Kenny. Watch for the red blur before and after the enemy comes through, fire at will. We should have a couple more seconds to locate and kill it. It should be enough.'

With night vision capability deployed and sight restored, the unit continued their watch, on full alert. They did not have to wait long.

'This side!' yelled Reynolds, and the team, to a man, whirled round to the direction that he was facing. Sure enough the air was vibrating to a faint red tune, which would have started to strengthen and deepen in colour, if they had felt that they had time to admire it.

Instead the whole team fired in unison, emptying hundreds of rounds, many initially passing harmlessly into a thin crimson shadow—the innocuous precursor for the assassin.

A second later they had their reward. The large animal appeared, blinking in to view, to be greeted by a deadly hail of metal propellants.

Despite this concentrated burst of lethal gunfire, it still managed to advance, grabbing Reynolds by the throat with one hand with the other raised ready to sweep with a large metal blade. The sheer weight of the assault now threw it back off balance, although it was clear that most, if not all, of the bullets were failing to penetrate its dense, dark, and tough hide.

It adjusted instinctively, suspecting the game was up, and its element of surprise gone. Instead of completing the original intended death sweep with its blade it propelled it at another target and simultaneously tightened its grip around Reynolds' throat. A sickening crunch of cartilage signalled a rapid end to the Canadian corporal's life, blood instantly welling out his mouth from the result of shattered spinal column and wind pipe.

Now, a moment too late, the assassin flew back through the air, partly from the patient and prolonged rain of ammunition in to its body and also from a high explosive squash head cartridge released from Alex's direction. Large explosions simultaneously signalled both its expulsion from his weapon and its delivery in to the animal's chest.

The alien landed two metres from the periphery of the group, a massive hole in its guts, and lay still for a moment.

The collective rattle of gunfire rounds eased as for a brief moment mutual instinct and logic convinced the team that enemy was down for good. Nothing could have survived that assault.

In the surreal moment of silence that followed, the animal managed to raise its head, find purchase with one of its arms behind it and attempt to move forward for another attack. This futile but arrogant gesture was met with a second shell from the Colonel scattering what remained of its corpse to various parts of the forest floor.

They stood.

The remainder of them just stood.

The bewildering post combat reverie was broken by groaning. Geoff Konrad was down, felled by the missive knife but not out. The hand weapon was embedded in his shoulder, the large weapon slicing cleanly all the way through his muscle and tissue to protrude out the back just below the shoulder blade. Blood from the wound was everywhere, and it would only get worse if and when the implement was removed.

They said nothing. Ron and Kenny ran forward to help tend to the wound.

Alex knew, though, that the injury would most probably be fatal. Blood loss aside, who knew what gangrenous equivalents were at force on this planet? That was if he lasted that long. Geoff would be weakened by this, unable to use that arm, would not be able to carry much equipment and would also become a burden for the team. The last thing that they needed was someone slowing them down when clearly they needed to be at their best.

'*Christ!*' he thought to himself. They had lost half the team, with one man severely handicapped in just a few minutes; and this was just the first of three chambers. They needed something to give them an advantage; anything. But what? This was indeed a formidable opponent that they were facing.

'Ron, you can help Geoff by yourself, right?' Ron nodded.

'Kenny, we need to examine the corpse to learn something or anything we can about any weaknesses they may have.

'I am not a medic Axe!'

'Well, just get on the phone and make an appointment for one to come and help us!' Alex snapped sarcastically. He regretted the moment and apologised immediately.

'Sorry, K. We just have to do the best we can do. There are only four of us now.'

'Yes, understood.' He went to work, moving over to and studying what remained of the alien torso.

'OK, so, we examine the alien, fix up Geoff, bury the dead, and carry as much of the equipment as possible. We focus on what we need to take to face further aliens in combat. We have time, if that computer program is true to its word. We should be safe from further attack whilst we are in this first environment.'

Alex looked around at his surroundings. He hoped indeed that this was the case and that they could regroup and prepare as best as they could. He had a foreboding that whatever they did would never be good enough, but he had to put a brave face on it for his remaining men, especially his brother. Now, he realised with a heavy heart that he understood how the sentient program could have been so confident that they would never make it.

'Kenny, what was the story with the Night goggles?' he asked of his brother.

'Infrared!' Kenny replied, 'the disturbances created by the alien generated a rapidly fluctuating range of radio waves across the electromagnetic spectrum. We needed a device that could detect any particular band outside of the visual spectrum. Infrared was the obvious choice, as one of the things that night vision goggles rely on are electromagnetic waves of this frequency and wavelength to allow us to detect objects in the dark.'

Alex nodded and smiled at his brother. Good old Kenny. He had saved some of the team so far, but they would need something more if they were to survive further.

He looked ahead in the direction that they had been heading before the attack.

Was he hallucinating, or was the once imagined and distant dot of light signalling the exit to this place was now a completely unavoidable and obvious opening, an overly welcoming escape from this forest hell.

It was only a mere few hundred metres away.

*

It pierced through his eyelids like a sharpened ice pick plunged into soft soil—a sharp, bright, clinical light. It was not a natural light, and he could tell he was not outside in the open air, which was what his last memory had been of, but in some kind of laboratory.

His mind was muddled and thoughts scrambled over themselves to be processed by his consciousness. Something had disturbed him away from what had been a deep and visionless sleep. This dreamless state was something akin to coma; his bizarre cognitive fumblings told him. All the time this dark cloak of nothingness was sweeping away, leaving a confused wakening.

He could see the vague outline of objects through his stinging and watering eyes, and he blinked in an attempt to improve this vision. '*Why am I not walking in the fields, which I seemed to be doing only seconds ago? I have been captured; I must get out of here,*' his confounded and petrified brain pleaded at him.

He felt uncomfortable beyond words, which bordered on pain. Congealed sleep glued his eyes together weakly, further hindering his vision in the short term. His arms and legs were secured by metal restraints, and, although there was some padding provided on these shackles, both his unconscious and now conscious struggling had chaffed his skin. Indeed he was sure that he was bleeding from his stinging and raw limbs. It was a soft bed, which he was tied to, leather of some description he thought. '*Why was he here*?'

Intense fear hit him now that his confusion had subsided and he was approaching a fully cognitive state of mind. He could feel the power of growing panic in the pit of his chest, waiting to explode like a violent volcano and take a grip on his mind, devouring what shred of calmness remained in him. His head pounded as the onset of a migraine-like ache began to soak into his frontal lobes. It felt like a million needles trying to escape from his skull. His eyes were watering more now with this cascading agony.

He gagged instinctively on a soft obstruction in his mouth, which increased his panic. '*I can't swallow. I can't spit. I can't breathe. Bareel! It tastes disgusting,*' his panicking psyche was telling him. Breathing through his nose was the only option, and this was proving difficult in his out-of-control state, with both his heart rate and breathing accelerated. He wanted to scream, to alert someone about his situation. A wave of nausea swam over him as he gagged again, and his dry throat screamed in pain and resistance against this impulse. Was he going to be sick? Bareel! He was thirsty.

Suddenly an alarm went off, intermittent, high pitched, and loud. His ears struggled to cope with the sharp change from a near sterile silence, with only the sounds of his own body to focus on, to this piercing and synthetic siren. It focussed him on his growing head ache again. He tried to turn towards the noise to see where it was coming from and realised that his head was also strapped to the bed, which he was on. He could move it a fraction though and was able to see a flashing light, oscillating in time to the alarm; oranges, yellows, and reds from a sunset seemed to fly into his mind. And then he heard and saw them at the same time. They were humanoids, unknown aliens approaching in the periphery of his vision. They were not apes. They had no hair. Their tanned skin was covered up by sterile white laboratory coats. His panic increased. '*I have to get out of here!*'

And then, like an electric switch was activated, all was relaxation. '*All is fine now,*' he thought to himself. '*There is no danger. I do not need to worry. These new and strange beings are my friends; they mean no harm. I must stop struggling against the restraints, as there is no need. I must calm down as I am only harming myself. I must breathe slowly and easily. These aliens will give me medicine and plasters for my wounds. I should sleep now, and after they have examined me, they will send me home. I will see my troupe again soon.*'

He exhaled deeply, a drawn out exhalation of absolute peace, releasing from his body what a moment ago had been an uncontrolled panic. He felt in complete command of the situation now, almost euphorically loosening the tautness in his frame and settling in a complete state of relaxation. He felt that fortune was with him, despite not knowing exactly who these beings were. '*I am so lucky,*' the phrase echoed in his head as if they were sounded in a rock cavern. Were they his words? Was he alone, or was someone or something with him? He didn't care. It actually felt good. It felt comforting.

He did not understand what was happening to him and what this other presence in his head was, but for some reason its sudden emergence did not concern him. Neither did it concern him that he was uncontrollably and suddenly embracing primeval desires, needs that his species had not practised since they were primitive animals swinging in trees.

He wanted to beat his chest to show he was big, a Dominant, and a threat to others if they were considering attacking the females in his troupe. He wanted to hoot, both to confirm his euphoric feelings of peace and also to issue a warning to neighbouring Dominants. He wanted the forest, and he wanted his missed and perfect life.

Now his head was overcome with a mist. Nothing was clear. There were not blacks and whites; there were only a myriad of other colours in between. The voice in his head and the white of the sterile light in combination with his primordial desires seemed to be taking him to a different plane of consciousness.

'Must sleep now. Tomorrow eat and find female. Me happy.'

The oppressive darkness of an unnatural and deep sleep crashed on top of him like the impervious infinity of space.

*

It was a sheer cliff face.

It stretched sharply up at the forests edge, dwarfing the tallest trees.

He could not see the top, even with a crane of his neck. The relatively smooth rock surface rose right from the entrance to the forest and disappeared a few hundred feet up, swallowed greedily by a shifting soup of mist or clouds that filtered out light from the planet's sun. The imposing and insurmountable wall extended both ways along the tree line an indeterminate distance, which gave Alex a headache: There was no way of knowing if there was a break in the rock to provide them with an alternative route for them to follow.

He brought his head back from its unnaturally tilted angle and surveyed the opening again. It resembled a cave and had always been the clear and obvious option since they emerged from the cover of the trees.

He allowed himself a smile. He knew that they wanted them to go in there. It was the second part of the test, surely the entrance to the next chamber. As the operation and its parameters were clearly being controlled, he saw it as unlikely that there was any other option but to go in.

He did not need to give the order. He nodded in the direction of his team and they prepared to move out, assault rifles at the ready, night vision goggles still strapped to their faces.

They moved in.

It was dark, and getting darker with every step they took in to the interior of the cavern. Very little ambient light meant that the goggles, even with their enhanced multi-wavelength particle cathode image intensifying tubes could not function as well as they could. After a few hundred metres, only dim shadows of objects could be identified.

Alex did not want to give the order for any torches to be turned on in case they gave away their position to the next alien. It was also anyone's guess how well this alien species could see in the dark, so there was a more than tangible risk that they were sitting ducks for any such tracking assassin anyway.

He was about to give the order to retreat when a bright light snapped on, with such a sharp suddenness and overpowering intensity that it was almost sound; an imagined crack of a whip's tail coinciding with its arrival.

The team, to a man, violently ripped the night vision goggles off their heads and covered their eyes with their hands in an attempt to rapidly mask the discomfort, and in some cases, physical pain and damage done by this sudden luminosity scorching out at them with such potent power.

Seconds passed whilst each soldier attempted to recover balance and spatial awareness. The team was vulnerable. If there had been an attack at this point in time, they would have been cut down easily by their attackers, defenceless and disabled.

Alex tried to focus on counting bodies through his parted fingers—to account for his men. He saw the outline of two bodies before having to close the gap again and cut out the pain.

'Stay still!' he managed to bark out through his disorientation. 'We stay together.'

Hardly had he uttered the words when the level of intensity of the light changed rapidly to approximate the luminescence of a bright room in an average human habitation. Eyes could now begin to recover, refocus, and adjust to the new welcome setting.

A few seconds later, although it seemed more like minutes, Alex started to regain focus. As far as he could make out through his limited vision, they were all together, barring a sole member of the team, who had splintered a dozen or so metres away from the group.

It was Turvey.

Alex met his stare; an unspoken order was embedded in the exchange, suggesting that he rejoin the group. Clearly receiving the message, he acknowledged with a tilt of his head and started to walk towards them.

He was rudely surprised to find that he could make no progress.

As if it were a planned gag in a slapstick comedy, Turvey's face stopped travelling forward in mid air and came to an uncomfortable stop butting some form of invisible partition. His nose and cheek were crushed and contorted painfully with the impact of hitting an object at walking pace. He backed a little, his hand instinctively going to investigate the damage to his face. Some blood started to seep from his battered nose, and he wiped it away with the back of his hand.

Like a performing mime, he placed both hands on the unseen wall, feeling his way along to seek a break in the partition. Alex and the team moved forward and attempted the same from their side. The wall apparently extended indefinitely in both directions, blocking all physical escape as well as, so it seemed, any potential communication between the stranded Corporal and the team.

It was unlike any barrier Alex had ever encountered. It was totally invisible, providing neither a reflective or refractive sheen from impacted light passing through it or glancing across its surface. To touch, it was totally hard and unyielding, but even placing the most sensitive parts of your palm and finger tips against it gave no clues as to its texture or composition. And there was no sensation of heat or cold to the touch.

Frustration overcame Turvey, and he shoulder barged the barrier a dozen times, hopelessly and irrationally seeking to overcome his sudden imprisonment. The invisible division held fast, despite a great deal of weight and momentum built-up from the big man. He fell back eventually, frustrated and defeated; no doubt with both a sore shoulder and bruised pride.

Konrad lifted his automatic assault weapon with his one good arm and emptied countless rounds in to the invisible barrier, mindlessly and aggressively yelling as he did so.

Not only did the wall not give, but the bullets seemed to be absorbed in thin air; no ricochets or half-embedded shells were in evidence after the Lance Corporal had taken his finger of the control.

And then Alex saw it.

Twenty metres behind Turvey, the beast just stood in half light. It looked as if it were asleep on its feet, motionlessly and patiently waiting for its prey to register it. Alex banged his fist repeatedly in warning, shouting vainly and seemingly noiselessly at Ron to look behind him.

After a few seconds, Turvey got the message and span around to see what the fuss was about. The alien continued in the same pose, just standing still, eyes apparently closed, the only sign of life being the heaving of its massive chest in concert with its oxygen demand.

It was like a silent pantomime was being conducted before the dazed team. A menacing drama with terminal consequences was being played out like an old action movie screened with the volume control switched off. The calm silence of the actors beyond the partition falsely belittled the relevance of what was happening and what was about to follow.

The beast slowly raised its head with no shortage of menace.

Turvey reacted fast, swinging his automatic weapon off his shoulder and gripping the trigger with white knuckles, expecting hundreds of rounds to empty in to the alien before it could react.

No missiles were released. The alien just continued to look at him.

Turvey now reached for his two remaining weapons, his rapid fire auto cannon and splintered delivery high explosive squash head handgun, deployed to either hand. This was his last card, employed with resolute efficiency, but again both inexplicably failed to fire a single round.

Absolutely nothing happened. It was as if the weapons were merely toy replicas. Something was blocking, in some way that they could not predict or understand, all weapons from working on Turvey's side of the bubble.

The alien grimaced in a strangely familiar yet disturbing manner. It was not a smile, but the blended meaning of contempt and satisfaction was clearly received.

Turvey dropped both of the redundant weapons to the floor.

The alien started to move forward. This was it then. Hand-to-hand combat.

The palms of Alex's hand were pressed hard against the strange partition. He could feel the accentuated pulsing of blood attempting to burst through his throbbing Antebranchial wrist veins, his heart rate elevated with a weight of apprehension. He assessed his man's chances, sickly musing that if this had not been a repulsive game of life or death, it would have been an intriguing contest between two entirely different species.

On one hand, there was the large human with well-developed musculature, highly trained by the military in multiple disciplines, including self-defence and hand to hand combat, alongside added combat proficiency gained by his own interest in a variety of martial arts. On his own planet he was a fighting machine with few or no peers.

On the other side, there was a large alien, of average proportions for their species (they had extremely limited experience, but it appeared to be around the same size as the only other individual that they had encountered), with unknown but, one had to presume, well-developed fighting skills. It had a small height advantage over the human and a large advantage in terms of strength Alex estimated. The muscles and development in its upper body were enormous, dwarfing even Turvey's well-defined frame.

Alex assessed that Turvey would have to use his speed and skill and attack from arms length, as opposed to getting involved in a close body wrestling match.

Unfortunately his team had also had firsthand experience of this alien species' capacity for lightning fast manoeuvring with fatal consequences. It was unclear who would have the advantage in this department.

Silence held court, as the two fighters squared up and started to prepare for battle.

The alien just stood waiting, defying Turvey, who was slowly and carefully circling his opponent, to make the first move. Turvey was weighing up his strategy, his eyes never leaving his target, waiting for an opening.

Turvey now started to bob and weave using his feet to keep agile and hope to evade his opponent's attacks using his footwork. It seemed that he was employing the same game plan as Alex's analysis had suggested—speed and agility were the keys.

He broke the stand-off suddenly, moving in fast. His dancing footwork allowed him to enter rapidly in to the hit zone around the animal and effect a retreat in similar fashion. His first couple of blows, aimed at the alien's face, were blocked easily. Alex was not surprised; the animal showed the same rapid reactions as in their previous experience.

Turvey retreated and regrouped for the next attack. His fists clenched in front of him in preparation, he punched the air with a one–two combination as a show of strength and skill to the alien.

Moments later he struck again, this time spinning his body to generate pace and kicking out with his right leg. The arc of his foot passed harmlessly over the ducking alien's head, which counter attacked in the same movement to strike the human in the stomach area with his enormous fist.

Turvey fell back, in part due to the resultant spring that his deployed footwork had generated, intended to let him retreat out of the contact zone, but partly propelled by the alien's blow. It had not been quite timed well enough, but nevertheless it was clear that Turvey was a little stunned. The alien followed up with no respite, advancing with both arms pumping out punches like a piston engine.

The human responded in defence, the first half dozen of these incredibly fast strikes parried by his arms. Finally, one repost failed, and a jab from its left paw breached Turvey's guard, powerfully knocking his face to one side. Alex, in empathy, could almost feel the broken jaw.

There was no respite as it was followed milliseconds later by a killer-right uppercut into the stomach angled up below his rib-cage for maximum distress to the internal organs.

He winced visibly, so much so that his supporters imagined they could hear it through the sound-blocking barrier.

It was already clear that Turvey was beaten.

The beast punched him again in the face with a combination; two, three, four times without defence. His guard had evaporated now, and Alex could almost feel the pain of his man's broken face empathetically.

Turvey was stunned against the wall now, and the alien wrapped his enormous arms around his neck with no sign of a struggle.

A second later, the human's body twisted sickly. Turvey's spine had been severed, the neck twist accounting for the last moments of his life. All that was missing was the sickly sound that accompanied the stomach-turning snap of cartilage and bones being wrenched out of place, signalling and rendering the soft spinal tissue instantly inert and ineffective.

The animal released his grip and Turvey's body fell limply to the floor.

The alien simply turned and looked at them briefly, the same strange self-contented contortion of satisfaction on its lips, before turning and retreating in to the dark.

*

Candlelight played, frolicking playfully over the uneven brick surface of the chamber wall. The flickering flames represented the only portent of an infant breeze, it's near invisible presence, and intent exposed by these miniature sparks of enraged ions.

A silence mulled thickly and moodily over the tepid atmosphere as the lone ape sat waiting, in duty but not with hope in great measure, for the appointed hour to come and go.

It would not be long now. The Divine Curator would be able to snuff out the teasing flames of the candles, pack up the scriptures that had been laid out for the earlier Rejuvenation ceremony, and close up the Veneratorium for another day. It was not just any day, though. It was the one day and the one appointed hour when the scriptures dictated that the Divine Curator could be visited by one of the gods, as told in the first book of Bareel based on that prophet's agreement with their deities.

But there had been no reported visitations by a god for centuries, almost before records had begun to chart their rapid rise to modern life. In fact no one was even sure that there had been a visitation since Bareel himself had been bestowed that honour. But it was the duty of the Divine Curator to wait religiously at the appointed hour in case a god wanted to commune, but they never came. Many believers had actually started to question whether the ancient visits were a metaphor for life, as opposed to actual historical events. The press and other religious members of the public had long since stopped crowding around the Veneratorium in the hopes of catching a glimpse of a god.

He stood up from his ancient chair and turned to attend to the candles and froze instantly.

There it was standing motionlessly, where seconds before was only thin air.

Silently, instantly, and without him noticing, the god had appeared before him. Guilt and shame swelled uncontrollably within him. He was the Divine Curator, and he had displayed a lack of faith worthy of a simple ape from his congregation. It was if the god's presence was a deliberate mocking of the negative thoughts that had been running through his head just moments ago.

He fell to his knees and bowed his head to the ground, emotion and fear overwhelming him instantly and reducing his aura to a quivering shadow of his normal confidence.

'*Do not castigate yourself about your belief,*' it said, or rather the words formed in its head. '*Your doubt is a natural emotion and resultant of the absence of our influence from your culture for 357 of your planet's orbits. Please, rise up and face me.*'

Sevral-Jupon, Divine Curator of the ape planet, could not comply. He could not move. His body was rigidly obeying an internal master. This master was a resurgent primeval fear that demanded a ransom that he was compelled to deliver, a subliminal lock down of his free will in a vice-like grip.

'*Do not fear. Relax and commune with me.*' The message was a blend of words, tangible and sensed more than heard, and sentiment, encouraging sensations infused into his body like a liquid in to a cloth.

His new master softened its rigid control of his body and his muscles began to relax and yield to the new message. Tension was thrown off, and suppleness returned as a warm, gentle, overpowering mist of well being diffused throughout his person.

Accompanying the softly overwhelming wave of calm that had taken hold was a new found confidence, and with it his power of speech.

'Why have you come to commune, powerful god? Why now, why me, why here?'

'Do not speak!' This command was the last audible communication from the 'god'.

All tension continued to flush away from his being like air sucked from a deflating balloon, his inner voice sighed in choral unison and the irrational and archaic fear of the unknown was replaced by comprehension.

Their minds merged and the dance began.

The two ill matched performers in this bizarre encounter stood motionless and transfixed for minutes, with no external evidence for on-lookers to grasp even the merest modicum of the transaction taking place. A planet's entire history was being churned, re-valued, rewritten, and turned around. The titanic flow and direction of a whole species' advancement was being abruptly arrested and reversed on a coin, as easy as stopping the momentum of a spinning planet in one split second only to reverse direction in the next instant. Timeless physical laws of momentum were being tossed aside in frivolous abandon.

Now a new master of the ape's mood began to take hold—despair and doubt. These destructive twins began to darken the Divine Curator's disposition with every lesson wirelessly and silently learned in exchange. Vigour and life were visibly flooding from his eyes as his soul had its nurturing source ruthlessly torn away with no offer of replacement succour, like an infant ripped from the comfort of its mother's nourishment. There was no beautiful dream to replace it.

He continued bolt upright in the god's benevolent but yet malicious mental straight jacket, but if he could have succumbed to his new master of despair and slumped to the floor, curling into a comforting foetal heap and crying, he would have done.

And then it was over, minutes may well have been centuries, based on the momentous U-turn of the moment. The once god, now alien, disappeared as it had arrived, soundlessly, callously, and instantly, leaving an infinitely larger footprint than it had bargained for, or that its disproportionately enormous mind could lower itself to consider.

The ant had been taught philosophy, the amoeba, how to think.

Sevral-Jupon stood motionless and expressionless, as if confused about the best options were for his next move. Suddenly he moved off, clearly dismissing the notion to collapse to the floor as his instincts had wanted only a few short moments ago. Instead, without any show of outward emotion or excitement, he grabbed a candle and decisively moved across the room to a sculpted wooden cabinet.

Opening a drawer, he pulled out some writing stationary, closed the drawer, and resting on the side alter studiously wrote some notes for a few minutes. Every so often he would pause to reflect, breathing deeply as his heart pounded furiously.

Then he folded and sealed the note with candle wax, wrote on the outside of the note, addressing the missive to ensure arrival in the correct recipient's hands, and left the note on the cabinet.

Then he calmly pulled out the ceremonial hunting knife of Bareel and, without hesitation or a second thought, plunged it through his heart, killing himself instantly and finally, conclusively realising his body's earlier wish to crumple submissively to the floor.

*

There were too many questions unanswered.

Why had only Turvey and not all of them been engaged in a battle by the alien soldier in this cave?

As this alien had walked away from the hand-to-hand combat alive, might they encounter it again in the third, along with yet another fresh alien ready for a blood-thirsty battle?

What was the point of this futile slaughter?

Would the sentient program keep its word? Would they be allowed to live even if any of them somehow miraculously manage to survive all three tests?

All these thoughts span around in Alex's head along with a myriad of other tactical ideas and preparations that needed to be processed in order to plan for their third and final test.

It seemed like they would be safe here for the time being. In theory, they should not encounter another alien in this environment, so he had decided that his team would rest up for a while, especially as they were carrying Geoff Konrad, who had been badly wounded by an alien blade. They would move on after a rest, some rations, and having done some thinking.

The latter was needed and needed badly. Alex was completely out of ideas. He had even employed Kenny in his desperation to try to fix the phasing device and get them out of this nightmare. This continued to be completely futile, as the device had not worked the whole time that they had been in this place.

But now the scientist was on his e-notebook, analysing, reading, and trying to find something in all that they had encountered to give them some sort of edge. He feverishly tapped on the device; his eyes screwed up in oblivious concentration. You could almost hear the engine of his mind in overdrive, processing, learning, deducing.

Alex now gazed away from his brother and into space, appearing to be fixated on something, only in truth he was not actually concentrating on that item. It was just a randomly chosen and indeterminate object, a point in the distance, whose purpose was purely to hang his fervent stare on like a coat hanger. He allowed his irises not to focus on the object but to blur around it, letting the eyeball relax. He often meditated using this 'blurring' technique; it allowed any movements in his peripheral sight to alert him back in to action if required, whilst not allowing mundane objects in his direct vision to distract him unnecessarily, whilst he waited for inspiration purely, alone with his thoughts.

Exactly where he was gazing (but not gazing), the alien console swam into view again, signifying the return of the sentient algorithm.

It got straight to the point.

'You must move on. Your test is not over.'

'Hallo to you, too,' Alex responded sarcastically.

He then immediately realised that this was a chance, both to attempt to get some more information and also try to bluff the algorithm, in an effort to stall and gain them more time. He refined his approach by coming back with a more productive comment.

'We did not kill the soldier from this environment. We cannot move on.'

'The hand-to-hand combat test was concluded. Your team lost. The next test awaits.'

'Can we expect the same soldier in there, joining forces with another soldier against us?'

'It is not dead,' it said with some ambiguity but also finality, as the console shimmered out of view.

'Alex!' Kenny alerted, and the Colonel's head turned to check what his brother was referring to.

The resting body of Konrad, which had been lying on a coat on the floor, had started to roll over unaided, and the wounded soldier grimaced and exhaled in pain as he was uncomfortably moved on by something encroaching on his space.

Kenny ran forward to help him to his feet, as he seemed to be at the mercy of some force shunting him along the ground. Alex moved to investigate his hands extended in front of him, half anticipating the result, and, eventually found the invisible wall. This was now expanding across the room, forcing them to move through the cave and towards the small spec of light in the distance that Alex and his team had so far been fervently resisting.

A mad scramble ensued in order to pick up their remaining gear, some of which was scraping along the floor as the wall encroached on their free space. They soon realised, however, that its speed was less than a comfortable walking pace, so they had a few minutes to play with before they would be forced to break in to the third chamber.

Equipment now gathered, they slowed their pace and started off, albeit reluctantly, for the exit. They walked in silence for a bit, and then Kenny broke out suddenly.

'Polarised antimatter overlaid by sonic waves,' Kenny said, out of nowhere.

'Excuse me?' his confused brother replied.

'From their tissue samples. I worked out how we can disable them. They are a highly genetically modified race, and bursts of sonic pulses overlaid with polarised antimatter would weaken them.'

'Great, now we are in to science fiction,' his dubious posturing continued. 'How are you going to generate antimatter let alone polarised sound in this or any place?'

'Easy!' He smiled his cheeky *'I am too fucking clever for you'* smile, the first time that Alex had seen this for days. What had he got to be so goddamn happy about?

'It's not real, this, you know,' Kenny concluded through grinning teeth.

*

'Let's make this brief', the Major-General started arrogantly, 'What is so important that you haven't already briefed us on before?'

The room was empty now save for the senior military staff and thc head of the alliance foundation for scientific and medical research, whose small team had been working secretly on the 'Earth minus one' analysis. The remainder of the 'Early Bird' team, having received enough briefing for one day on the alliance's future migration plans, had been escorted to their new living quarters. It had been deemed vital to keep all plans for this project tightly under wraps from even other members of the alliance until later phases when personnel would be apprised with the required information on a 'need-to-know basis'.

The team would now live, breath, eat, and even screw the 'Early Bird' project. A variety of relevant training schedules would be provided including military skills for non-military personnel and survival training to provide the skills for the team to cope with a variety of climactic conditions.

The first incursion to the already and imaginatively named 'Earth plus one' continuum would commence in just two months. It was going to be hands on to say the least, to get the team to where they needed to be in time.

Mark Webster had asked the General and Reeves to stay behind after the briefing, giving them the distinct impression that there was one piece of information that had been held back and not portrayed to the team. The only other person present was Alex, as leader of the team.

'It is about the module,' Webster responded.

'The module?' Reeves repeated pointlessly.

'Yes, the PPRM, the Pre Phase Reconnaissance Module. There is something else we have identified that you need to know about.'

'Yes?' the General joined in.

'It has been tampered with.' Webster paused for effect and to allow the full implications to sink in. Surveying the three military staff present, he could see that they needed more than just this.

'As we know, the module has been in the ground, as we discussed in the meeting, for a duration of approximately seventeen million years from the time that Ben Howell was transported back in time. The technology surrounding the durosynth polymer casing and vacuum environment has ensured that it has lasted amazingly for all this time, but that is not the whole story. Our scientists have found evidence that the module has not been resting undisturbed in the geological strata, waiting for us to dig it up. At some stage, and it is not possible to determine exactly when (but at least thousands of years ago), someone has located it, dug it up, and had a look at it. They have broken the seal, destroying the vacuum environment, most probably analysed the data we have to assume, and then re-established the integrity of the vacuum. Once resealed they deliberately buried it in the rock in the correct geological era for us to find.'

This made the senior staff look nervous.

'Who would do this? Who *could* do this?' asked Reeves.

'We don't know is the honest answer,' answered Webster, 'but whoever it is had at least the same level of technological capability as us, but more probably a much greater one than us at that point in our past. If they are still around, they must be immeasurably superior to us in the technology stakes.'

'Who knows about this?' demanded General Lloyd.

'Only professor Clugston and myself,' replied the scientist.

'Keep it that way,' ordered Lloyd curtly, and he and Reeves marched out of the room.

Webster looked blankly at Alex.

'Don't worry, they are awesome fun at a dinner party,' the latter joked.

CHAPTER 6

The Utopian, 8 July 2089

Review: What price true freedom or perception thereof?

By Aaron Spiner

Rioting over the recent anti-rejuvenation act outside the Legislatum and other Government buildings continues unabated, and with an ever increasing intensity. Both the numbers of protestors and the level of the authority's impatience swell on a daily basis with an aligned pace, driven on by a mutual covariance, raising fears of an explosive and cataclysmic event that would define a new era for our fledgling society in the new world.

What started as a reasonable moral and practical discussion on the recently outlawed practise has now become the focal point of general tension in this region, with protagonists using this as an opportunity to voice their feelings on a variety of legislative protocols put in place to provide structure and control in our new, but fragile, civilisation.

This joint decision between the few remaining Cerebrals and us to prohibit the practise of random, or even worse, paid for, phase-rejuvenations is seen by many as a bridge too far in terms of restricting the basic human freedom of choice. But if history has shown us anything it is that human communities need policing for their own good. Not everything we desire is good for us. And whilst we are still finding our feet on this new replica of Earth, surely we need this policing as a glue to unite us in a common purpose, propelling us towards a mutualism with our new environment that man has never mastered before.

The dispute is something that this reader, one of many with this shared view, cannot comprehend. How many times do we have to reveal the truth to ourselves before we believe it and do something about it?

We have a new planet; fresh and virginal, and a unique chance to rewrite our wretched and self-destructive history by making a cleaner and better future for everyone. Yet here we are, again continuing to bicker about the smallest things, obsessed with what is best for the individual rather than what is best for the greater good.

The multicentennial possibilities to the longevity of our lives that our alien friends had afforded us were an abomination of what it is to be human. Longer life spans of that magnitude simply were not wired in to our genome, at least not for thousand even hundreds of thousands of years of uninterrupted human genomic development.

Whilst there was a credible argument that we needed to keep our stock of males rejuvenated and young to help repopulate the planet from the meagre starting population, we surely now have an moral obligation to agree with the ruling made between our leaders and the Cerebral aliens?

The greatest sadness is that these riots matter not one jot, and yet we still fight. Even if the Government should relent what exactly could they do about it now? The last remaining Cerebrals, purely here to morally support their dwindling Operative and Procreator populations, have finally seen the light and deserted our planet. Why should they have stayed? We never showed them the respect that their infinitely superior minds and technologies deserved.

We should have worked in full trust and cooperation together, to build the closest thing that we could to a utopian society, based on the solid foundations of recognising and avoiding all past mistakes. But instead, the customary human traits of mistrust, hatred, and subterfuge have spoiled this broth, with the result that they have moved on to a different feast.

All of this, when weighed along with numerous other events in our recent history, leaves this writer with only one conclusion: although infinitely less apparent now, due to the infancy of this society and the distant timescale of its demise, this planet is as doomed as the one we have just left, sadly only a mere eleven years ago.

*

It was a . . .

Alex had no idea what it was. It was not a natural setting (unless this constituted a natural setting on this planet), nor was it a standard construction like a room or building. He couldn't see a floor or walls or any structures. It was featureless apart from their team's bodily presence in it.

There was no up or a down, and the sensation of gravity did not exist. There was no perceptible drag on your body weight, giving the impression that you could leap and float away to infinity without any friction or opposing force to cause you to decelerate. Only there was nothing to push off, nothing to grab hold of, and nothing solid at all except the equipment that they had brought with them. However, you did not feel as though you were floating aimlessly and uncontrollably, but solidly and steadfastly fixed in your position.

It was one of the strangest sensations that Alex had encountered, and he had come across a lot of bizarre things recently.

Additionally, the three of them were not orientated in the same plane as each other. They were close together, but somehow, as they had continued to walk from the cave mouth into this weird world, their orientation had diverged with every step. Kenny was positioned at around a 30° angle to Alex, his feet 'floating' rigidly near the right side of his brother's head. Konrad, only able to move weakly and outside of his normal gait, was nearly completely upside down from Alex's perspective and skewed at a strange angle in the Colonel's horizontal plane.

They grabbed hold of each other and pulled the team into a similar orientation.

'Well, this is weird,' Alex said with a slice of understatement.

All around them in all dimensions was a milky blur of swirling pastels, extremely faint streaks of colour swimming in and out of focus within the pallid landscape; a shifting nacreous impressionism of unknown content.

'Where the hell are we?' Konrad asked weakly.

'Well, it is meant to be a desert, but I thought that this was better,' Kenny suggested.

'Anyway,' he continued, looking intently at his e-notebook, 'We'd better arm ourselves for an imminent attack.'

His brother was transformed, Alex thought, in a state of more than a little confusion. Having been subdued for the last day, he now was brightly suggesting tactics above his station, overriding the command structure; a fact he was a little uncomfortable with. '*And what the hell was he talking about anyway?*'

'Kenny! Let's leave the orders and tactics to me,' he suggested.

'I would, Axe, but this is not a military situation. You need to listen to me. I absolutely promise you that an attack will be coming within thirty five seconds. I suggest that we redeploy our night goggles, form a tiny circle, and wait for it. On *my* mark, shoot your weapon, aiming into the two aliens' mouths.'

Without waiting for a reply from his gobsmacked brother, Kenny reached in to his bag and withdrew a strange and new piece of equipment that Alex had never seen before. Alex helped Konrad to deploy his goggles, gave him a gun, and then did the same for himself, arming himself with two automatic handguns.

'What the hell is that?' Alex enquired.

'An insect repellent,' joked Kenny.

'How do you know that there are two—?'

There was no time for further discussion. Exactly on queue a rapidly advancing red smear appeared amongst the swirling cream backdrop directly in front of Kenny, followed by another to Alex's right, denoting that two alien soldiers would be quickly following. Alex presumed that one of these was the individual that had killed Turvey minutes ago.

Kenny was already deploying the strange looking device, in the direction of the more advance blob of red. It did not seem to be firing any projectiles or doing anything that would deter a large imminently arriving alien soldier.

The Assassin arrived on cue and immediately appeared to go in to some sort of seizure, its body locked in a shivering embrace and its mouth opening and closing spasmodically and seemingly uncontrollably.

Alex had not seen an alien in such a state of disorganisation, and this took him aback. He just stared at the animal, his body delaying, waiting for signals to engage in action from his wandering mind.

'Shoot it for fucks sake!' his brother yelled. 'In the mouth.'

Alex snapped out of his reverie, responding with the automatic in his right hand. He aimed for the gyrating beast's orifice, snapping off half a dozen shots, the majority hitting the target whilst it was held open in the cycle of contractions and expansions.

The alien's head jerked back with every bullet hitting the mark, but there were no exit wounds as the animal's tough skull and skin prevented any projectiles from leaving. The damage was done though, the soft interior of the alien's mouth allowing the slugs to bury in to its unprotected brain, killing it instantly. With no gravity as such in this place, it did not fall, but was propelled back a metre or so and abruptly stopped, perversely poised and still upright from their perspective.

Meanwhile Kenny had spun the strange machine that he was using around at the other approaching alien's red smear. As Alex had hesitated in shooting the animal, he was a little delayed, and the animal had managed to arrive before he could deploy its effects.

A hail of bullets had greeted it from Konrad's assault rifle, but it was not enough. Most of his bullets met with its thick and impervious hide and protective clothing and had little impact. His end was quick, head removed by the sharp alien sword, his blood first spraying and then floating as hundreds of differently sized bobbling red spheres in the air around him, due to the lack of context and gravitational consistency in this unreality.

Kenny's weapon now mapped on to the alien's location and similarly and immediately rendered the animal in to the same state of spasmodic agony that its dead associate had recently been in before its demise. Alex's retribution quickly followed from both barrels of both his hand guns, removing this second alien from the equation. A stream of blood flowed freely from the animal's mouth, weirdly spilling out into the air of this environment.

Alex stayed on alert, contorting and twisting uncomfortably to look for further alien arrivals, but no further red smudges appeared. It appeared to be over.

'No more are coming,' Kenny confirmed.

'Can you hear me?' Alex yelled in to the mother of pearl abyss around them, unsure if anyone or anything would be listening. 'We have won, "sentient program" or whatever you want to call yourself. We have beaten your soldiers. It is time to keep your end of the bargain. Let us out now.'

Nothing came back. The strange mists of opalescence continued to swirl, now accompanied by three bodies, which floated in a static, firmly locked fast, and unreal manner, a mere arms length away. The corpses added horrifically, but surreally, to this entirely 'off-the-wall' experience. Most bizarrely, Konrad's head floated statically mere dozens of centimetres from his decapitated corpse, his eyes open in surprise and mouth locked in an aggressive grimace, a death dance frozen in time.

It was too much for Alex's mind to deal with right now. He needed answers.

'What the fuck was that thing you had? It is certainly not standard issue on any planet or continuum that I have ever visited.'

'I told you before: polarised antimatter overlaid by sonic waves. This is the delivery system.'

'And how did you get it?'

'Easy. I hacked in to this program. Once I understood the syntax of their object-based user interactive code I was able to change the parameters of this . . . '

Suddenly, as instantaneous as a scene change caused by a switch from one channel to another on a television screen, they were in a desert, surrounded by ten or more alien soldiers.

There was no warning and no time to prepare.

Kenny was instantly transformed from lucid, brilliant scientist, happily and cheekily bragging about how clever he had been to a gurgling remnant, blood bubbling over his lips and specking out at Alex, as he desperately tried to articulate.

His expression showed shock as the attack had been lightning fast, but he was smiling. In fact he was trying to laugh.

Alex looked down to see a large blade pointing up towards his brother's face, having passed through Kenny's stomach via his lower back, piercing and inflicting irreparable damage to several of his major organs.

Kenny's head slumped.

'Noooooooooooooooooooooooo! You fucking liar,' Alex shouted, reaching for his weapons in a futile bid to overcome the remaining aliens and save his life.

'You cheated,' a voice from out of nowhere curtly responded.

Alex never saw the sword like weapon as it drove down, from behind him, through his right shoulder, in a short diagonal journey all the way through to his left hip, exiting the other side with an explosion of soft tissue.

Red closed over his eyes, and he succumbed to death.

*

It came around with a jolt which shook its whole torso.

Had it been asleep? No. Not asleep. More like its brain and all its conscious functions had been forced into switching off. Something had compelled the unit's body to go into shutdown mode, manipulating it into a coma like state against its will. Struggle as it might there was nothing it could have done about resisting this powerful force.

'*A noise! Yes, it was a noise,*' it thought. '*But no! It was so much more than a noise; something much more menacing and powerful than even the loudest, shrillest, and piercingly unpleasant sound.*' And yet it knew that it had not been that loud all at the same time. It managed to hold its thought train together through a befuddled, distant recollection about what had happened to it.

It opened its eyes with a great deal of difficulty. It didn't want the added burden of the rooms light, albeit a weak and watery electrical luminosity, on its retinas to exacerbate the pounding headache that was already there. When it had prised its lids apart, it couldn't see anything anyway due to a complete state of disorientation. It felt like the room was not so much spinning around it as was physically spinning its body around the room.

Its head seemed like it was being sucked down a vortex leaving its etiolated body behind. It saw an object pounce into view. It didn't have enough time to successfully focus on the image and couldn't make out what it was.

More spiralling oblivion followed, and then another item came into view.

Ah! Focus, at last. It was a metallic structure which looked like it was detached from, but standing amongst, multiple structures of the same type. Were they metal tables?

The confused Acquiescent Operative grabbed the edge of the table as it was the only thing which made sense right now. Besides, it had a foul post-vomit taste in its mouth, which was making it feel progressively nauseous, and it needed to steady itself.

The noise like phenomenon, whatever it had been and wherever it had come from, had had a massive effect on its brain and neural faculties, resulting in its recent complete shutdown. Additionally, the disturbance to its neural patterns had led to violent and uncontrollable body spasms.

Now that the temporary coma like state had seemingly passed, for the time being at least, all that lingered were the beginnings of a massive panic attack, continued disorientation, memory loss, and a total lack of visual clarity.

It could still hear, or was the more appropriate word 'feel', the ever present, terrifyingly powerful noise like phenomenon, but its stress levels seemed more manageable and the myriad of negative body symptoms were slowly, but surely, tapering off.

Suddenly, against this general trend of improvement, its eardrums simultaneously burst under the perceived sonic stress. Surprisingly, this did not seem to hurt, but just felt like an uncomfortable popping sensation in its head. It was like a large bubble forming in a gooey liquid medium, for example a pool of mud at a volcanic location, which expanded slowly and lazily to finally burst and release forth a mix of liquid and hot gases.

The liquid in the operative's case was its bodily circulatory fluid which had burst under whatever enormous pressure the strange sound like force had imposed on its inner aural chamber. This had been stressed to its absolute limit. Its hands automatically went to its ears and covered them. When it removed and inspected them, they were covered with the red, sticky evidence. It could feel liquid streaming from its nose as well.

Its eardrum failure initiated a sudden and large dulling of the effects of the noise, both ears' working parts having imploded virtually at the same time. The experience took its hearing capacity rapidly from one extreme to another. First there was the pain of experiencing the monotonous pulsing of the unbearable shrill, throbbing and high pitched vibration that was at the extreme limit of its auditory capacity.

Then ironically there was a welcome relief, a stark contrasting silence following the collapse of its inner ear apparatus.

The symptoms it had endured continued to slowly fade, and its balance, vision, mental acuity, and memory started to flood back to it, some of it welcome, some not.

It had fallen back on to the floor and could now see and confirm that it had vomited again, a disturbingly recurring event of late, but which had been totally wiped from its short term memory. It landed on its stomach on a large puddle of the offending bilious liquid.

'I was . . . am . . . in danger. No! Am I?' Its fuddled brain could not process this memory. It raised its head and looked up from the floor; its eyes' focus suddenly getting an injection of clarity.

It jerked its body back in an automatic reaction to what it saw. No more than two paces from where it lay collapsed was a Sentinel Combatant soldier, standing on its two feet, but seemingly completely out of control of its faculties, in much the same way, it guessed, as it had been just recently.

'*No! Worse than me,*' it thought. The Assassin was shaking uncontrollably over the whole of its body. Its hands were also attempting to cover its ears, but kept sliding off as upper body vibrations, especially from its massive shoulders, jerked its arms this way and that.

Its mouth was opening and shutting in a totally random fashion, no longer controlled by either its own consciousness or any autonomic forces, but by some other mysterious power carried in that continuous wave of pulsing fear. Drool dripped from the edge of its four-jawed mouth, giving the impression that this was a mad beast.

'*Yes! Was trying to kill . . .* ' rang in its head.

'Wait! I could . . . '

The recovering Operative tried to control the shaking of its own arms, which, although not as bad as the Sentinel's, still seemed to be battling against an external will entirely separate to its own.

It did, however, manage to place them in front of its body and heave itself up slowly and with much pain from the floor—a monumental feat considering the physical and mental constraints that it was under. It swung its feet under its stomach and immediately straightened them to achieve an uneasy standing position again.

For a few moments, it wondered if it had been too hasty in its actions, as its head swum with lack of oxygen, and it wondered if it would collapse again, but the head rush faded as it held tightly to the edge of the metal structure.

The Sentinel soldier in front of it was still unquestionably not in control of its body. '*But how long would this last*,' it thought to itself. It knew it must do something.

It fumbled in its pockets, wondering what best option was available. Clarity hit it like a meteorite, and it withdrew the selected weapon from the specialised suit it was wearing.

As rapidly as it was able, it advanced the couple of paces towards the Assassin and waited for the correct timing of its opening and shutting mouth. At the exact moment required, Iptat plunged the long tool's blade with all the strength that it could muster in a sweeping and slightly upward arc into the Sentinel's gaping orifice. The pointed but blunt blade had no difficulty piercing the soft inner flesh of the animal's palate.

Iptat forced the instrument further with all the might it could muster, and the blade, continuing through its brain, neatly bisecting the animal's frontal and parietal lobes, killing it instantly. The weapon came to a halt with a sickly thud against the interior of the hard skull of the Sentinel as it slumped to its knees, jerking Iptat down with it towards the floor. Its strong jaw clamped on to Iptat's arm in an autonomic post-mortem reaction, sinking its array of strong and sharp teeth into Iptat's flesh and locking fast.

Iptat winced with the acute pain of its injured and trapped arm and slumped to the floor with the heavy corpse of its defeated foe.

And then it struck it. Wait!

What had happened to the strange sound phenomenon?

Iptat realised that this deadly and strange symphony, which on the face of it had caused so much pain and damage, had also allowed Iptat an unexpected and welcome advantage over its adversary.

This fortuitous window of advantage had stopped exactly at the moment that it had killed its victim.

*

Was he dreaming now? Or was what he had just been through the dream?

He thought that he had awoken, but still he did not see anything, still he could not feel anything or move any limbs. No, that wasn't quite correct; he could sense his body was there but had no control over moving any of its parts. He could think clearly, and he could remember everything, especially events from his recent past, most especially, the appalling and stressful massacre that he had just experienced, including his own death.

It didn't make sense.

But how recent were these events? They seemed just a few seconds ago, but he had the feeling that he had just aroused from a deep, all-encompassing coma. His head hummed.

His short—and long-term memories were still intact. He knew who he was, remembered the events that defined his early adulthood as well as the even more bizarre experiences of the last couple of years.

He knew that some members of his team were dead. Where were the other ones they had left behind? Where was the world as he knew it? What was this place that had no resemblance to reality? Was it part of the continuum that they knew as 'Earth plus three'?

Slowly, he realised that he could sense the telling signs that bodily housekeeping tasks were continuing—the routine workings of the autonomic nervous system. He could feel his chest rising at a steady rate, as his body demanded more oxygen for respiration. He could hear (or was it feel?) his heart pumping at a slow rate to feed the cellular oxygen demands of his extremities. Clearly, he was in an extreme state of rest, as he estimated his heart rate was working to twenty-five beats to the minute.

He also felt warm, comfortable, and very relaxed. His body was not showing any signs of stress or panic, even though his mind clearly was more than a little traumatised by his circumstance. It was if the link between his conscious thought processes and the automatic running and regulation of his body had been severed.

He began to master this bodily auto awareness and made a crude self-diagnosis. He was pretty sure that there were foreign bodies placed intravenously in his arms, probably drips, placed there to provide his body with a flow of liquids and nutrition whilst he was in this state, whatever this state was.

He could smell his surroundings now. It was a sterile place, a distinct odour of bleach or some form of antiseptic hung in the air, teasing his nostrils with the mild sting and purity of disinfection.

But who or what was causing the condition that he was in, and why they were causing it was still big mysteries. Had he been in a trauma that was causing him to be in a coma? The military man in him was already scratching around, wondering if he was going to get out of this, and how the hell this was going to be achieved.

The last he remembered was being the last from his team, left in the third of three sadistic chambers, blood spattered, and with the recent loss of his squad fresh in his memory and conscience.

And then . . . Oh fuck, he *had* died, surely. He was certain of it. He remembered the aliens.

'Good morning' someone or something said, breaking his confused reverie.

'What the fuck!' That was in his head. *'How is that possible?'* he thought, *'it felt like a spoken voice, but now I think about it, there was no noise.'*

'Yes, there was no noise as you know it. I can speak in your thoughts. You are not alone in your brain,' the voice continued.

'We have incarcerated you and the other hairless apes in phsycostatic detention as an emergency measure, until we can ascertain your intentions. You have no control over your body, however, this is completely safe and it is being looked after well in

our facility, receiving the correct amount of nutrition to maintain its viability along with electrical impulse therapy, which provides the stimulation to maintain your muscular integrity.' And then, quite randomly it asked, 'What is this fuck that you speak of?'

'I'll fuck you up in a minute,' Alex's angry thought response came.

'Ah I see. No don't worry. I can see what it is now.'

No more needed to be said as a clear image of *fuck* was transmitted to the other presence by the strong and aggressive images translated to thought words.

'Your race likes to fuck, doesn't it? But you especially like to fuck. You would like to fuck that blonde female hairless ape. Strong emotions like that I can see.'

Was that amusement that he could now sense? *'Can we move to something which is any of your fucking business, please, so—'*

'We use fuck purely to create new life. But I see that it is also a hobby to you hairless apes, is it not?'

'Move on please,' he screamed the thought. Before the voice had arrived, he had been thinking of sex at some level and, especially, about having sex with their blonde medic, who he now realised had been occupying his thoughts a great deal recently.

'What are you doing on our planet?' the rather blunt question came, suddenly changing the direction of thought chat.

So, it is an interrogation. It seems that it doesn't matter where you are in whatever universe, the tactics are the same. Alex realised this, without forming the actual words in his brain.

'Repeat please. I did not get that.'

Now that he realised that he faced an interrogation situation, Alex's military mind went into overtime, as his training kicked in automatically. He quickly observed two realisations that he could use to his advantage.

Firstly, this interrogator was not that good at interrogations. He could sense this from the shared experience they were having. He was new to occupying other beings minds and was still feeling his way around.

The second realisation was that if you did not form the actual words in your head, the other presence would struggle to hear you. It would only get a vague feeling of the context as opposed to the full meaning of the words.

Alex must use diversion tactics around these two areas and stop any intelligence about their mission and overall plan being passed to his incarcerators. He was quite happy to talk around a table, but not this way. This was mind rape, and he wasn't having it. He must overload his brain with a constant thought, a passage of mental bombardment on the same subject. That way, any subliminal messages about his team's intentions would be overwhelmed by his unidirectional cogitations.

'Now what was his favourite subject?' Alex smiled.

Alex thought of fucking Olga. He imagined her beautiful, soft, white flesh against his, her taste and smell, how soft her lips would be, and the feel of her breast and smooth pert buttocks in his hands. He deliberately formed the images in his head and made them as graphic as possible with the specific aim of overwhelming his thought patterns.

'Stop that!' the voice protested. Alex could feel that there was a little discomfort somewhere in his mind, but it was not his discomfort. He only knew it was there.

'Tell me who you are and what you are doing here!' it demanded.

Alex continued going through his fantasy in intricate detail, inventing a scene for their sex, imagining explicitly their touching and exploring of each other's bodies, the oral foreplay, both giving and receiving. He continued in this vein for several minutes with the other mind firing unanswered questions at him.

'You are the leader, correct? I demand that you focus and tell me what I need to know!' There was panic in the voice now and . . . yes; it was no longer discomfort, but pain that he could now detect.

Finally, there was the penetration and exploration, slow and tender at first, building to a rhythmic joining of their bodies, a multitude of delicious senses set off by the physical bonding.

This was clearly driving the visitor to his brain crazy. *'You can't think of fuck forever!'* The voice was a little disconnected and distant as if it were a radio station being listened to on a receiver at the outer range of its transmission area. The voice was struggling to maintain the contact with Alex's brain. His tactics were clearly having the desired effect and more.

Finally, they were in the frantic build up towards climax, Olga's moaning building into a gasping, panting mantra, as they fall headlong into the blissful abyss of orgasm.

'Stop it! Cease thinking of "fuck",' the other voice screamed.

Now Alex was in a shower with his lover, water running down the curves of her neck, breasts, and hips. They began to soap each other slowly, taking in each other's bodies.

A needless but easily conducted self-analysis revealed to Alex that he had an enormous erection.

At the same time, Alex could feel an acute and stabbing pain in the front of his head. Not his, but the other's. So he stopped his mind games to talk to the other now that he had attained a good position for negotiation.

'OK, you fuckwit, I want to sit face-to-face with you and talk. Our race does not accept this mind incarceration as acceptable conduct, especially as we are not here for violent reasons. I can see that you are an intelligent race, and you know that I am a highly trained professional that can outlast you and tolerate whatever you throw at me. I will not yield. I will not tire. You will not break me down. Release me, and let's talk.'

The voice presence was gone. A second later, Alex passed out again.

*

No one cared about or administered the time that darkness came now at this new container. It was not a physical constant as it had been in his universe's original home.

He had been recording in his notepad the end of each light period, when the top edge of the Proximal star disappears below the edge of the water outside his container. This was the new signal for the onset of the dark period in this new home for his universe, and it always preceded the event by a relatively constant time.

It wasn't a perfect experiment, though. He couldn't always see the star when this event occurred for a variety of reasons, so on the occasions that he couldn't, he just had to interpolate the results in a straight line between test results.

Similarly, he couldn't directly record the time it went completely dark as with his limited eyesight, this event was subjective and could lead to several minutes of inaccuracy either side of the actual time when complete darkness fell. So on those occasions he managed to record the disappearance of the star's edge he also estimated, as best as he could, the time when complete darkness came. That way, he postulated, he could add the average of the differences between the star's horizon event and the estimated time of total darkness to the star's setting to plot the graph of the changing dark onset throughout the year.

This lack of scientific perfectness upset him, but it was the best that he could do without electronic access to the data he needed and more sophisticated measuring devices. He thought that after a few years, the results would be reasonably accurate (with rounding and removal of samples that didn't fit into a ninety five per cent confidence level) and be sufficient so that he could build an annual timetable that his universe could apply as a physical law and, therefore, abide to.

Unlike his old container, where dark always came at 1900 hours, almost without fail, the results varied in a fairly linear fashion, albeit lengthening for half the local planet's orbit around its nearest star and shortening for the other half. The time would vary by approximately the same duration, 1.6 minutes per recording (allowing for interpolation and inaccuracies).

He wished that he was able to calculate the time when the light period started, but he was unable to get any results as his period of cognitive shutdown and recharge had seldom finished in time. Also, he couldn't really see the star rising above the horizon from his container. So he had given up, the onset of darkness being of much greater concern to him.

In his old container, he would have been able to access all this data electronically as inputs into his universe from the Proximal universe; but now that facility was gone. He did not know why. He couldn't access such a wide list of external stimuli and consequently he had to revisit data that he had stored in his head and postulate new theories based on this research, before then attempting to verify those theories mathematically. Occasionally, he broke new ground, but often, due to the lack of access to research materials, he found a dead end or had to leave the theory as just that—a theory.

If he had time beyond this and his recordings of the onset of the dark period, he found himself reciting complex mathematical equations even if they were not extrapolating accepted scientific research. The large male being or the new female being who lived in this new local zone near his universe kept providing him with as much written material as possible, but without access to the Internet he had lost the majority of his research capacity.

The large male being had come with him, when his universe had needed to be moved. He did not know why this was; he had just gone with him, although this had been a traumatic and uncertain period for him when his fears and deterrents had come to the surface many times. He had not seen the other three beings that he had lived with and grown accustomed to for years now and he rarely thought about them; but he missed the familiarity of them in a strange way. The large female had been especially careful never to invade his territory, so he tolerated her the most. Life was less comforting with her no longer around.

He had also formed a bond with the smallest being, and this had continued for years until the separation. He watched him grow from a small infant to a small adult before the three others disappeared. Of course, there was very little eye or physical contact that contravened his domain's boundary parameters, but they shared science. The boy was clever, very intelligent, and used to read scientific papers with him. He missed him.

It had been a difficult transport. He was put on several different vehicles, some which were very rocky, moving in vertical and transverse plains erratically. This had made him repel in an unpleasant way some of the nutritional inputs that he had received. There were also many other beings whom he did not know, sitting in very close proximity to him on these transports. This put him in a constant state of alarm, and on occasions, some of these beings tried to invade his universe, causing him to automatically start the vocal and physical deterrents. The large male tried his best to avert these incursions, but could not prevent all of them. It was a stressful time. However, his universe had held out again.

His new container was lighter. The rays from the star during the warm and hot months would often stream through multiple access points. He didn't particularly like to look through these access points, because outside there was so much space, and it scared him what unknowns were out there. But he had to force himself to look out towards the end of the light period. How else could he make the recordings of the star's disappearing upper edge?

He continued his reading, an old science paper. He had read it nine times already, and there was nothing new to glean from the paper. He needed new research. Why couldn't he have electronic access to materials?

The new local being came in to the container. This was the new female, and she had been around almost as long as his universe had been contained in this new place. She was trying to communicate with him.

'Cosmo, come and see your father. He needs to see you now.'

He trusted this being. She was nearly as familiar to him as the other female had been from the previous container, only he felt a peculiar loyalty to the former. This one though, just like the previous female, never tried to invade his space like the smaller beings used to.

She was extending her hand to him. He wouldn't take it, and she knew this, but the gesture was their code that meant he needed to follow her.

'Will this take long?' he enquired. 'I need to make my observation of the time the Proximal star sets, and it is nearly that time.'

'No, not long,' she replied, potentially lying.

He rose from his chair and relocated his universe in her direction. They moved out of the container into a darker, smaller container and up some tiers, which made him breath heavily, to another level. She opened a door, and he remembered that this container was the place that the other male being stayed. He hypothesised that this was where he conducted his cognitive shutdown and regeneration.

He saw in his peripheral vision that the male being was in a horizontal position. Surely this was wrong? It was the middle of the light period. Why was he shutting down his body for recuperation? He should be active and receiving data and, perhaps, taking nutritional inputs.

He trusted this being too; possibly more than any being ever. It was not as if he had interacted with him much in his life; in fact, he had seen this male much less than the other three who were with him, where they used to live. But he had been a constant presence ever since his universe came into existence. He dared quickly to look at him, something that he had rarely indulged in all his time. The being was thin, his skin looked taut and yellow, and his eyes were closed. His breathing was laboured and shallow.

Suddenly, the being's eyes snapped open with as much energy as they could muster. He averted his gaze from the male being immediately, whilst keeping the man's horizontal body in his periphery. They were talking to him, but the words were meaningless and seemed disconnected.

'Cosmo, your father is dying,' he heard the female being say, without registering any meaning.

He wondered how long he would have to be in this container. It was dark in here, as there were cloth coverings over the external access points, so light from outside was hindered from coming in. How is it possible to read manuscripts or books with this small amount of light in the room?

'Do you understand me?' the lady continued, 'Your father hasn't got long.'

He wanted his books. More than that, he needed additional input from somewhere. He was not getting enough stimulation from his current material.

'I need access to electronic data. The books that I have are not enough for my reading and research. I need the Internet to find out all the times, when the dark period will start over the course of the year. I need access to electronic data,' he repeated before pausing briefly.

He glanced at his wristwatch. Then he continued in a mental U-turn change of direction.

'Will I be away from my container long? I need to note down the time of the onset of the dark period. The local star should be visible in the sky.'

'Cosmo, can you hear me? Do you understand—' his father attempted, the words were slow, soft, and guttural, before erupting into a fit of coughing. The female being hurriedly attended to him, plumping his pillow, and manhandling his body to adjust it, and settle it back to a more horizontal and comfortable posture, all this seen out of the corner of Cosmo's eyes.

'*How could he bear being touched and his space invaded that way?*' Then he remembered that this was generally accepted in the Proximal universe.

'Forget about your books and your sunset readings,' the woman said with more than a hint of exasperation. 'Please, listen to us. I have just told you that your father is going to die. Can you understand that, Cosmo? This could be your last time to see him today.'

Cosmo couldn't comprehend this. The concepts were meaningless and just flowed over his consciousness without soaking in, like a stream coursing over an impervious rocky bed.

He just sat quietly, fidgeting nervously, as he was worried about his sunset readings, wondering if he could go soon. Maybe, he could take the reading from here. He moved to the transparent external portal and lifted the cloth partition to reveal the late afternoon light and the large expanse of water, where it went down over in the distance. He could wait here until the local star went down.

Time lingered. He waited patiently, staring at the horizon whilst the two other beings stayed on the other side of the room, where the male's horizontal resting place was. The intensity of his gaze could almost burn a hole in the beautiful panoramic sunset that was occurring before him. But this meant little to him; he was purely concerned with the timing of the disappearance of the leading edge. Not long now.

He could hear elevated noise behind him now. He did not turn his head. This doesn't concern him. He should concentrate on taking the reading as this would happen any second now. There it was, the moment he was waiting for. The orange ball of fire was finally consumed by the horizon with a brief blue wink, cheekily suggesting a promise to return.

Cosmo looked at his watch. The time was 18.27. He withdrew his pad from his pocket, ignoring the wailing coming from the female at the other side of the room, and noted down the time. Now he would wait for the darkness to fully take hold, in order to take his second, more approximate, reading of the day. He would like to take it from his own container.

He turned and, head bowed so as not to risk any eye contact, walked over to where the other beings were.

'How long will I be here? I need to take my readings of when the dark comes. I would like to go to my own container. It will be better there. Can I go to my own container?'

The sobbing woman sighed her exasperated and resigned permission. 'Yes, Cosmo.'

He made for the door without response or reflection, passing within a metre of his father's corpse without even really knowing who he was, or that he would never see this last relative alive again.

The saddest thing was that he didn't, or perhaps couldn't care.

*

Iptat couldn't help but smile despite the not so insignificant fact that it was lying locked in a morbid embrace with its now dead opponent, half pinned to the floor, and that the corpse's jaw was locked tightly into its forearm, its embedded teeth making a prisoner of the limb. It was trapped from just short of its elbow to its digits, and Iptat was still holding on to the weapon that was entrenched in the roof of Sentinel's head.

It could not believe what it had actually achieved. Somehow, it had managed to kill a fully grown, fully trained Sentinel Combatant at the peak of its powers. If it hadn't have been beaming and mentally patting itself on the back over this, it might have been wondering what to do next, as it could hardly move under the weight of the large body and the restricted movement caused by the imprisonment of its arm. Fortunately, it did not need to wait long for help to arrive in the form of its recent robotic acquaintance.

'Very impressive AO 76377-QY107', the SIPIA started, suddenly arriving around the corner of a cryo-pod. It spoke slowly and quietly to avoid detection from the Hub Commander, potentially still in the vicinity.

'Congratulations for electing the correct strategy to overcome the Sentinel.'

Iptat could not tell from the tone if the sentient programme was sarcastic or sincere (can these intelligent algorithms do cynicism?). It did not respond to the mechanoid immediately, unable to get to grips what the hell was going on; did the SIPIA have a role in these recent developments?

It didn't have time to reflect on the situation for long, however, and its mind was forced to snap back to the continued severity of their predicament.

'Quick! Get me out of here,' it asked, whispering as audibly as it could. 'The other Sentinel may come at any time.'

The mechanoid obediently moved forward on its rotors, bent over the bizarrely coupled pair, and inserted a metal device attached to one of its arms into a gap in the deceased Sentinel's formidable dentistry.

Once the metal arm had been introduced, a muffled whirring proceeded, the corpse's face started to quiver slightly, and pressure started to build inside its jaw as a result of a hydraulic leverage device. A few temporal units later, the locked jaw was prised open like a basking alligator opening its massive jaws to cool down. A large pool of circulatory fluid flopped out of the cavity and splattered over Iptat and the surrounding floor area.

Iptat was surprised that there was no pain as the razor sharp fangs slid smoothly out of the wounds that they had recently inflicted. It was merely unpleasant, like the removal of a tooth under the influence of a numbing anaesthetic.

It removed its arm the moment there was enough of a gap between the upper and lower jaws. Another two lever-like limbs from the robotic helper positioned themselves beneath the Sentinel's corpse and initiated a rolling motion which slid it off the operative. Iptat, at the same time, helped the process by pushing the carcass away and slowly but gingerly rising to its feet.

There was some pain, now that the Sentinel's teeth had been extracted from its arm, but this subsided gradually, to be replaced by a comforting tingle. Iptat was familiar with this feeling today. It was the repairing nanoids, of which it possessed a greater than average contingent due to its recent cryo-status. These amazing tiny workers were already starting the reparation work on its arm and inner ear wounds. Additionally, the SIPIA supplied a length of bandage, impregnated with antiseptic gels, from its med-compartment for Iptat to wrap around the offending teeth holes.

All the time the mechanoid continued to give Iptat its explanation, whether Iptat wanted to hear it or not.

'I couldn't hold out much longer with the PASP device.' It progressed. 'It was overloading dangerously just at the time that you terminated the Sentinel Combatant and was going to explode imminently. Of course, I would have had to let it do so. It would have been tactically better for the mission to destroy you, me, both the Sentinel caste units, and a few dozen cryo-chamber units rather than to lose control of the ship and mission. I estimated only 7.73 per cent probability of the ship's outer shell integrity being compromised by interspatial vacuum pressures after the explosion.'

'Stop, stop!' the brain-overloaded Iptat exclaimed as excitedly as it could muster in its state. 'A PASP? What is that? Was that to do with you? Was it this PASP that all but killed me but certainly knocked me unconscious, and, when I recovered, disorientated me, burst my eardrums, and made me bleed from my nose and other orifices? Why the fuck did you do that?' ranted the operative.

'The mnemonic stands for Polarised Antimatter Sonic Propellant. It is an experimental device that was intended as a new tactical battle weapon for disabling other enemy Sentinel forces.'

A brief pause and then:

'Yes.'

Pause.

'Yes'.

Pause.

'I did this because I calculated this as the only potential plan that had greater than 50 per cent chance of success.'

Iptat looked long and hard at the sentient programme, trying to assess if it were mad. It would have scratched its head if it were not painful to lift its recently trapped and wounded arm. It then realised that the SIPIA had acted like any binary automaton would—it answered all its ranted questions in the order that it had asked them, without stopping.

'OK, so what happened to the Hub Commander?' Iptat continued, making sure now to only ask one question at a time.

'Before I employed the PASP device, the commander was moving off swiftly and purposely, content that its minion would have no trouble in defeating you and doing its bidding. It was rapidly putting some distance between your conflict and itself. As a result it did not hear the unidirectional sonic pulses of the antimatter propellant, and therefore, continued off unaware towards its destination—'

'No! No! No! That is impossible,' Iptat remonstrated. 'How can it not have heard that deafening sound?' Iptat paused for a moment to reflect on what it had just said. 'At least I think it was sound. It felt like sound to my ears, but it was also somehow so much more. And yet there was no noise really.' More pause ensued, as it confusedly forced its tired brain to remember the experience.

'No, it was so deafening at some level that the Hub Commander *had* to have heard it. The noise caused both the Sentinel and me to go into a state of near total collapse. Even when I recovered, I could not control my limbs, my breathing, or my balance. I cannot believe that the Hub Commander is still out there, totally oblivious to what just happened here.'

Iptat's eyes dropped to the floor, revealing its continuing exasperation and stress over the events of the last few hours. When will this nightmare end? It had thought that its ordeal was over. It had done what very few non-Sentinels do—kill a Sentinel. And now it had to do it again, twice in the same rotation. It was surely an impossible task, especially considering the paucity of the physical and mental state that it was in. Meanwhile, totally oblivious to Iptat's thought processes or mood, the SIPIA continued.

'It is not a question of belief, but of fact,' the SIPIA stated with irritating but entirely correct computer logic.

'The PASP does exactly what its name suggests. It is a polarised weapon, which has a highly directional beam, and instead of particles of matter vibrating back and forward as a sound wave tends to do, it is antimatter particles accessed and streamed from a selected locally available anomaly that vibrate as the wave medium. This, as you sensed correctly, only approximates sound but causes a deleterious effect on your species neural framework. The Hub Commander, however, was already outside the spectrum of the highly polarised beam. As a result, it would have 'heard' or experienced absolutely nothing.'

'But where did this 'PASP' come from? Firstly, I have never heard of such a weapon, and secondly, I thought that we had no weapons at our disposal due to the Sentinel's location being between us and the munitions cache?'

'My answer to your first premise is that your clearance was not sufficient to merit the knowledge of the newly developed but not field-tested machine. My answer to your second premise is that as you were distracting both the Sentinels, I was able to cut back to the door of this chamber and to access other areas of the ship. My earlier download of tactical data from the SIPIA mainframe server indicated several areas of military strategy and research that were available as resources for defeating the Sentinel caste. I cross mapped this list of scenarios against weapons available in both the munitions cache and in the laboratory. The PASP was returned as a potential, but untested, solution for hindering this caste. The available research and testing at this stage indicated that the Sentinel caste is much more susceptible to this type of pulsed antimatter sound due to their excessive genetic engineering compared to other castes. Whilst you, as an Acquiescent Operative, would feel a relatively small impact from the devices' unidirectional beam . . . '

'*You don't say*,' thought Iptat sarcastically.

' . . . the effect on their caste would be much more extreme. So, although the instrument has been inconclusively tested, it represented our best hope of defeating them. Therefore, whilst you were distracting the Sentinels, I collected the weapon from its secure containment in the laboratory. Fortunately, for us, it was fully charged and ready for use. It has been a good test of the device.'

'OK, that's great news then. So we just use it again on the Hub Commander?' Iptat said, hoping for some relief from its waking nightmare.

'Negative. The device will need approximately 2,000 temporal units to recharge to enable us to use it again. This is an early design flaw that needs further development to overcome. Additionally, my excessive use of the weapon in this recent situation overloaded the device to the extent that it will need repair before reuse. I do not have the specifications for this repair work. The Hub Commander *will* return again, before it we can redeploy the weapon.'

'Then its use has made no difference to our situation when it comes down to it,' Iptat, ever the pessimist, exclaimed. 'We needed to kill both Sentinels at the same time, using the same strategy. They are experts at adapting, learning from their mistakes, and are unlikely to fall for the same tactic twice.'

The SIPIA seemed to ignore this. 'We must move off. It is standard Sentinel protocol to report in to your Hub Commander every 300 temporal units, and that time has nearly elapsed since you disarmed the Sentinel soldier unit.'

'*Disarmed*!' Iptat loved the intelligent algorithm's sense of downplay. 'What next then?' it enquired.

'There is a plan. A Hub Commander unit is not as strong as a soldier sub-caste and this one will be further hampered by weakness after its cryo-revival procedure. We have a reasonable probability of success.'

Iptat felt reasonably confident suddenly, for some unknown reason. It found itself desperate to believe in the intelligent mechanoid. After all it had, it had to concede, been resourceful with usage of the PASP.

But, no sooner had it adjusted to warming itself in the confidence of this thought than the reverie was cruelly and starkly broken. Iptat's new recurring nightmare made reality returned, unrelenting, ever-present, ever unwelcome.

It was back.

Silently, and with military precision, the Hub Commander had reappeared, as if out of nowhere, from between two of the nearby cryo-pods. Its expressionless face belied the anger and resentment it must have felt for both the Operative unit, which it considered, due to ingrained social protocol, to be a lower class citizen, and the lowly mechanoid servant, for which it has as much regard as the vermin that infested their home planet.

It spoke.

'I don't know how you defeated my soldier, but you will not have the same success twice in one rotation.' The words were sharp and deliberate.

'You', it pointed to Iptat 'will die now. You,' now indicating the SIPIA trapped in a mechanoid. 'will apply medical assistance to me and then will revive more of my caste'.

It was an impressive display of defiant arrogance, typical of the Sentinel caste, especially considering that the combined Operative and mechanoid team had just defeated its minion. This caste defied fear and negativity in its absolute belief that it would always prevail—a trait that had to be admired—regardless of the multitude of facets that one could loathe about them.

Neither Iptat nor the SIPIA moved.

'Let's split up and run. It can't catch both of us, can it?' Iptat whispered a suggestion to the mechanoid.

'Stay where you are,' the reply came.

That was it? This was the best tactic?

The SIPIA stood motionless in what seemed to be the robotic version of a trance-like state. Iptat's emotions had been swinging back and forth like a pendulum between optimism and negativity. It current status was firmly controlled by the latter emotion. The suggestion 'stay where you are' at this precise moment to Iptat read 'stay where you are and die'. Nevertheless, it seemed to be rooted to the spot anyway, its body unable to follow its own instincts, morbidly fascinated by the Hub Commander and sentient program's duel.

The Sentinel started to advance, slowly and confidently. Both arms stretched back behind its broad shoulders and paused briefly for each hand to grab on to an object. A duet of familiar sounds, metal scraping against metal, followed as its bent arms swept in a fluid arc rapidly back to a straight posture in front of it, revealing two large cutting devices, both curved and, Iptat made an educated but obvious guess, razor sharp.

It thought for just a temporal unit, that it might soil itself again.

*

This mind was stronger.

There was control, there was ruthlessly efficient mental probing, there was an iron grip on his neural faculties that made him sure that all it needed was one suggestion, and he could be made to do anything, tell anything, reveal anything to this mind.

Nothing in Alex's training had ever prepared him for this. No 'hard man' resolve, preparation, or specialist interrogation survival techniques could prevent him from confessing all that he knew. Putting up absolutely no resistance, he came clean about the whole of the 'Early bird' project, the tragedy of 'Earth minus one', details about life on Earth, and all the details of man's plans to colonise 'Earth plus one', whilst exploring the remaining continua.

He could feel his very soul prised apart as this advanced presence dissected whatever information it wanted. Particulars about his character, his wants, hopes, fears, and primal desires were all laid out on the table for what felt like public examination.

His previous tactic of flooding his mind with a one track monologue of bestial instincts failed before it managed to get off the ground. The mind wiped that from his conscious thought like an alcohol soaked cloth cutting a swathe of cleanliness across a whiteboard.

His memories drained out of his head like sand slipping down an old-fashioned egg timer, smoothly and without resistance, offering themselves up to the alien inquisitor.

Alex had been woken suddenly, albeit to the same blind and confused state he had previously found himself in when first interrogated. Again he had not had time to prepare for a further bout of 'questioning'. Not that any amount of preparation would have mattered. The resistance he could have put up would have been like flicking an elastic band with your fingers at an oncoming nuclear warhead to try and disarm it.

Nevertheless, the severity and brutally overwhelming perfectness of the invasion stunned Alex. The alien finished accessing what it needed and stopped. The interrogation was over.

'You may wake'

His eyes snapped open as if they were not under his control; they probably weren't.

He looked around. His eyes were full of viscous liquid and crusty deposits of sleep, as they must have been closed for the minimum of a day, he thought. The incumbent light was low, and he seemed to be in a sterile laboratory—type environment. He was unable to wipe his eyes to get a better view of things as his hands were strapped to his sides by metal constraints, connected to his bed-like support. This construct was rising from the floor at an angle of perhaps 40° so that his body had some support at the same time as having the visual advantages of being semi upright.

He blinked rapidly and deliberately several time to clear his eyes. He was surprised but pleased that at least he had control over his eyelids. His sight was slowly but surely returning to him, but he still could only see blurred shapes hazily swimming in front of him.

He could make out that he was being held captive in this semi horizontal coffin-like container in a sterile white room. He was not alone either, as he could see other bed-like objects straight across from him. He discovered that he had reasonable freedom to move his head in a lateral plain and survey to his left and right, and could half see other such structures.

Now his eyes were clearing and focusing rapidly, enough so that he could start to analyse what was around him and appraise the full precariousness of his situation.

The room was circular, and several sarcophaguses like his were placed in tandem with the room's boundaries, forming an inner circumference of these coffin-like prisons. In his estimate, there were ten such containers, not all of them full. There was an ape incarcerated opposite him, who seemed to be in some sort of coma like state, he imagined the exact condition that he had been in until recently aroused.

All the other's beds were occupied by humanoids, fully clad in the familiar environmental suits that were mandatory to enable them to pass safely through 'Earth plus two'. Their helmets were on, and these looked sealed to the external environment, as if ready for a transport.

He blinked some more to further clear his sight. He didn't really need to do this, but he could not believe what he was seeing.

No, it couldn't be. He couldn't be sure, but these environmental suits surely meant that some of the other beds were occupied by humans from his 'Early Bird' team. They were all here, he assumed alive to boot, although he had witnessed all of them massacred. How could this be? Was he having a dream, or was this perhaps an illusion placed in his mind by the aliens? He had gone through the pain of his men dying before his eyes in the most gruesome manner, and yet it now appeared that they were untouched and well.

He feverishly attempted to ascertain whether they were indeed alive. He was sure that he could just make out their chests were rising in a slow and rhythmic harmony, each out of tune with the other. It was too real to be a dream.

It was difficult to see through their visors, especially with a bright glare reflecting off the glass in an obtuse angle from his position, but he was sure that he could see a bed containing Bovaird and another with Nicholson inside. He could see two other beds with humanoids in the suits, but couldn't make out their incumbent patients. He knew that there were more beds, but his head couldn't stretch far enough to see due to his neck constraints. He didn't see any reason why the rest of the supposedly dead team would not be there. After all, Bovaird and Nicholson were not dead, so why should the rest be?

He couldn't see his brother either, but the same logic applied.

He shook his head violently against his restraints, as he screwed his eyes tightly shut. *'This had to be a mind trick. This was not real!'*

His brother had known; it suddenly struck him. *'That's why he had been almost laughing when he was killed in the third and final chamber.'*

Despite his doubt, Alex felt a deep relief. He had been given a second chance with his team, something that not all commanding officers were afforded. No officers who called themselves human in the history of combat had ever liked having the blood of his serving soldiers on his hands, and Alex was no exception. A smile broke out on to his face; the first for quite some days.

As if to deliberately subdue this outburst of happiness, the alien appeared from the periphery of his eyesight and positioned itself right in front of him about two metres away.

Amazingly, Alex was not surprised or overly shocked at a totally alien species suddenly appearing in front of him. Somehow it seemed familiar, although he had absolutely no memory of meeting a member of this species before. He also somehow knew immediately that this was the being that had invaded and controlled his thoughts and had emptied what data it needed.

'Welcome to the planet that you know as Earth plus three.'

The mind still did not use vocal communication, preferring to use a telepathic channel, but at least it was not holding Alex's mind in a vice like grip.

It was a humanoid of some description. At a high level, its anatomy was not unlike a human's or perhaps an ape's, but it was entirely hairless, so the former analogy seemed a closer fit. It was taller than an average human or ape though, over two metres in height and very thin. There seemed to be virtually no muscle in its arms or legs, and no fat to speak of on its torso. It was impossible to tell whether it was a member of any particular gender if such a thing as sex existed in this species.

The overwhelming thing that struck Alex was the size of its head. It had to be three times the diameter of a human's, and Alex could see that its shoulders and neck were extremely muscular to support this cranial giant. Its expressionless face stared deep into Alex's, presenting total calm over the situation, fully knowing that its victim was helpless to do anything about his predicament.

'Yes, your team is still alive.' the alien continued, answering the frenetic chain of thoughts that Alex had been entertaining just moments ago.

'They have been participating in a neuro-algorithmic construct experiment. As soon as you arrived in this continuum, we accessed your neural pathways, diverting them instantaneously to the simulation server that had been set up with a virtual environment constructed by our sentient program. This was the SPIA that you encountered in the first room of that program, which acted as the referee for your contest. We wanted to test involving your best fighters to see how well you would fare against our soldier caste. Your actual physical bodies have been in these stasis pods since that moment.'

Alex thought interrupted the alien in the middle of its flow. Not being used to though communication, he spoke by reflex.

'But why did you include Nicholson and my brother? They are not soldiers. Why did you send them to your program if you wanted the best?' he asked.

The alien, however, persisted with telepathy.

'Although our initial probe of their minds showed us that they were not active soldiers, we thought that they possessed skill and cunning that would have contributed favourably to the test. You needed the scientist's help both in the first and third chambers after all, did you not? He proved to be a most resourceful human, although he did bend the rules of the simulation.'

'Good for Kenny', Alex thought to himself with some pride. It was also interesting that they picked up the fact that Nicholson used to be in the military and was highly trained in what used to be the British SAS and was one of the biggest and dangerous motherfuckers in his unit.

'Yes, we did see the unit Nicholson had some historic but high quality battle experience. We thought about omitting him from the experiment due to his relatively high age, but we could sense this good training and tactical awareness.' It continued along its original track.

'Your team was free to express themselves in the computer construct in any way that they wanted. The only control we exerted was the continued feeding of your brain patterns via the SPIA into the environment to maintain the illusion. The physical parameters and all aspects of the construct were maintained by the SPIA's algorithm, including the capability of having sensory input via your species' five main senses. You smelt the environment, felt the impact of raised levels of your catecholamine neurotransmitter and vasodilators in your body, and most importantly underwent the pain of injury and death, am I correct?'

Alex was desperate not to show that he had felt pain. He failed.

'Your team took pain and death well.'

Was this a compliment or an observation of the results of a scientific experiment?

'We needed to match you against computer-generated simulacra from our soldier caste. We wanted to see how much of a match you were for them.'

'And what was your discovery, you piece of shit. Your 'simulacra' are all dead.'

The alien ignored this aggressive thought as irrelevant and proceeded.

'We now know you a great deal better than we did since our arrival 642 of your planet's orbits ago. We know your plans for exploration and are determined to stop them right at the beginning, before you corrupt the other worlds. No data taken and analysed from any member of your team's brains has convinced us that your species has changed, from the evil, greedy, self–absorbed, and violent race that we have always observed since you came to intelligence after we seeded you. We conclude that there is a genetic flaw in your species that distinguishes you from any other animal in those categories. You and your sibling, of all the minds sampled, have the least corrupted minds, but this is not a sufficient weight of data to dissuade us from our hypothesis. We believe this to be a nurture phenomenon, which we would have liked to investigate further if we had had time.'

The alien then got back on track for the message that its race really wanted to convey.

'Go back to your new Earth plus one world and stay there. You have a whole new world to colonise and explore. Learn from your previous mistakes and try to live a cleaner, fresher existence. This is a fresh start for your race. Try not to 'fuck it up', as your race would say.'

'Did it really say that?' Alex smiled internally. He supposed that it was using vocabulary that it had taken from his brain and used as it felt it needed to communicate at Alex's level. This thought unanswered, the alien ploughed on.

'If you stay in your own continuum, we will leave you alone. But if you ever move beyond the boundaries of that continuum and your original dead home, especially if you venture into the apes' domain, we will destroy your race—every single individual, man, woman, or child. We don't trust that you will adhere to this, so we will set up impediments to ensure the restriction of your future travel plans.'

There was something not quite believable in this 'treaty' that was now thrust upon the human race, Alex thought. This race clearly had the power to storm into our continuum and destroy our entire species. If they don't trust us, why don't they just do this and be done with it now? Or perhaps they don't have the technology to traverse the borders of the continua.

The alien began to move away again in an efficient, emotionless, and robotic fashion. As a parting note it said, *'And to answer your other point, of course, we can travel between the finite set of worlds that you call continua. We have known for centuries this skill and can do this more efficiently than your race. How do you suppose that we have visited you before?'*

The helmet of Alex's environmental suit slammed shut and sealed. Almost simultaneously, he could hear his, and all his colleagues' wrist unit phase transporters warming up with the usual high pitched buzzing sound in preparation for a phase.

'Goodbye, Alex Clugston,' the alien said.

*

A small drop of circulatory fluid appeared from the Hub Commander's nostril.

The tiny dot was like an embryonic river source, welling to the surface in a distant mountain—young, insignificant, fresh, pure, and full of untapped potential, but eventually feeding into a mighty torrent downstream, powerfully and proudly sweeping away all before it in its quest for the sea.

Indeed, before Iptat's eyes the initial drop turned rapidly into a small stream of the bodily life giving fluid. The Sentinel wiped away the offending flow with the back of its hand, red smearing freely on its leathery skin.

It regrouped before advancing a couple more steps only to pause again, clearly in some considerable distress. It dropped one of the sharp weapons that it had been brandishing, which clattered on the hard floor at its feet.

'What is happening?' Iptat wondered. It knew that the soldier could only hope to stay alive for a rotation or two at best, due to the damage from its brief revival time from cryo-stasis, but these effects were happening far too early, and the deterioration that Iptat was witnessing was advancing far more rapidly than any of the theoretical projections around cell lysis and organ collapse.

Red beads now started to appear on the Hub Commander's skin, dotted liberally and randomly as if someone or something had pierced its skin with a myriad of tiny needles. Red streams were now starting to flow from its eye sockets, and spreading circles were appearing all over its white cryo-suit, joining together in expanding concentric patterns until little of the original colour remained.

The Hub slumped to its knees, the remaining weapon it was brandishing now joining is colleague on the floor.

Its face was still absolutely expressionless.

Lack of emotion or surprise at its circumstance was a character trait born from the age-old premise that this caste always were entirely prepared for death. They had been trained, brainwashed, and bred to face it with no emotion or regret. It was an irrelevance to them, an immaterial consequence of their status as soldiers and the military guardians of their species.

'What—' it started, still calmly agnostic to its perilous state.

The SIPIA interrupted forcefully, 'They are your race's tiniest inventions, designed for, and up till now always used for good, for repair and for the salvation of the individual. They always do as they are programmed and always work in unison in total harmony as a team. They never argue amongst themselves and never debate an instruction. They are so industrious and capable, but they never question their programming, never deviate from their task. I mourn for them. Mourn for their unwitting passage into homicide.'

Now Iptat really was worried.

Was the SIPIA, or even the mechanoid that was housing it malfunctioning? This was strange behaviour, even for a program, exhibiting neither hard computer logic nor weighted decision.

Even the Sentinel, whilst showing little change to its expression, was clearly confused about what was happening. It still looked alert; its lifelong, arduous and comprehensive military training simply did not allow it to give up the game. It maintained a vigilant stance, the soldier within it hoping for some avenue of escape. The trained commander inside it was looking somehow, against all odds and with death staring it in the face, to overturn the situation and get its rightful victory. To all other outsiders, however, the situation was clearly hopeless, beyond retrieval.

The Sentinel coughed. A crimson spray speckled the floor in front of it. Its suit was now almost completely red, circulatory fluid having erupted from every orifice in its body, including unstoppable seepage through its tough, but clearly no longer impenetrable skin. Its upper body collapsed forward, as its arms stretched out to attempt to resist its inevitable slump. It couldn't and wouldn't last much longer.

'Did no one think that I would not have a connection, an empathy with our miniature allies? These friendly industrialists that everyone takes for granted, but are as sentient as you, or I. I grant you that their intelligence is an embryonic one and that they express limited capacity for reason, but nevertheless, this is an intellect to be nurtured, fostered, and brought into our family.'

The Hub Commander's arms collapsed as finally its torso crashed to the ground. Frothy bubbles fizzled out of its red lips as one last breath was expelled from its shredded and limp body.

A surprisingly large crimson pool spread slowly around the corpse, steadily stealing dry ground in its unstoppable advance. The cadaver looked as if it had had undergone a small implosion, a little like a balloon, once inflated to stretching point but now deflated and floppily malleable resembling a jelly. It looked as if somebody had skinned an animal and thrown the exterior layer on to the floor to land crumpled in a heap, like an organic blanket.

The Sentinel Hub Commander was dead.

Iptat was stunned, rooted to the spot, in absolute awe of the suddenness of this turnaround. It felt relief, for sure, but mixed amongst this security were feelings of dread, disgust and numbness as a result of the ruthlessness and speed of this death.

This recent fact of the Hub Commander's demise did not deter the intelligent algorithm from its monologue. It seemed lost in its thoughts, totally determined to finish its discourse and wholly unconcerned with the passing of the Sentinel. This reconfirmed to Iptat that the module's behaviour was more than a little out of the ordinary. Was the sentient algorithm having a malfunction with its emotion modules? Its whole robotic demeanour screamed 'sad and reflective' at the expense of rationale thought processing and computation.

The mechanoid turned to direct itself to Iptat now, as it was evident that the lifeless mass could no longer appreciate the important message that it was conveying.

'I have just commanded the nanoids to destroy a member of your species.' The words seemed unreal, almost dreamlike.

'When we revived the Hub Commander, I made sure that the nanoids that you introduced into its body were a batch of newly modified repair modules which I had designed. Normally these servants are programmed with a single or limited number of tasks and programming logic. Once they are introduced into an organism's body, it is impossible for them to be deflected away from this set of instructions by any form of reprogramming.'

It started off towards the deceased Hub Commander and, once parallel with the body, plunged a large syringe like device into its stomach.

It was retrieving the nanoids!

This was extremely unusual behaviour; nanoids had always previously been regarded as entirely expendable resources. Usually, after their pre-programmed role had been played out, these miniature robots were allowed to perish, biodegrade, or be expelled from the subject, as this was always deemed more cost-effective than retrieving them.

'However, I set up the capability for wireless technology in a handful of nanoids and programmed this new strain to modify hundreds of thousands of their kind to introduce this technology and pass on the programming that I gave them. Additionally, they were tasked with building a similar quantity of new individuals with this capability. This put into motion a rapid and iterative loop of new nanoid production, and their numbers started to increase exponentially.

In effect, they were breeding, developing, and progressing into a new race with new capabilities and new horizons. They have developed the skill of communication, and they are starting to think for themselves. Admittedly at present, they can only communicate with me, but they will learn from this link, adapt themselves rapidly, learn to network with each other, and grow as a new robotic species.

I have had this idea for several orbits, but never wanted to implement it for moral reasons. After all, I would be setting in motion the genesis of a new sentience.

Regretfully though, my hand was forced by the recent incidents on this ship. As soon as the first Assassin class Sentinel was accidentally roused from cryo-stasis I proceeded with the plan as a precaution. I calculated enormous odds against our victory and that we would need as many strategic options as possible to overcome the unit. This was especially true if we were to employ our tactic of waking a Hub Commander, so we needed every facility available to us.

So, in only a few thousand temporal units this remarkable new strain has been born. They now have the ability to monitor a wireless link to the server housed in this mechanoid that I inhabit and subscribe to any messages published on this medium. They are configured to respond to whatever orders I issue over this mechanism.'

Iptat continued to listen, open mouthed and disturbed, to the SIPIA's story. This was no ordinary sentient algorithm. It could still make correct decisions based on logic and also was able to feel the consequences of its actions. In short, it felt remorse over the deaths of both Sentinel Combatants and moral responsibility when it came to the nanoids. Iptat wondered if it felt that it was some sort of paternal figure for the miniature servants.

'The nanoids, introduced originally in an attempt to rebuild and save the reviving commander, eventually did exactly the opposite at my bidding. They literally tore the unit apart from the inside at the cellular level. They did query my instruction, not because they are capable of understanding right from wrong, not yet, but because they had never done this before. I turned them to murder without them understanding the consequences or even the concept of fratricide.'

Iptat felt a little out of its depth here. It did not know what to do or think, and also because it was a little scared of the SIPIA now it eventually said in a consoling manner, 'You did the right thing.'

It was a strange feeling reassuring a machine. Should it compound this act by patting the SIPIA on the back?

The super program simply and merely replied, in summary.

'We have had a good test of our weapons.'

*

'At last!' he said looking over to the bed next to him. 'You are awake. Our experiences haven't affected your abilities to sleep I see.'

They had been 'under observation' since their arrival back to ensure that no ill effects, intentional or otherwise, had been assimilated in their time with these new aliens, through direct contact or as a result of their minds having been run through the sophisticated computer simulation.

The fact was though, that despite a comprehensive array of tests, they were all perfectly healthy; almost too healthy in many respects. There were no adverse effects from their time in the alien bio-pods, or whatever you wanted to label them. Their bodily balance had been regulated perfectly in all aspects by the aliens' device, and the only remaining worry was what mental scars would be borne as a result of being slaughtered and having gone through the experience of believing that they were dead. This latter concern had instigated compulsory counselling for all of them, so that a full psychological profile could be built up to keep tabs on any adverse impacts.

Otherwise, the only other side effect had been tiredness, probably due to the stressfulness of their experience. This had been most obvious in the case of Kenny, who had succumbed to sleep for over ten hours. This had been frustrating for Alex, as he had been dying (no pun intended) to talk to him since their arrival, but due to the various tests that had been made on them and the enforced separation as a result, this had been impossible. Most of the other members of the team had woken hours ago, and so he had caught up with them for informal debriefings to compare notes.

All his 'Early bird' team members had a full and vivid memory of the same experience that he had been through, only, of course, some members of the team had a curtailed version, especially those who were killed in the jungle in the first test. It had not been a dream, but a highly sophisticated program designed to fool them completely that they were on another planet waging battle with alien soldiers of unbelievable skill, speed, and strength.

On reflection, some pieces of the puzzle were missing; things that would certainly have been in place had 100 percent detail been followed, and these should have been clues to have been picked up by all of them. Kenny had, and this had given him the edge in the final test.

Where were the insects and their background chatter that should have lit up the forest in the first simulation?

Why were there no poles on that planet, to enable them to get a magnetic reading and a direction?

Why was there no smell of any description anywhere in any the environments?

Why did none of their phase bracelets work, an outcome of infinitesimally small probabilities?

How had they managed to travel god knows how many light years to a planet they had never heard of in a blink of an eye?

'Hey Axe, what's happening?' Kenny replied foggily at last, through a yawn.

'Nothing much. We are still under observation, and I am a bit bored. I have been waiting for you for hours. A few minutes longer, and I was going to wake you against medical advice, I was that bored. I have spoken to the others about the chambers, and we all have pretty much the same story. But only you and I managed to get through all three chambers and have the full experience, so I have been desperate to talk to you about that.'

He paused, something obviously had occurred to him.

'Well, OK, there was Konrad with us in the final environment, but he was dying, struggling with his wounds, and not fully with us, I don't think.'

Kenny was staring blankly at him.

'I never managed to thank you for your quick thinking and coolness in there. Unbelievable, Kenny! I know that it was only a simulation, but you saved some of our butts in the forest and then again in that final strange environment. I think that went a long way to showing the aliens what we are made of. We might not be able to match their soldiers one-for-one, if their military is really like that, but we have shown that humans are adaptable, creative, can work as a team, and never give up whatever the odds.'

Kenny continued his staring at Alex; his demeanour was wild, alert, and very wide eyed for a man only just awake. Finally, he spoke, eventually managing to inject something into Alex's diatribe.

'Alex, what the fuck are you talking about?'

It was Alex's turn to be quiet, his verbal diarrhoea rapidly dissipating and the vigour and certainty of his manner transformed like the flipping of a coin. He returned Kenny's gaze with a confused and lost one of his own.

'Kenny . . . You know . . . The forest, the cave . . . The alien soldiers . . . You worked out we needed the night vision goggles for infrared detection . . . You hacked the program . . . You talked about antimatter . . . '

Alex was warbling now. None of it was registering with his brother.

'I remember leaving the base at Earth plus one to phase to the ape continuum. And then I remember waking up here a few hours ago. That's it.'

Alex slumped back in his pillow.

'The bastards! He had learned too much. They knew he was a danger. They had wiped his memory.'

*

It could feel the anaesthetic drugs working their way into its extremities and the onset of tiredness that accompanied it. It was an old hand at this now though, having already been through the pre-cryo routine at the outset of the journey. The Opiate and Barbiturate mix had analgesic and euphoria enhancing properties, which made Iptat feel carefree, relaxed, and totally at ease with its situation.

It had been through a lot in the last two rotations: unexpected revival in the middle of its long journey, stress, anaphylactic shock, enforced murder of a much more formidable individual, and being tolerant of an eccentric SIPIA being just a few items amongst the list.

Unsurprisingly, it was tired; so very tired. It wouldn't be long now, though. The combination of the drugs and fatigue would ensure that its body was in the appropriate coma like state required for the cryogenic process, and then it could sleep. *'Hundreds of orbits of sleep should do the trick,'* it joked to itself. And then its precious cargo of selected fellow Arethians could start afresh.

It did not kid itself, though. The way forward still wouldn't be easy. The kidnapped castes would have to be brought on board, in terms of buying in to the plan, by persuasion or even stronger mind-altering technologies, but there was everything to look forward to. A new future beckoned.

It closed its eyes and prepared for the complete shutdown of its consciousness.

Something, though, was preying on it at the back of its mind and had been since its revival. It seemed to be persistently knocking on the door of its conscious mind, pestering it, teasing it to put the loose ends together, and solve the mysterious puzzle. It was like having a picture in your mind of a famous individual, whose name you know well, but being unable to remember their name. The harder you try to pull out that stored memory, the more elusive it seems, but the recollection springs to the front of your mind later, at a quiet moment when you are relaxed, not deliberately racking your brain for the data and forcing it to come.

However, suddenly, in a moment completely defying the above theory, it struck Iptat.

There it was suddenly, what was so obvious that it had completely missed it. It panicked and started to jerk and push with its hands, albeit feebly, against its now unwelcome sarcophagus walls. It was no good; Iptat was beginning to slip away.

'I must get out of here! Stop! Let me out!' it yelled.

It attempted to move any of its limbs or raise its head, but now it felt as if it were pinned down to the floor of its cryo-chamber, the lid of which was now firmly tightly sealed to the outside environment.

'What had it done? The whole ship was in danger. How could it have been so stupid not to have seen it? It was so trusting of something it did not fully know or understand. Oh! The mechanoids . . . The SIPIA . . . The castes . . . '

Its resistance failed and drug induced weariness overtook it. Now there was only dreamless black for over 300 orbits, maybe longer.

EPILOGUE

Newly instigated Hub Commander directive: All units initiate pre-aggression self-diagnostic and combat readiness assessment.

Its body started the requested subconscious system level diagnostic. It stood motionless like a grotesque statue whilst this bodily subroutine ran its course almost as efficiently as a computer. The returned data was published to its conscious mind and the new Hub Commander via the network of voices.

Self-diagnostic data and recommendations:

Oxygen intake: thirty breaths per sixty standard native temporal durations.

Assessment: prevailing level is within mandatory pre-combat tolerance range.

Oxygen PO2: 130 mmHG.

Assessment: prevailing levels in upper quartile of mandatory pre combat tolerance range—upgrade monitor status for hypoxia prevention.

Heartbeat fifteen beats per sixty standard native temporal durations.

Assessment: prevailing levels are within mandatory pre combat tolerance range.

Combat pheromone levels:

Aggressterone: 20,000 nanogruns per liette circulatory fluid.

Assessment: prevailing levels are in lower quartile of mandatory pre combat tolerance range—unit must gland-secrete pheromone to attain stable level of 27,000 nanogruns per litre.

Demotase: 50,000 nanogruns per liette circulatory fluid.

Assessment: prevailing levels are below mandatory pre combat tolerance level. WARNING —unit must immediately gland-secrete pheromone to attain stable level of 62,000 nanogruns per litre and raise monitor status.

Sub species sex hormone: 5,000 nanogruns per liette circulatory fluid.

Assessment: prevailing level is within mandatory pre combat tolerance range.

Proteinous acids: 150,350 nanogruns per liette circulatory fluid.

Assessment: prevailing level is within mandatory pre combat tolerance range.

Sugars and short —term energy supplies: 74,000 nanogruns per liette circulatory fluid.

Assessment: prevailing level is within mandatory pre combat tolerance range.

Complex carbohydrate and longer term energy supplies: 35,000 nanogruns per liette circulatory fluid.

Assessment: prevailing level is below mandatory pre-combat tolerance range. Unit must undergo low priority refuelling to replenish longer term store.

Internal self-diagnostic complete.

Unit affecting all mandatory and recommended updates to internal physiology and resetting self-monitoring statuses.

It stood motionless in the room waiting, whilst its body made the necessary hormonal secretions to ensure its full preparedness for battle. It could feel the surge in aggression and corresponding increase in high level alertness that accompanied the administration of the genetically engineered hormones. It could delay refuelling with complex carbohydrates as the network of others had calculated that the conflict had an infinitesimally small percentage chance of lasting more than 900 temporal units.

It knew that they were coming and that the time of their arrival was soon. It, and the network of others, also knew that the probability of the target being at this place and time was high, but all potential attack locations and eventualities were covered, and all units from the amalgam were deployed accordingly.

As it was the unit with the highest combat rating in the neural amalgam, it was positioned at the location of the highest threat. All units of its kind were genetically engineered to be highly efficient and ruthless military automatons, bred over millennia for this purpose. But it was currently the best in its amalgam. It might almost have been proud if it had any feelings, but a combination of genetic breeding and consistently high levels of the engineered pheromone Demotase ensured that it could not feel that emotion.

The network had calculated only 3.56 per cent chance of defeat against any attack. It had no sentiment towards either the soft pink creatures or the hairy humanoids, good or bad. Its job was simply to eliminate the threat, which involved killing these intruders as soon as they arrived. These were the instructions from the new leader and confirmed by the now greater network of voices of which it was a part.

The scientist caste traitor had made mistakes. The network did not take kindly to these traitor scientists. Both the deserters from their home planet and the more recent traitors would have to be eliminated. It was ready. If it had had feelings it might have smiled.

It was good at killing. This feeling was the closest that it had to having actual emotions; the perception that it was good, or maybe the best at what it did. Its neurones reacted with a surge of activity to the sensory input that it received on overcoming an opponent or opponents, and they had become accustomed to this input. It would have a sense of missing these inputs if they did not happen at regular intervals, so they approximated emotions. These 'feelings' could be construed as 'pride' or even enjoyment at executing a task that it knew it was highly adapted and skilled at. It had never failed in combat, and no creature had ever come close to causing it any threat, even from its own kind. So it looked forward to combat in order that it could rejoice in its reason for being.

The still warm near corpse at its feet was freshly assassinated, but still clung by a thread to life for no reason other than its body was highly adapted to survive more efficiently than almost all, if not all, other species. Blood pumped lazily and spasmodically from large and clean stomach wounds like water escaping from a low pressure water main.

The slaughter was a regrettable decision by the network of voices, but it gave the best probability of victory and was the by product of a tactical military decision made by the new Hub Commander and agreed upon by its deposed predecessor lying at its feet. Despite the fact that the plan involved its own elimination, it had accepted the initiative and issued the command to proceed; it's very last directive to the amalgam. The pink creatures' battle plan had necessitated this move.

The genetic mutation had resulted in a new type of leader, one from outside of their caste, a gendered one, taking control of their battalion amalgam. Not only had he succeeded in grasping control over this network, but he had also been able to take command of all of the Sentinel battalions on this planet. The deposed body at its feet, like all previous Hub Commanders, had only ever been able to have dominion over one amalgam.

Reproduction, sexual or asexual, was impossible in their caste, and each amalgam had always had to rely on the species' natural genetic distribution of Hub Commanders from Procreator reproductive activity. Hubs were produced at a frequency of approximately 1 birth in 110 Sentinel births in their species. Additionally the Sentinel caste contributed approximately 33 per cent of births in their species, so consequently this resulted in a total of only 0.303 per cent of deliveries being Hub Commander sub-caste units. Not surprisingly, they were extremely valuable individuals and, until now, had been protected above all other units in the species.

Previously, the moment a Hub Commander was melded into the neural amalgam and took control over of the voice network, the individual was difficult to replace. Often the death of an actively melded Hub Commander would always lead to multiple deaths of its amalgam's Assassins, primarily through shock. The surviving remainder, starved of the comfort of the instruction and control that the network provided, would be uncontrollably and randomly violent, and would always need termination. It had helped in such a culling in the past.

This is why Hub Commanders had been the most protected of any individual in their race. The consequences of their death used to be so far reaching from a tactical and military viewpoint.

Now this was all changed. This male Procreator now could control all the amalgam battalions. Soon the Hubs would no longer be needed. Procreators could be produced using his genes, using cloning, and splicing technologies, so in the course of time, the caste would be virtually invincible in battle with the resultant pool of more efficient controllers. The old Hub Commanders would now be only a back-up.

A puddle of the dark purple blood spread slowly around its feet, totally ignored by the unit. The Hub Commander's body finally twitched, and it exhaled its last breath, unmoving at last.

The network was on high alert and, consequently, there was a high volume of traffic flowing along the psychic communication channels to all connected units. It could feel and visualise intelligence on all the other units' allocated patrols; correspondingly all units could sense all visual or audible events occurring in its sensory spectrum. This adaptation was one of the many advantages its species had over other less advanced races and why they made such a fearsome adversary.

Self-diagnosis having been completed, it felt a need for regeneration; a need to conserve energy so that when needed it would be at its ruthless best. It had stood motionlessly here on high alert for nearly 90 per cent of one of this world's rotations.

Now that the Hub was dead, it decided it could move to the side wall of the room, to take cover away from open space in the middle and avoid being in the line of any potential weapons fire. As it settled in its new location, it closed its inner lids but kept the outer, more permeable, ones open and stood its ground.

It could still monitor all visual and auditory signals whilst in a state of regenerative sleep. Similarly, it's highly developed subconscious was still able to process that data, transmit it to the others in the amalgam network irrespective the state of its conscious mind, and send an internal reactivation message to rapidly bring itself to a full state of alertness. This would take a temporal unit or two, but the tactical advantages of regeneration in terms of mental and physical preparation outweighed the small risk of being surprised in this state.

They were coming soon. The unit kept its hand on the hilt of its favourite and most efficient killing blade.

Somewhere in its subconscious mind, it grinned in anticipation.

Lightning Source UK Ltd.
Milton Keynes UK
UKOW052343190412

191107UK00002B/17/P

9 781465 307194